A PLACE OF SAFETY

In a village in 1950s South Africa, a civil war is looming. Mr Barlow has four children: Margaret, fifteen; Robert, fourteen; Stephen, nine; and Pauline, seven. Anxious for their safety, he bundles them out of school and sends them to live with their aunt in England. But when they arrive in London and their plans unravel, events do not run smoothly and the children are soon forced to hide a secret. Convinced that there is a great story behind the arrival of the Barlow family, the editor of the local newspaper is determined to discover the truth.

Books by Audrey Weigh
Published by The House of Ulverscroft:

SOMEONE TO CARE
A FUTURE WITH YOU
BALLET FOR TWO
TO BE WITH YOU
HESTER'S CHOICE
MOVING ON

AUDREY WEIGH

A PLACE
OF SAFETY

Complete and Unabridged

ULVERSCROFT
Leicester

First published in Australia in 2005

First Large Print Edition
published 2006

British Library CIP Data

Weigh, Audrey
   A place of safety.—Large print ed.—
   Ulverscroft large print series: general fiction
   1. Large type books
   I. Title
   823.9'14 [F]

   ISBN 1–84617–522–4

Published by
F. A. Thorpe (Publishing)
Anstey, Leicestershire

Set by Words & Graphics Ltd.
Anstey, Leicestershire
Printed and bound in Great Britain by
T. J. International Ltd., Padstow, Cornwall

This book is printed on acid-free paper

For
Laraine Ball
A friend who shares an interest
in books and theatre

Author's Note

This story takes place during the 1950s.

In England at that time, the official attitude toward juveniles was more authoritative.

Persistent truants, young beggars, homeless or neglected children and those deemed to be exposed to moral danger would be taken in by police or welfare officers and dealt with under the Children and Young Persons Act of 1933.

Children under the age of 16 years were also deemed to be in need of Care or Protection if they did not have a competent parent or guardian taking care of them.

Apart from well-known cities, such as London and Birmingham, all the places and characters mentioned in the story are imaginary.

1

Birds rose in panic and confusion as the shabby truck bounced and rattled along the unsealed highway, trailing huge clouds of dust. Barlow fought the urge to drive faster, warning himself to concentrate on the rough surface. Time was short, but reaching the village safely was more important than speed. He slowed as he neared the outskirts, aware of more hazards ahead. Chickens and foraging pigs tended to wander heedlessly on the road, and numerous young children would be playing in the dirt outside their homes.

The schoolhouse lay at the far side of the village beyond two rows of dwellings and small workshops. Barlow jolted to a stop outside the thatched building and clumped up the wooden steps, leaving his cab door hanging open. Every child in the crowded one-room school turned towards the doorway, surprised by the unexpected visit but glad of any change to routine.

Margaret Barlow looked up from the book she was reading aloud and stared at the man who was edging towards the head teacher at the opposite end of the room. Why was her father in the village at this time of day, and whatever had made him interrupt classes like this? A vague sense of alarm passed over her as she watched the two men turn away to talk, but she shook the feeling off and called her pupils' attention back to their work.

'I shall be coming in a minute to see if your handwriting is good today,' she warned the two upper sections. The children grudgingly turned their attention back to the work on their slates and Margaret continued with the passage she had been reading to the third group.

Rustlings and excited whisperings made her look up again and she saw that her father was threading his way between the crowded desks towards her. His tense expression warned her of trouble, but she calmly read to the end of the paragraph before moving into a corner so that they could talk more privately.

'You must come at once,' murmured Barlow. 'Bring Pauline and Stephen.'

'What's happened?'

'I can't tell you here. Just leave everything and come with me.'

He headed for the doorway and Margaret laid her book down on the rickety table that served as her desk.

'Pauline and Stephen, you are both wanted

outside,' she announced.

The two youngsters scrambled out of their places on the long benches, delighted by the diversion, and Margaret clapped her hands to bring her class to order.

'I have to leave you for a little while,' she said. 'Get on with your next exercise quietly and don't interrupt Mr Askejinaki's class. When you have finished that work properly you can draw a picture about your favourite story.'

Her brother Robert had also been called out from his place in the group of senior students, and when Margaret hurried down the steps she found he was already helping Pauline and Stephen into the back of the open truck. Barlow started the engine as soon as the two older children had clambered in beside him.

'What's happened?' asked Margaret again.

Her father wiped the back of his hand across his forehead, leaving a dirty smear.

'War,' he said shortly.

'War?' echoed Robert. 'Where?'

'Right here in this country.' Barlow paused to consider his next words. 'You know there have been rumblings in the past weeks, politicians and chiefs arguing. Well, it flared into fierce fighting this morning. It won't go away. It will spread through the whole country this time.'

Memories of recent newspaper reports and political speeches on the radio flashed through Margaret's mind. Divided by different languages and traditions, the two largest tribes had been bickering for years. Petty jealousies had caused skirmishes and so-called rebels had challenged government troops over land rights and industrial developments but, so far, outright war had been avoided.

'How did it start?' she asked.

'Southern tribes finally got together. They invaded the north this morning. They claim the northerners are trying to take complete control and leave them with no assets and no rights at all.' Her father released the brake and drove towards an open space where he could turn the vehicle more easily. 'It really is serious this time. The Prime Minister has been assassinated and the Kukulinda copper mine has been captured. Some reports say they have already attacked the port.'

'But the port is only about a hundred miles from here,' exclaimed Margaret.

'Exactly. That's what all the hurry is about.' Barlow sighed. 'We've got to get you out of here before the airstrip is taken over. The Walker Company plane is going to wait until twelve o'clock.'

'That Walker plane is only a four-seater,' said Robert.

'One of you will have to sit on the floor. The weight won't matter. There won't be any stores on board.'

Margaret paled. 'Aren't you and Mum coming with us?'

'No.' Her father forced a smile. 'I'm afraid you'll be in charge of this expedition. We're sending you to Aunt Joan in England.'

'Can't we all stay together?' pleaded Margaret.

Barlow shook his head firmly and braked to avoid a hen that suddenly darted across the road. 'Mum and I can't leave. We're needed here. But we have to know that you are all safely out of the way of any trouble.' Moments later he pulled up outside their sprawling wooden bungalow and leaned his forearms on the steering wheel. 'Don't worry about us. The rebels probably won't come anywhere near a little village like this.'

'So why rush us away then?' demanded Robert.

'Things aren't going to be easy, and it will take a load off our minds if we're certain you're safe. Besides, white children could be tempting bait for kidnappers. Now don't make a fuss about leaving. We have enough to think about without any of that kind of nonsense.'

He gave another deep sigh as he watched

the two younger children jump down from the back of the truck and dash into the house. They were filled with glee at the thought of an unexpected holiday, having no inkling as yet that anything was amiss.

'Go and help Mum,' he instructed. 'We haven't much time.'

Their mother had already packed one suitcase. She tossed an empty case onto Stephen's bed and managed to smile cheerfully as Margaret entered the room.

'Oh, there you are, Margaret. Fill a bag with your clothes and then do the same for Pauline please. Try to put a change of everything in, and choose the warmest ones. You're going to find it cold in England.'

They were all too rushed to wallow in misery or despair. Pauline was bewildered by the hectic preparations, understanding only that they were going to England to visit Aunt Joan. Only seven years of age, her sole journey out of Africa had taken place when she was a baby, and she had no idea how far they would have to travel. Stephen was nine and he knew the meaning of war, but life in the village had always been simple and tranquil and it seemed impossible that violence could have broken out so close to their own home. Both children wanted to find out much more about the upheaval, but they realised this was not a time for questions. They must follow the hasty directions and not distract their parents.

There was no chance to say good-bye to any friends, or time to grieve at the prospect of leaving their dog behind. All the children gave him loving pats and he whined dejectedly, sensing trouble. His ears and tail drooped as their father ordered him back to the verandah, then Robert climbed into the back of the truck with the younger children and Barlow started the engine. They bumped back along the road, past the corrugated iron shacks, the wooden houses on stilts and the thatched schoolhouse. The street seemed strangely deserted, but a crowd of elders had gathered outside the headman's house. The men watched the truck in silence, none smiling or raising a hand in greeting.

When the last building had been left behind Barlow increased speed, driving as fast as he dared along the pitted dirt road. The pilot had promised to wait until twelve o'clock, but a distance of twenty-six miles lay between the village and the airstrip and if conditions had deteriorated he might not be willing to stay so long on the ground.

While he concentrated on driving, his wife occupied herself giving last minute instructions to Margaret, who was pretending to feel

7

calm and competent.

'Here are your passports. Your birth certificates and vaccination cards are inside.'

She waited for Margaret to unzip her shoulder bag and stow the documents in an inner pocket.

'Good. Dad will give you some money when we get to the airstrip. Remember that people are not always honest in big cities. When you get time later, see if you can put most of your money under your clothes. It will be safer there.'

'I can wrap it in a hanky and use a safety pin, like you did once.'

'Good idea. Now look, this envelope is very important. Give it to Aunt Joan as soon as you see her. It gives her authority to withdraw money from our bank account in England, so look after it carefully. She won't be able to get any money without it.'

To Barlow's relief, the plane was still standing on the primitive runway, its outline shimmering in the heat. He drove directly towards it across rough grass, ignoring the small office building near the road. As the truck drew closer to the aircraft, the pilot stepped out from where he had been waiting in the shade of a nearby tree. He had already decided that a lingering departure would be too much of a strain for everybody and he planned to act quickly before any member of the family became upset.

'Great timing,' he said as the truck came to a halt. 'Okay, let's go.'

Barlow stiffened. 'Have you heard anything?'

'Only rumours. Nothing much has changed. But we've got to get moving. If we miss that lift we've been promised, we'll be well and truly stuffed.'

Mrs Barlow fought back tears and hugged all the children in turn, determined not to give way to her emotions until the plane was out of sight.

'Give my love to Aunt Joan,' she said huskily. 'And write as soon as you can. I'm going to miss you.'

Her husband adopted a businesslike manner in an effort to hide his concern. The idea of sending his children alone to a strange country was hateful, but he told himself he had no other choice. Nobody could foresee what was likely to happen in coming days, but early reports alleged that hundreds of people had been killed already. This was the children's only chance of reaching a place of safety and they had to take it. He choked back another sigh as he watched them exchange hugs and kisses with their mother. Margaret had only just turned fifteen and, although she had grown up quickly in the

9

past year, she seemed far too young to be given such responsibility.

'Here's some money for you,' he said, showing her a buff envelope. 'Look, these are American dollars. You can change them anywhere in the world. Use this local money first. It's likely to lose its value, so exchange it before you leave Africa if you can.'

Margaret pushed the envelope into another zipped pocket inside her bag and her father patted her shoulder.

'Don't worry about your plane tickets. Mr Scott will fix those up for you when you land. Ask him to help you to send this cable to Aunt Joan as well. If we can get through, we'll explain everything to Aunt Joan on the telephone. Keep that copy of the cable. It has the address on it and everything.'

'We'll soon be together again,' said Mrs Barlow, blinking back the tears that were gathering despite her fight for control. 'Look after them all, Margaret.'

Margaret nodded, not trusting herself to speak again now in case she broke down. Her father gave her a comforting hug then put his arm across Robert's shoulders.

'You're the man of the family now,' he said. 'Help Margaret to look after the younger ones.'

Robert had celebrated his fourteenth

birthday less than two weeks before and had never travelled far from the village without at least one adult in attendance, but he straightened up manfully.

'Don't worry, Dad. We'll be all right.'

One last wave to their parents across the flat expanse of the airfield, a last glimpse of the truck and the two disconsolate adults standing beside it, then they were flying over an almost unbroken stretch of dense vegetation. Scott was heading north-east, away from the danger of armed conflict but towards a part of the country that none of the children had ever visited before. When the river disappeared from view they all felt as though their last link with home had been broken, and Margaret struggled bravely to stem her own tears as she comforted Pauline and Stephen.

They landed at a small airport near a range of hills, where men were hastily loading a cargo plane with drums and boxes. An official told them that all communications with the outside world had been cut and it was impossible to send a cable or book seats for a flight to England.

Scott took a deep breath of exasperation, then turned to the children and spoke nonchalantly to give them courage. 'Don't worry. Once you get over the border you'll be able to get everything done. Easy as sleeping in the shade. Just go to the desk in the airport and ask for someone to help you.'

He pulled a plastic folder out of his back trouser pocket and handed it to Margaret.

'That's the Company's credit card. Use that to pay for your tickets and any meals you need. You can even ask for some extra cash when you pay a bill. It's good for all the countries listed on the back. But look — you need this number to serve as a signature. Don't lose it. Memorise it if you can. But keep it in a separate place, not with the card.'

'Where are you going now?' asked Stephen nervously. He did not want to part from the last person they knew from their usual life.

'I'm going to fill up that big plane over there with as much oil and food as I can, and then I'm going to fly it up to our north base.' Scott looked around, wondering how to shed his responsibility for the family, and his eyes brightened with relief. 'Ah, here comes the pilot who's going to take you on the next leg.'

The supply plane that they travelled on next had no seats at all, while the passenger aircraft to which they changed afterwards was carrying three people more than the permitted limit, so they still had to take turns at sitting on the floor. Margaret pressed her lips firmly together, determined not to let her true feelings show and refusing to think of anything beyond their present situation. Discomfort brought one small consolation. It tended to distract the younger ones from thoughts of home and what might be happening there, and how long they would have to wait before they could see their parents again.

2

They landed at an airport in a neighbouring country, where the children had to answer strings of questions in French. They all spoke French fluently, but the only progress they seemed to be making was to move from one official to another. The head of the immigration section wavered over a decision to admit four unescorted foreign children. Such a strange situation had never occurred before. The group had no exit or entry visas from any other country, very little cash and no valid tickets. In his experience, young children were usually included in a parent's travel documents. He frowned as he fingered the large blue British passports.

'You are a long way from home. How can I check that you have your parents' permission to make this journey?'

'We have been evacuated,' said Margaret yet again. 'There is a war on and we have to go to our aunt in England.' She drew Pauline closer and hugged her in an effort to comfort her little sister and to give herself an air of competence. Three minor officers had already demanded an explanation and the hitch was beginning to worry her. While this kind of resistance continued they might miss a plane, and who knew when there would be another?

'According to regulations, you should have return tickets to your country of origin — or else confirmed reservations for onward travel. You have neither. You didn't even have any tickets for the journey you just made. You should also have sufficient money to pay for any living expenses that might occur.'

'I have a company credit card.' Margaret opened her shoulder bag and flashed the card just long enough for him to read the large print. 'We have to use this to pay for our tickets and get more cash. This airport is the first proper one we have been to. You can't buy tickets in our village. And there aren't any banks.'

'We can't go back, anyway,' Robert put in. 'There won't be any more planes going that way.'

The officer closed his eyes as if in prayer, thinking only of trying to avoid further complications, then came to a wary decision. If he could send the children to some other place, any place beyond his jurisdiction, someone else would have to deal with the problem.

'I'll send someone with you to the reservation desk. If they accept that card and issue tickets, I'll grant temporary entry permits.'

'Thank you,' said Margaret. She nudged Robert to remind him to add his thanks, then they were sent to wait on a wooden bench with their luggage around their feet until another man came to escort them to the departure hall.

'Look fine if they won't accept that card,' muttered Robert. 'What will we do then?'

'Don't even think about such a thing,' returned Margaret. 'Look confident, even if you're not.'

To their relief, the female booking clerk said she could make reservations for international flights and that a credit card was acceptable.

'I was told that I could get cash when I paid a bill,' Margaret ventured.

'Quite right. But I can only give you local money, no foreign currency.'

'Oh dear. Well, we'd better take some, just in case we need it.'

The clerk eyed the family and made a quick assessment. 'It won't be a simple journey. You'll probably have to buy food between flights. But four thousand should be enough.'

Margaret suddenly remembered her father's instructions. 'We have to send a cable to England.'

'Better make it nine thousand then.'

Their escort agreed that such an amount would be sufficient, provided that valid tickets were issued, and the clerk set about making reservations by telephone. The process seemed to take far longer than any of them expected and there appeared to be some difficulty, but at last she started writing.

'You'll have to go to the capital first,' she explained when she finally replaced the telephone. 'It's going to take quite a while, I'm afraid. There aren't any direct flights.'

Margaret nodded ruefully and the clerk copied details from the credit card onto a small pad of printed forms on her desk.

'Now I need the identification,' she said, looking up suddenly.

'Er — ' Margaret stared at the woman. She already had their passports, so what else could she want?

'You do know the personal number, I hope.'

'Oh, the number! Yes, for the signature.' Margaret fumbled in her bag. 'Yes, I've got it here.'

The clerk smiled, aware that the girl had never used the system before.

'I'm glad to see you're keeping that paper safe. Now put it away again carefully as soon as I've finished with it.'

Margaret followed the directions and held

her breath as the woman made yet another telephone call. What would they do if there was something wrong with the card, or if Mr Scott had given them the wrong number?

'Right, that's all set.' The clerk counted out nine thousand in local currency notes and handed both the money and the card to Margaret. 'Now I'll write out your tickets. You've got nearly an hour and a half to wait before your first flight leaves, then almost an hour for your connection when you change. When you get to the capital, you must ask which desk you have to go to. You will need seating tickets for your international flight.'

By the time they had received their wad of tickets, gained the necessary stamp in their passports and composed a cable to their aunt with the aid of another airport employee, they only had about ten minutes left before they were due to board their plane. Margaret declared they must all go to the toilet, glad to know they would not be hanging about at that airport any longer.

The aircraft was old, but the seats were comfortable and their journey seemed to be going smoothly at last. Their next plane was not punctual, however, and after they had been sitting for more than an hour on hard chairs, an airport employee informed them in French that their connecting flight had been cancelled. The plane had been delayed by engine trouble at another place and, because it would not be able to arrive before dark, it had not been allowed to take off from where it was now. Service would not be resumed until the following day. Gradually the children began to realise the consequences of the hitch, and they stared at him in dismay.

'Do you mean to say we'll have to stay here all night?' exclaimed Margaret.

'Not here. This place will be closed.'

Margaret gulped. 'We'll have to go to a hotel. Can you recommend one?'

'No hotel,' was the response. 'This is not a major port.'

An awkward silence followed and then the man said he would ask his boss for advice. Eventually, a senior official came to talk to the children. He had never had to deal with a situation like this and he was unsure what to do. He could hardly tell four young children to wait outside the building all night — especially young foreign children, and white ones at that.

'You had better come home with me,' he said at last. 'The terminal will close soon. My wife can make a meal, but we have no beds. You will be safe, but not comfortable.'

'We have been camping often enough,' said

Robert stoutly. 'We don't mind sleeping on the floor.'

The man's wife gave a startled exclamation when she caught sight of the unknown foreign children, but she quickly produced a smile and welcomed them into the tiny house. Her husband gave a brief explanation in their ethnic language, and she threw two more handfuls of rice into the cooking pot. Three young children gazed with awe at the unexpected guests, apparently too shy to speak, but by the time the simple meal had ended they were chuckling and talking happily amongst themselves.

Despite their gratitude and brave words about camping experience, the Barlow family spent a restless night, pestered for a long time by a persistent mosquito and missing their parents more with every passing hour. Margaret was also tussling with the question of payment for their board and lodging. She did not want to embarrass the father by offering money, but she guessed his wages would not be generous and having to feed four extra mouths would make an impact.

Soon after dawn, their host drove them back to the airport and Margaret quietly handed him some folded banknotes.

'Please buy a present for the children for us,' she said. 'And thank you again for all your help and your hospitality.'

He inclined his head with dignity. 'It was a pleasure. I hope your journey goes well from here.'

They had to wait two hours for their plane, but they finally landed in the capital. By following painted signs they found their own way to the reservations desk. The clerk was able to arrange for them to sit together in one row on the next flight, but there was another long and boring wait to endure first. The small cluster of airport shops had few items of interest on view, and the passenger lounge was sparsely furnished.

They slumped in well-worn chairs, all silent until Pauline and Stephen began to pester each other just for the sake of something to do. Margaret thought longingly of home. She would rather spend a whole week with thirty-seven wriggling children in the schoolroom than put up with two irritable siblings for the next six hours in this place. What day was it? School would soon be closed for the weekend, she mused. What would Mum and Dad be doing right now? Mum was probably getting lunch ready. That thought gave her an idea and she stood up again. Eating would help to fill in time and they would all feel better if they had a proper meal.

'Let's go and see if the cafeteria is open,' she said. 'I've got plenty of local money.'

At long last they found themselves on a huge international aircraft bound for London, feeling conspicuous because of the large cardboard labels attached to the front of their clothes.

'I'm surprised they didn't put us in the hold with the luggage,' quipped Robert. 'We must look like packages with these tags on.'

An air hostess had been delegated to look after them and she quickly brought pillows and blankets.

'You look worn out,' she said. 'Now just relax and go to sleep. If you need anything, press that button there.'

After their recent experiences, the children thought the upholstered seats were luxurious, and all four soon fell asleep. They were twice awakened shortly before landing. They had to leave the aircraft each time and endure yet another tedious wait while the plane was serviced and re-fuelled. They appreciated the comfort of reclining seats while they were airborne, and a second hostess decided not to disturb their sleep with offers of food. She raised the window blinds and served a late breakfast as they flew closer to their destination.

'Nearly there now,' she said. 'That's France

down below and we'll soon cross the English Channel.'

They looked out eagerly as they flew over the south coast of England, exclaiming at the scenery below, so different from what they had seen from the planes in Africa. Margaret felt no need to act like an adult and hide her own excitement, her spirits soaring higher at the thought of reaching their journey's end. Very soon now her duties would be over and she would no longer have to carry such a heavy responsibility. She leaned further forward when London came into view, enthralled by the sight. What a huge city it was! It spread for miles. It was a pity Aunt Joan didn't live in London. Still, even a small town in England would be a lot different from the quiet village where they had been living for the past few years.

They had been instructed to stay in their seats until everybody else had left the aircraft and, despite her impatience, Margaret was glad the hostess was there to guide them. She supposed they could have followed the other passengers, but the busy terminal building was huge and she could have been confused easily by all those doors, corridors and signs. Another hostess took over almost immediately and she escorted the children to the baggage hall, where their suitcases were the only items left on the conveyor belt. She helped them to load their luggage onto a trolley and they passed quickly through the Immigration and Customs Departments, coming out to find a large crowd waiting to greet passengers. The children stared at the mass of faces, wondering how they would find Aunt Joan amongst so many strangers.

'We'll put out a call for your aunt,' said the hostess. 'That's the easiest way to find her.'

She led the way to the information desk and moments later they heard their aunt's name booming across the huge hall. Several people came to the desk to make enquiries, the children gazing eagerly at anyone who approached, but Aunt Joan did not appear. The clerk asked one person to wait a moment and repeated the message over the loud-speaker.

Gradually the crowd dispersed. The four youngsters stood despondently beside the desk, their spirits sinking as the great hall grew emptier. Three more messages brought no response and the clerk leaned one elbow on the desk, scratching the back of his head with a pencil.

'Well, I'm sorry,' he said. 'It looks as though she's not here.'

3

The four children stared blankly at the clerk for several seconds, then turned to each other for comfort and reassurance. Margaret bit her lip, absolute despair creeping over her for the first time. She had never imagined that such a thing might happen. All through that long exhausting journey, when it had been essential to pretend that she had complete self-confidence so as to hearten the others, she had bolstered her own courage with the prospect of handing over her task. Boarding the large international aircraft had been a relief — an immense relief. She had convinced herself that all she had to do from then on was to look cheerful and wait for the plane to land. As soon as they reached England, Aunt Joan would take over responsibility for them and make all the decisions.

Pauline's lip began to quiver and Margaret hastily reached for her hand, smothering her own concerns.

'Aunt Joan is a bit late, that's all,' she said. 'We'll just have to wait a while.' She gave a wan smile to the hostess. 'Aunt Joan doesn't live in London, and she wouldn't have had much time to get ready.'

'Surely someone arranged all this with her before booking your seats!'

Margaret shook her head. 'We had to leave in a hurry because of the war. And communications with Gnujeemia had been cut, so it was ages before we could send a cable.'

'Oh, is that where you've come from?' The hostess and the clerk exchanged startled looks, recalling the glaring headlines they had seen over the past two days. The hostess resolved not to mention that country if possible, and to prevent the children from seeing any newspapers or television screens. The family had gone through enough distress already without hearing details about the attacks and alleged brutality.

'Where does your aunt live?' she asked.

'At Allingham. I don't know how far that is.'

The clerk gave a thoughtful nod. 'It's a fair distance. It would take about three hours by car, I should think. Possibly longer by train. I don't suppose there'd be a direct line.'

'That probably accounts for her being late,' agreed the hostess. 'Well, there's no need to stand here until she comes. Let's go and have a cup of tea or something.'

She led the children past shops and into a

large restaurant, choosing a table by the window and pointing out where Robert should park the luggage trolley.

'You all drink tea, don't you?' she asked and, as an affirmative answer seemed to be expected, they all agreed that they did.

The hostess chattered gaily as she poured tea and offered small decorated cakes, hoping that a steady flow of gossip would help to keep their spirits up. They soon lost interest in the one-sided conversation, however, and were almost glad when she rose to go.

'You must wait here until your aunt comes,' she instructed. 'The toilets are over there if you need them. Don't go away. Even if you hear your names called, you must stay right here. We will bring your aunt here to you. Will you be all right on your own for a little while?'

Robert stiffened at the implication that a babysitter might be required, but he held back a caustic comment. 'Yes, thank you.'

'Good. I'll see you soon.'

Silence fell at the table as the woman walked briskly away. The children looked around the restaurant in the vain hope that Aunt Joan might be sitting at one of the other tables, then they stared out of the window. There was nothing much to see. Two workmen were slouching under the wing of a huge aircraft, apparently waiting for further orders. A heavy drizzle was falling and the vast runway beyond the parking bay looked bare and depressing. Tears gathered in Pauline's eyes again and she wiped them away with the backs of her hands.

'I don't like England.'

'You'll feel better once Aunt Joan gets here,' replied Margaret, and sought quickly for some encouraging words. 'She'll take us to a nice big house. We'll have a wonderful time here. Just wait and see. We'll go shopping in big stores and go to the cinema. We'll ride upstairs on a big bus. It's ages since we went to a city, and cities are bigger and much more exciting in England.'

'I'm cold.'

'You'd better put some more clothes on.' Margaret searched in Pauline's case for a jacket and helped her to pull it on over her cardigan. Silence fell again. Stephen showed no sign of tears, but he was listless and withdrawn, clearly suffering from homesickness. Robert tried to interest him in the planes that were landing and taking off at regular intervals, while Margaret fixed her attention on the door of the restaurant. She soon found herself recalling her father's instructions about changing their African money. *Do it as soon as you can. It's quite likely to lose its value*. Should she obey him or the hostess? Surely it wouldn't matter if she left Robert in charge for a few minutes while she went to find a bank? In a big airport like this it should be easy to exchange money.

'You stay here with the others, Robert,' she said at last. 'Dad said I must change our money as soon as I could. I won't be long.'

'That lady's coming back,' said Stephen.

They all looked around eagerly, but they could tell by her expression that the hostess had no good news for them.

'I'm afraid we haven't heard anything yet,' she said as she reached the table. 'We shall have to start planning our next move in case your aunt doesn't arrive today. Have you got any other friends or relatives in London?'

'Not that we know of,' answered Margaret.

'Oh dear. You can't spend the night in the restaurant.'

'We have plenty of money.' Margaret drew herself up with a show of maturity. 'We can go to a hotel if Aunt Joan doesn't arrive before dark.'

The hostess pursed her lips doubtfully. 'I don't know whether that would be the best idea. How old are you?'

'Fifteen.'

'And I'm fourteen,' added Robert. 'We're both past school-leaving age. And we've all stayed in hotels before.'

'We'll have to change our money into English first,' said Margaret. 'I was just thinking of doing that when you came back. I might as well do that job now while we're waiting.'

The woman dithered over her response to that suggestion, wondering what might go wrong and whether anybody could raise any objections to the plan, but she finally assented.

'The rest of you must stay here in case your aunt arrives while we are away. We won't be long.'

Margaret thought the main hall looked busier than ever and she was glad the hostess was there to lead the way. The teller at the counter of the Money Exchange smiled a welcome as they approached, but he looked disconcerted when Margaret laid down the small bundle of African notes.

'I don't think I can accept those,' he said hesitantly. 'There's a war on, you know.'

'Yes, that's why we're here. We had to leave. Can you change just some of it?'

'Just a minute, I'll check up.'

The teller held a muttered conversation with another man behind the desk, then came back shaking his head. 'I'm sorry, we can't take it. We don't know how much it's worth.

Rates change rapidly after a political upheaval.'

'Can't you telephone someone and ask?'

'It's Sunday. Everything is closed for the weekend. I'm sorry, but we can't do anything about it until the banks open again.'

Margaret re-folded the notes slowly, feeling that their difficulties were mounting with every minute. She did not want to offer the American dollars. She only had a few and her father had told her to keep them as long as possible. In the meantime she had better keep the African money safe. When she opened her handbag another solution occurred to her and her eyes brightened.

'I've got a credit card!' She pulled the card out and turned back to the clerk. 'I can get some English money with this, can't I?'

The man turned the card over then frowned, and again he shook his head. 'I'm sorry. It's not valid for England,' he said. 'Look at that list. It only has African names on it.'

'Well, that settles the question of going off to a hotel,' said the hostess as they moved away from the counter. 'I must say I was not very happy about that idea in the first place, and I doubt that the airline officials would have agreed. It might have been difficult to find a hotel that would take you, anyway. You are all very young.'

'Where *can* we spend the night then — if Aunt Joan doesn't get here soon?'

The hostess suppressed a sigh. She would be glad to see the end of her part in this affair, but it was a relief to know that finding a solution would not be her responsibility.

'We'll find a place for you. Don't worry.' She paused and then nodded as though she had just reached a decision. 'I think the best thing to do now is to get you a hot meal. You can take your time over it. In the meantime we'll fix up accommodation for the night. If your aunt hasn't arrived in the next couple of hours we'll go there. We mustn't keep the younger ones up much longer. You've all had a very tiring couple of days.'

The children had little appetite, but they were glad of some activity to keep them occupied. They lingered over the meal, hoping Aunt Joan would reach the airport before they were whisked away to some other place, but nobody came for them and eventually the hostess ushered them out to the car park.

'You're going to spend the night at a hostel,' she explained. 'It won't be as luxurious as a hotel, but you will be safe there.'

'It's only for one night, anyway,' said Robert staunchly.

'Exactly. They don't usually take children

without an adult to look after them, but Matron decided that if you could travel half way across the world by yourselves, you'd be all right in the hostel for one night.'

Driving through the busy London streets should have been a thrilling experience, but the youngsters felt chilly now they had left the airport buildings and they were too weary to appreciate new sights. Margaret did her best to show some interest, but her spirits drooped again when she noticed they were travelling into a less attractive area.

The hostel was a tall drab building in a narrow and uninviting street, but the Matron looked kind and friendly.

'You poor mites,' she exclaimed, looking from one to the other. 'Fancy coming all this way and then finding nobody waiting for you. Never mind, tomorrow's another day and we'll get everything sorted out.'

She noticed they were all clutching the necks of their jackets in an attempt to keep warm and her eyes widened.

'Haven't any of you got coats?'

Margaret shook her head. 'Only plastic raincoats. We never needed warm clothes at home.'

'Oh dear. We'll have to fix you up with some before you go outside tomorrow. You're going to catch your death of cold if you're not careful, coming from the tropics to a climate like this. It's only March, and not even as warm as it should be.' She pressed a button on her desk and soon afterwards an elderly woman in a grey overall came into the office.

'Take these children up and show them where everything is,' said Matron. 'They've had a very long journey, so they'd better all go to bed straight away.'

The hostess bade them farewell, unable to conceal a note of relief in her voice, and the children followed their new guide up a flight of concrete steps guarded by green painted iron railings. On the second floor they turned left into a corridor with a bare concrete floor. Dark green walls stretched ahead of them, dimly lit by small electric bulbs. Each light was screwed into a ceiling socket and protected by a wire cage. Pauline and Stephen drew closer to Margaret as they passed the first of the closed brown doors to either side of them, and Robert had difficulty in maintaining his brave stance. The building was cold and cheerless, looking more like a prison than a homely place to spend the night.

At last they reached the far end of the passage and the woman opened the door on the left.

'I think the girls had better sleep in here,'

she said. 'We're letting you use the little room opposite so that you'll be close together, but it was used as a storeroom for a while so it's not properly equipped. No curtains or lockers, you see.'

Margaret and Pauline peeped into the first room as she switched on the light and saw two canvas camp beds with a low wooden locker beside each. Well-worn blankets were folded at the foot of the beds, with a pillow and bed linen.

'Leave your cases out here for a minute,' said the woman. 'All of you come in and I'll show you how to use a sheet sleeping bag, just in case you haven't seen one before.'

She shook one sheet out and they saw that it was stitched into a bag with a pocket at the top.

'You put the pillow in here,' she explained, pushing one into the pouch. 'Just the one piece makes a top, a bottom and a pillow slip. This saves a lot of laundry, you see. Now then, the other room is right opposite.'

She crossed the corridor and opened the facing door, fumbling inside for the light switch.

'Ah, that's it,' she said as the light flashed on. 'As you can see, there aren't any lockers and there's a stack of buckets and things over there, but I expect you'll be too tired to notice, anyway. The bathroom is half way along. You'll see the sign on the door.' She pointed back along the corridor and then turned to go. 'There's only women up here, by the way, no men. Oh, and you can have breakfast from half past seven on. Make sure you come down before quarter-past eight in the morning. Just go down to the office and someone will show you the way to the breakfast room.'

She walked back towards the staircase, her heels clicking on the concrete, and Robert gave a rueful grin.

'Well, it certainly isn't luxurious, but at least it's free.'

'We don't need luxury,' answered Margaret. 'And we managed well enough on the floor the other night. Now then, Pauline and Stephen, to the toilet. And then you'd better get into bed as quickly as you can. We all want to look our best when Aunt Joan gets here tomorrow.'

She escorted them to the bathroom, where they found four toilet cubicles facing a row of six wash-basins, then led the way back to the small bedrooms. Pauline undressed rapidly and slithered into her sheet bag.

'I'm cold,' she complained as Margaret tucked the blankets around her.

'You'll have to put your cardigan on again.'

'I'm cold all over the rest of me.' Pauline wriggled part way out of the bag, thrust her arms into the sleeves of the cardigan and slid down under the covers again before starting to fasten the buttons.

'That's better, isn't it?' said Margaret.

'Not much. I'm freezing all the way down from my middle. These blankets are too thin.'

'I'll give you one of mine.'

'Then you won't be able to sleep all night. You'll be frozen.' Pauline began to shiver violently. 'I bet Robert and Stephen are cold, too. Why don't you ask for some more blankets?'

Margaret thought of the friendly Matron downstairs. She would surely understand if they complained about the cold.

'All right. I'll go down and see what I can do.'

As she moved towards the door, Pauline started up in alarm. 'Don't leave me here by myself.'

'You'll be quite safe. Wrap yourself up before you get colder than ever.'

Pauline was longing for more blankets, but she was terrified that something dreadful might happen if she were left alone in that strange gloomy building.

'Let me go in with the boys until you get

back,' she pleaded.

Moments later she was huddled in Robert's bed and he stayed to comfort the younger ones while Margaret went on her errand. She retraced the route along the bleak corridor, twice hearing a murmur of voices from behind closed doors, and hurried down the two flights of stairs. The office door was slightly ajar and she heard the clink of teacups as she approached.

'The Children's Office was closed and nobody else had any bright ideas.'

Margaret stopped abruptly as she recognised the voice of the woman from the airport.

'You did what the law required,' answered Matron calmly. 'You put them in a Place of Safety. It's irregular for us to take them here, I'll admit, but you have to stretch a point now and then. After all, they are evacuees, aren't they? And they're much too tired to be bothered with formalities just now.'

'But what happens tomorrow?'

'We'll have to hope that the missing aunt really is a responsible person and that she turns up. If not, they'll have to go into Care.' Matron gave a noisy sigh. 'Then I suppose the next problem will be deciding which Council should take them, yours out there at Heathrow, or ours.'

'Will they be kept together?'

'I doubt it. That's the most unfortunate aspect of these cases. It's difficult to place a family of four in the same Home, and with these particular children there's such a wide difference in ages.'

Margaret stood stiffly just outside the door, listening to the discussion with mounting horror. They were talking about her family — making plans to put them into some kind of institution; even taking it for granted that they would be separated. For more than three minutes she remained motionless, learning that even she was too young to escape the same fate, but clicking footsteps from a nearby passage suddenly reminded her that she was eavesdropping. She must not be found there, listening to that conversation behind the partly open door. She must not let it be known that she had overheard what was being said.

She rushed for the stairs, her sandals barely making a sound on the concrete, and did not slacken her pace until she reached the landing on the second floor. She leaned against the dark green wall while she recovered her breath, closing her eyes in the hope of being able to think more clearly. Before morning she had to decide what to do. She must not allow these people to take over her family, especially if they would be separated. Her parents had placed her in charge of the others and she was determined to stay in charge until Aunt Joan took over. Nobody else must be allowed to interfere.

4

Slamming doors and rattling buckets wakened the four children early the next morning. For almost half an hour last night they had shivered in their beds, wondering if they would ever feel warm again, but they began to feel better after pulling outdoor clothes over their pyjamas. Fatigue had finally overcome their anxieties, and they had all slept well on the narrow cots.

'Come on, Pauline,' said Margaret, easing her way out of her sheet bag. 'Get yourself dressed properly while I make sure the boys are up.'

'Is it very cold?'

'Not really. Once you get moving you'll find it's all right, and I'm sure you'd like some breakfast.'

The boys were still huddled under their thin blankets and they were reluctant to stir.

'Come on,' urged Margaret. 'Don't be so lazy. It's time to get moving. Put your warmest clothes on.'

Robert lifted his head and gazed searchingly at her, relieved to see that she was looking more cheerful. Last night she had definitely been upset. She had tried to brush aside his concern, claiming she was merely disappointed by her failure to get more blankets, but he did not believe that story.

'You're looking better this morning,' he said.

'Yes, well I feel better, too. I've had a good sleep and even the weather has improved.' Margaret wafted one hand towards the uncovered window. 'Look, real English sunshine. I told you it didn't rain all the time.'

'What do you think they'll give us for breakfast?' asked Stephen.

Robert sniggered. 'Probably dry bread and water.'

'That would be better than nothing,' snapped Margaret. 'Just be grateful, and don't expect too much. We're not at Buckingham Palace.'

An elderly woman and a much younger obese woman were busy at the chipped wash-basins in the bathroom. The younger one ignored the new arrivals, but the older one stared in indignation. This floor of the hostel was reserved for females. No one could really complain about little boys, so long as they didn't make a nuisance of themselves, but one of these boys looked much older than usual. Why had he been allowed in?

'Good morning,' Margaret said brightly before the woman formed the words to grizzle. 'It's a lovely day today isn't it?'

'Mm,' came the grudging reply. 'How long will you be here?'

'Only an hour or so. We're on our way to Allingham, but we couldn't get there last night.'

'Huh.' The woman turned away and Margaret led the children to the last two basins in the row.

'Make it quick,' she hissed. 'We'll have a proper wash later.'

At the foot of the first flight of steps they met a middle-aged cleaner, who directed them to the basement. On the way there Margaret cast a guilty look at the office. The door was ajar as before, but no voices could be heard this time. At the far end of the large basement room the children found a counter, where they received a light breakfast of tea and toast. At least thirty men and women of various ages were seated at the bare wooden tables, but they all kept their heads down as if determined to ignore every other person. The sombre atmosphere inhibited the children so they dared not chatter.

'They're not very friendly, are they?' whispered Robert.

'They must be very unhappy people. I

expect they're here because they have no home to go to.' Margaret looked down at her mug of tea and concentrated on her own family's predicament. She had to prepare herself to hear that Aunt Joan had not come to the airport. If that were the case she must make sure they got away from here quickly, before the Matron had a chance to contact any of the council people she had been talking about to the air hostess last night. A vague plan had occurred to her before she fell asleep, but she had not worked out the details and she could only hope it would be successful.

'Listen carefully,' she said as she began to gather up their empty plates. 'I'm hoping that Aunt Joan has arrived in London by now. But if she hasn't, we'll have to make our own arrangements.'

'Like what?' asked Robert.

'I'll tell you later. Just keep quiet all of you, and don't ask any questions, no matter what I say. With a bit of luck, things will already be sorted out and we won't have to do a thing.'

Stephen helped her to carry the crockery back to the counter and she led the way up to the ground floor. The office door was now wide open and Matron gave a friendly smile as she looked up at them from behind her desk.

'Come in. I hope you all rested well last night,' she said. 'Look what we have picked out for you.' She stood up and pointed to a collection of warm clothing spread across a table near the window. 'They might not be exactly the right size,' she continued, 'but they'll put you on till you can get fixed up properly. Come over here and see.'

Margaret and Robert exchanged glances and flushed with embarrassment. They had donated clothes to poor people and had often helped to raise money for community projects, but they had never expected to be on the receiving end of such charity themselves.

Matron guessed what was running through their minds and she spoke gently.

'These are all given to us for people who need them, and who needs them more than you at this moment? It's sunny out there today, but there's a nippy wind. None of you wants to be ill, just because you haven't got the right clothes.'

'Thank you,' murmured Margaret. She moved forward and allowed Matron to hold a jumper and skirt up against her. She had to agree that they needed heavier clothes, but she must make sure the family was not placed under any obligation.

'We won't need them for long,' she

asserted. 'I'll send them back as soon as I can.'

'There's no need to send them back here, dear. You can pass them on to another organisation if you like.'

When she had distributed clothes to each of them, Matron consulted her watch.

'Time I telephoned the airport, I think.'

From her end of the conversation it was obvious that Aunt Joan had not arrived there, nor sent any message. Matron shook her head sorrowfully as she turned back to the children, but Margaret spoke first.

'It's quite possible that the cable was never even sent,' she said. 'Someone was going to do it for us, but if he got busy after we left he might have forgotten all about it.'

Matron thought of stories that were circulated so frequently in news reports. Corruption was rife in developing countries, and it seemed that the young girl had found a polite way of saying their 'helper' had pocketed the money instead of sending the message.

'I expect we can find out. And we could get onto telephone enquiries. We'll send a telegram if your aunt is not on the phone.'

'There's no need for that,' said Margaret quickly. 'We'll go straight to the Walker Engineering Company. They've got a big

46

office in London. They made all the arrangements for us to come to England, so they'll know what to do next. We couldn't go there yesterday.'

'Ah, Sunday. The office would have been closed.'

'Yes. I don't know where the Manager lives.'

Robert stared in surprise, wondering what Margaret was planning to do. She must have worked out some scheme, but he couldn't help. She had warned them all to keep quiet.

'If they arranged for you to come to England, they must know what is to be done next,' said Matron thankfully. If that were so, she would be freed from responsibility sooner than she had dared to hope.

'May I use your telephone please?'

'Of course. Yes, of course.' Matron pushed the instrument closer and took the telephone directory from a handy shelf behind her desk. 'Walker, did you say? What's the full name of the Company?'

Margaret rested her hand on the receiver, determined to make the telephone call herself. If the woman spoke first she would ruin everything.

Matron smiled to herself at the display of independence. 'I'll just look it up for you.'

She found the entry in the directory, wrote

the number in large figures on a sheet of paper and passed it to the girl. 'You have to dial the letters as well as the numbers. Do you want me to do it?'

'No thank you. I'll manage.' Margaret looked for the letters before starting to dial and managed to complete the task smoothly. She was rewarded by a ringing tone, followed by a sharp click and an answering voice.

'Walker Engineering Company. Good morning.'

'Hello. It's Margaret here.' She rushed on before the other person could ask questions. 'Yes, Margaret Barlow. We all arrived from Gnujeemia yesterday, but nobody met us. I think something must have gone wrong.'

She ignored the startled response, nodding as though in agreement with some statement. 'Yes, yes, I know. Who's there now? Yes, all right . . . We'll come right over . . . Yes, of course we can carry our luggage, we haven't got much.'

'You must have got the wrong number. I haven't the slightest idea what you're talking about.'

'That's all right. We'll find the place. Thank you. We'll see you soon.'

Margaret replaced the receiver and smiled triumphantly at her audience.

'There you are. Our troubles are over. We're to go to the office right away with all our belongings.'

'How are you proposing to get there?' asked Matron.

'By bus.' Margaret was improvising rapidly. 'Buses go everywhere in London, don't they? We'll have to go to a bank first, though, to get some English money.'

Matron chuckled with amusement. 'My goodness, you don't seem to worry about being strangers in a foreign city. Are you quite sure you'll be looked after properly when you get to that office?'

Margaret put her right hand behind her back and crossed her fingers. 'Absolutely sure. Would you please tell me where the nearest bank is?'

'There isn't one close by.' Matron took a deep breath. 'I can't allow you to go off on your own. You don't know where anything is and it wouldn't be safe.'

Margaret's shoulders drooped. It seemed that her plan would fail before they could even attempt to leave this place. Matron, however, had other ideas.

'I'll send someone with you. In the meantime, you had better get into those warm clothes. Make sure you don't leave anything behind in the rooms.'

As they mounted the stairs, Robert nudged Margaret.

'What was all that about Walkers? They

don't even know us.'

'Sh! I'll explain later. Just agree with everything I say.'

When they returned to the ground floor, warm and comfortable in the winter clothing, they found the caretaker of the hostel waiting for them.

'Mr Parkinson will drive you to that office,' said Matron. 'I can't allow you to go wandering off on buses by yourself. Now, are you sure everything has been arranged?'

'Absolutely sure,' said Margaret again. Her own arrangements were the only ones that mattered, she told herself, pushing aside a sense of guilt. 'Thank you very much for all your help. Give me the address of this place please, so that we can send the clothes back.'

Matron wrote the address and Margaret tucked the paper away in her handbag. 'Thank you.'

'You don't need to send the clothes, but I would appreciate a note to say that you have arrived safely at your destination. This has been an unusual turn of events, to say the least.'

'We will write, I promise,' said Margaret. 'Thank you again.'

The drive through the crowded streets aroused an excitement that had been missing during their journey yesterday. The largest town that the children had visited during the previous few years had been small in comparison with this huge city and they stared up at the massive buildings with awe. Their enthusiasm delighted Mr Parkinson and he took long detours to show off some of the more important sites.

'That's the Tower of London. Built by William the Conqueror. Lots of history there, of course. Kings beheaded and goodness knows what ... Now you see that name — The Royal Mint — that's nothing to do with sweets or mint sauce. A mint is where money is made.'

The bustling pavements, the strange black taxi cabs and the huge red buses all attracted the children's attention and even Margaret forgot her worries for the time being. They drove along the Embankment beside the River Thames, admiring the unexpected number of bridges, then entered a maze of narrower congested streets. Mr Parkinson announced that they were now in the commercial area, filled with business premises and bank headquarters. Margaret drew in her breath. If he insisted on coming into the office with them to make sure that proper arrangements had been made, he would find out that she had not been truthful.

'You'll have to hop out quickly when I

stop,' he said suddenly. 'As you can see, I won't be able to park around here. Make sure you all get out on the pavement side.'

A few minutes later, he pulled up behind a stationary bus and the children scrambled out of the car. He climbed out, too, gave a conciliatory wave in answer to the impatient tooting from another driver and hauled the suitcases out of the boot.

'The place you want is just around there,' he said, pointing to a nearby corner. 'Mind how you cross the road. You must go down to the traffic lights.'

'We'll be all right. Thank you very much,' said Margaret.

The others added their thanks and they all waved as the car drew away from the kerb and was quickly surrounded by traffic.

Robert picked up his suitcase, then changed his mind and set it down on the pavement again. 'Now tell us what's been happening.'

Margaret told them about the conversation she had overheard at the hostel.

'So far as adults are concerned, we are all under-aged and can't look after ourselves. Apparently there's a law that says if no adult is with us we should go to an orphanage or a State Home. But we don't want to be split up and put in their Homes. I spent ages trying to work out how we could get away from there.'

'So we're not really going to Walkers after all,' said Stephen.

'Yes, of course we are. I didn't want to tell lies if I could help it. Besides, that Matron might telephone to make sure we really did get there.'

'What happens after that?' asked Pauline fearfully.

'We'll get a train and go to Aunt Joan's house. She probably never got the cable and doesn't even know we're in England.' Margaret patted her little sister on the shoulder and pointed to a large sign, pretending to be totally sure of herself. 'Look, there's a big bank just along there. We'll get our money changed before we cross the road.'

They stopped short just inside the main door of the bank, overawed by the splendour of the building. Marble pillars rose to a ceiling decorated with multi-coloured frescoes, and a bronze statue of some dignitary stood in a commanding position on a stone plinth. A uniformed attendant went over to the children, thinking they had wandered into the wrong place by mistake, but he nodded when Margaret explained their errand.

'You need Foreign Exchange. Go down to the first teller along there.'

When Margaret laid her African money on

the counter the teller shook his head.

'I'm sorry,' he said firmly and with total lack of sympathy, 'I can't accept that currency. All assets have been frozen and no payments can be made for the present.'

The four children left the counter and gathered in a dejected group near the front door.

'Now what?' asked Stephen.

'We've got American money,' said Robert. 'It seems to be the only real money we have got. Why didn't you ask him to change that?'

'I don't think we should yet,' replied Margaret. 'We ought to keep it for emergencies.'

'This is an emergency, isn't it?'

Margaret sighed. 'We haven't got much, you know. We shouldn't spend it all on something like train tickets.'

'Well, we need money,' retorted Robert. 'How are we going to get some if we don't use that?'

'We'll ask the Walker Company.'

A startled silence followed her words. Pauline and Stephen were too confused to make any suggestions, while Robert felt completely baffled.

'The Walker Company?' he exclaimed at last. 'They don't even know us. We can't just go in and ask them for money.'

'We won't ask them to *give* it to us. We'll

ask them to lend us some. Or they might change our money for us, seeing as they have branches in all parts of Africa.'

Robert looked down at his feet. 'I don't think we ought to do anything like that. What would Mum and Dad say? It's like begging.'

'They would be pleased to know that we were using our initiative.' Margaret paused. 'It's either that — or go back to the hostel.'

'I don't want to go back there,' cried Pauline. 'I think it's a horrible place.'

'I don't want to go there either,' said Stephen. 'And I don't want to go to one of their beastly Homes. It'll be just like that place.'

'Well then . . . '

The prospect of returning to the drab hostel settled the question for Robert. 'All right,' he agreed reluctantly, picking up his suitcase once more. 'Let's try it and see what kind of reception we get. They can only say no.'

The receptionist at the Walker Engineering Company raised her eyebrows at the sight of four children straggling in by the main door, all carrying luggage. She gave a condescending smile, expecting them to make a quick retreat once they had taken stock of their surroundings, but the taller girl came directly towards the desk and the others followed close behind.

'We want to see the Manager, please.'

'I'm afraid the Manager is very busy just now,' said the receptionist. 'Can I help you?'

Margaret knew the woman would fob them off if she could. Their father always insisted on speaking to the headman whenever he visited a village on business, and she decided she must do the same now.

'We must speak to someone in authority,' she replied. 'The Walker Company arranged our transport here. We have just arrived from Africa.'

'I see.' The receptionist asked for their names, then excused herself and disappeared into an office behind her desk. Robert and Stephen wandered to a nearby wall to look at photographs of heavy mining equipment, while Pauline stared glumly at her feet and Margaret tried to compose a suitable speech.

When the receptionist returned she gestured towards a row of upholstered chairs.

'Mr Hogan will see you in a minute,' she said. 'Do sit down.'

Margaret suspected that they would be subjected to a long wait, but only a few minutes later they were led into a large room with dark panelled walls and a thick red carpet. They approached the immense desk near the window, where a stout middle-aged man sat watching them, and Margaret's courage began to falter. His expression

56

looked stern and she doubted that he would be generous.

'Now then, why did you want to see me?' he asked gruffly. 'We don't have any Barlows listed on our staff overseas.'

'Well, our father isn't exactly employed by you,' answered Margaret. 'But he buys a lot of your machinery, and goods are delivered by your supply plane.'

'I see. He's an agent. Well, what do you want here?'

Margaret's hands and knees began to tremble and she swallowed nervously. Only the threat of the family being separated prodded her into speaking again.

'We need some money at the moment,' she blurted.

'Money?' Hogan's eyebrows shot upwards and his face reddened. 'You want me to give you money?'

'Not give it,' corrected Margaret. 'We would like you to change some for us.'

She produced the African notes and he shook his head.

'Banks are not accepting that currency at present. They don't want any from neighbouring countries either.'

'We know. That's why we're in such a fix.' Margaret's eyes misted and she quickly blinked the tears away. 'We were sure you would help us. We only need a loan. We had to leave in such a rush, you see. Your pilots arranged everything for us.'

'Did they indeed?' Hogan wondered if the pilots had collected any fare, and whether it would be worth anything if they had.

'We have one of your firm's credit cards, but it's not valid in this country.' Margaret handed the card to him and he ran one hand through his hair before he leaned back and expelled air in an exasperated sigh.

'You certainly seem to have received excellent service. Is there anything else I ought to know?'

'It's just possible that the Children's Officer, or somebody like that, will telephone here to make sure we are all fixed up.' Margaret plunged on while he was boggling over that snippet of information. 'You see, we told them that your firm had made arrangements for us to come to England.'

'We're surely not expected to take responsibility for you now that you are here!' protested Hogan.

'No, of course not,' declared Robert firmly. As man of the family he ought to be giving his sister some active support. 'We only need some English money, nothing else. We have an aunt at Allingham, but we have to get there. If you can change some money for us we'll be able to buy tickets.'

Margaret laid her worthless currency on the desk. 'If you can't change it, perhaps you would lend us the money,' she suggested. 'You can keep this for security.'

A fine security that would be, thought Hogan. He hesitated for several moments then pushed his chair back from the desk.

'I can't see much difference between changing that and lending you some. But I suppose a few more pounds on top of all the property we have already lost over there won't do much harm. I'll give you the old exchange rate for it.'

He counted the notes quickly, then walked across to a wall safe concealed behind a large portrait and pulled out a black metal cash box. The children watched as he counted notes and picked up three silver coins.

'Here you are,' he said. 'Twenty-eight English pounds and five shillings. Be careful how you calculate. An English pound is worth nearly three of those notes. Two eighty-five is the nearest round figure.'

Their relief and gratitude made him unbend a little and he gazed at them with more sympathy. They were well-mannered, and they hadn't asked for much really. They stood in a row before his desk, looking extremely young and not as healthy as he thought they should. All of them were thin, with straight blond hair and fair complexions that had developed a slightly sallow tinge from years spent in a hot, humid climate. Their clothes were warm and sensible, but they looked as though they had been bought in a hurry by someone who had made a guess at their sizes. He had little contact with juveniles, but he could not help wondering how he would feel if he had children of his own and they were suddenly sent off to a foreign country alone. The little one had looked close to tears when they came in, but she was more perky now and the oldest two seemed sensible enough to cope with problems. If they had come this far safely, they should be able to find their way to their destination.

'Look, here's an extra ten pounds,' he said impulsively. 'You might find you need that for something important. If not, just treat yourselves and have some fun with it.'

Their effusive thanks embarrassed him and he lifted one hand to silence them. 'Don't mention it. Are you sure you don't need any more help?'

'Could you tell us where the railway station is?' asked Robert.

'Hm. For Allingham. That's north. You'll

have to go from Euston. Ask Miss Prince in the front office how to get to Euston Station. I'm afraid I don't use public transport myself.'

Miss Prince wrote instructions down for them and they left the building with the airy feeling that all was well at last. A bus with the right number on the front came along only four minutes after they had found the correct stop, and Robert took Pauline's suitcase from her before she mounted the back platform. Carrying two pieces of luggage up the stairs was more difficult than he had expected, but he persevered. Nothing must prevent them from climbing up to the top deck of a famous London bus.

The view from the upper deck was better than any of them had imagined, and they were all sorry when the conductor called to say they had reached Euston. A middle-aged man carried one of the suitcases down to hasten the children on their way, and directed them towards the station entrance. On the forecourt they met a heavy stream of newly arrived passengers, everybody seemingly in a great hurry. The children halted, feeling overwhelmed by the rush, but the crowd quickly dispersed and Margaret was able to find the ticket office without needing to ask for help.

'There is a direct train, but you'll have to wait a while,' said the ticket clerk. 'It leaves at two twenty-five from platform seven.'

'We could see more of London!' exclaimed Stephen. 'Let's go to Buckingham Palace.' He had regained his spirits and was eager to explore.

Margaret and Robert looked at each other thoughtfully, but the ticket clerk quashed that suggestion.

'You shouldn't go away. If you get stuck in traffic somewhere you'll miss your train.' He issued their tickets and pushed them across to Margaret, together with the change. 'Stay on the station, that's my advice. You'll be able to board the train at about quarter past two.'

'I'm sick of sitting around for hours just waiting,' complained Stephen as they left the counter. 'We did enough of that in those airports.'

'There's plenty to look at here,' said Margaret. 'And it's not much more than two hours. Let's find the right platform first and then watch some of the trains.'

They wandered about the station, intrigued by the automatic information boards, the slot machines and the sight of uniformed schoolchildren in a long crocodile being herded through one of the ticket barriers. When they found an escalator leading down to an underground region, they could not resist the temptation to ride up and down several times.

'Oh goody, this is exciting,' said Pauline. 'Do you know, I think I'm going to like England after all.'

5

'We're coming up to Allingham in a few minutes.' The ticket collector eyed the young passengers with some amusement. He had feared the worst when he first caught sight of the group hastening along the platform at Euston. With their mismatched clothing, high excitement and total lack of adult supervision, they threatened to be an unruly bunch. Much to his surprise, they had proved to be extremely well-spoken and well behaved. He had come through the train several times to keep a watchful eye on them, staying to listen to their comments on the passing scene. Everything had been new to them — the closely packed houses in long rows, the multitude of chimneys sending smoke into the air, and then the green meadows with frisky young lambs or sleek well-fed cows and the surprisingly short distances between towns.

'Make sure you don't leave anything behind,' he said now. 'I hope you enjoyed your trip.'

'We have enjoyed it very much. Thank you for your help,' said Margaret. 'Put your coats on, everybody, quick.'

They all left most of their buttons undone, too agitated to concentrate on such mundane matters when they were about to catch their first glimpse of Allingham. That town was to be their home for an unknown period of time. What would it be like, having to live there for weeks, possibly months?

'It's a big place, isn't it?' murmured Robert as they rode through the outskirts.

'Just look at all the television aerials!' exclaimed Stephen. 'Do you think Aunt Joan will have television?'

Nobody paid heed to any remarks or questions. The ticket collector looked around to check that they had gathered all their belongings, and when the train stopped he opened the carriage door for them. They lingered on the platform to watch the train leave and he gave them an answering wave of farewell.

'Now what?' said Stephen. 'How are we going to find the house? I hope we don't have to carry these bags much further. I'm worn out.'

'Let's take a taxi,' suggested Margaret. 'We've got that extra money and it feels as if we've spent a week or more asking how to get to places.'

'Suits me,' responded Robert.

They grew tense with excitement as their taxi drew away from the stand at the front of the station. At long last they were nearing the end of their journey. What was the first thing Aunt Joan would say when she saw them?

While Mr Parkinson had been talkative and eager to point out landmarks in London, this driver was silent, his expression sullen. He drove them through the town centre along a busy road lined with shops, then into a quiet residential area with well tended gardens and green roadside verges. He made a quick U-turn and drew up outside a large detached house, clicked his fingers impatiently when Margaret took longer than he expected to count out money for the fare, and drove away without wishing them goodbye.

The four children stood in a row before the wooden front gate, looking at their new home with a sense of awe. A wide driveway led to a huge black garage door with small frosted glass windows, and a narrower path continued from there past a high black fence to the front of the house. An arched porch sheltered the doorway, on the further side of which a large bay window looked out over the garden.

'It's like a hotel,' cried Pauline. 'Look, it's got an upstairs as well.'

'Yes, it's a big house,' agreed Margaret. 'Come on, let's go in. I can hardly believe we really are here at last.'

Stephen hurried ahead of the others and rapped loudly on the heavy wooden door, which was painted black with red trim. Almost immediately afterwards he noticed a white bell push and pressed that as well, but nobody answered and another spate of knocking brought no response.

'She's not in,' said Pauline unnecessarily.

Stephen banged again, then noticed the letter slot. He pushed it open and peered through.

'It's just empty in there. There's just a sort of passage and the bottom of a staircase.'

'Let me see.' Robert elbowed him aside and looked in. He could discern a floral patterned carpet that ran along the hall and continued up the stairs. 'It's fairly dark in there. It — er — looks a bit — er — well, it looks as if no one has been around lately. It looks kind of too tidy, if you know what I mean.'

Margaret lowered her suitcase with a groan of dismay and Pauline's lip began to quiver again.

'I thought we'd be all right once we got here,' she fretted.

Margaret remembered that she must remain calm and soothe the others. 'We are all right,' she said firmly. 'Don't worry. Aunt

Joan could be back any minute.'

'Look fine if she's gone to London to meet us,' muttered Robert.

'She might have gone away for the weekend,' said Stephen.

'This is the beginning of the week.'

'Well, a long weekend then. If she has gone away, that could be why she didn't know about us. What are we going to do?'

Robert hated the idea of standing about doing nothing. That would only add to the growing sense of helplessness. He looked at the narrow strips of decorative glass at either side of the solid wooden door, then walked back to the fence between the house and the garage. A large gate obviously gave access to the rear of the premises, but it was securely locked. The others could give him a leg-up and help him to climb over, but there was no telling what lay on the other side and getting back again could pose a problem. He gave up on that for the moment and turned his attention to the ground floor windows instead. The sturdy wooden frames had been painted black and red to match the front door. A wide expanse of glass filled the centre of the bay, but the nearest side held a casement window topped by a transom.

'We could break in easily enough.'

'Break in!' gasped Margaret. 'Don't be ridiculous.'

'Well, we can't stand out here all night. We'd freeze to death.'

'Aunt Joan might be back soon.'

'And she might not. I tell you, it doesn't look as if she's just gone out to the local shops.' Robert went back and peered through the slot again, craning to see a wider area. 'No. I don't reckon she'll be back soon.'

'We can't just break in. It's not our house.'

Robert shrugged and leaned against the side of the arch. 'So what do we do? Can you think of a better idea?'

Several moments passed as they stared first at the door and then at the darkening sky. A sharp wind was making itself felt and they longed to be indoors, safe from the oncoming night and the unaccustomed chill of the English climate. Margaret clenched her fists, willing herself not to break down and show her despair. Her worst fears had materialised. All afternoon she had been pushing away the dreaded thought that their aunt might not be here when they arrived, clinging to the hope that a missing cable was the only reason for Aunt Joan not coming to the airport. She had saved her family from the clutches of those officials in London, but perhaps that success had been in vain. Everything had depended upon Aunt Joan being at home. How was she to deal with the situation now? After all her efforts, they were likely to end up in Children's Homes anyway.

'I'm hungry,' Pauline complained.

'Me, too,' said Stephen. 'It must be long past tea-time and we didn't have a proper lunch. Aunt Joan would be here by now if she was coming.'

Robert could see that Margaret was weakening. If he sounded emphatic enough and persisted with his idea, he could persuade her that it was the best thing to do.

'I could break just the little window up there,' he said, pointing to the transom on his left. 'Stephen is small enough to squeeze through that and he could open the door for us from the inside.'

'It's a terrible thing to do, break someone's window.'

'I'll only knock out that small one. It's plain glass and I can mend it easily enough tomorrow. It won't be difficult to get glass in England.'

Margaret still hesitated and they all followed her gaze towards the large house opposite. It stood at the corner of a T-junction, slightly higher than their aunt's property, and a wide bay window faced the porch where they were clustered.

'There's people in there,' said Pauline. 'They'll be watching us.'

'It doesn't matter if anybody sees us do it,' argued Robert. 'We're not criminals. We're *supposed* to be living here now.'

'That's right,' agreed Stephen. 'Aunt Joan won't mind a little piece of glass being broken. She'd rather that, than have a lot of doctor's bills because we've been stuck out here in the cold. It might start raining again soon.'

Pauline gave a dramatic shiver as a stronger gust of wind shook the branches of some nearby trees. She thrust her hands deeper into her pockets and glared at the door again.

'It would be silly to come all this way and then not even get in,' she grumbled. 'We'll have to do something soon or people will start asking us what we're waiting for.'

'If they find out that we haven't got an adult with us, we'll be back in the same fix as before,' added Robert. 'And if it goes dark while we're still out here, we'll be in a real mess. It will be harder to do anything then. I don't care what you think. We'd better get in pretty soon.'

Margaret hovered indecisively on the edge of the porch step and then went back to the gate to look along the road. Two cars passed by, but nobody was walking along the footpath in either direction. The neighbouring houses were screened by tall privet hedges and only the windows of the building opposite stared at them accusingly. She took a deep breath and muttered a brief prayer.

'Please help me to do the right thing.'

No sign came in response and after another moment of uncertainty she went back to the others.

'Go on then. I suppose we'll have to do it. But be careful. Glass is very dangerous. And mind you only break that little one.'

Robert's first tentative strike had no effect. He looked for a larger stone and the resulting noise of smashing glass made them all look around in alarm.

'Go on,' urged Margaret. 'There's nobody coming. You'll have to get every bit of glass out before Stephen goes near it. Mind you don't cut yourself.'

She and Stephen hoisted Robert up and helped him to balance on the windowsill so that he could reach the broken window more easily, and he gave a cry of delight.

'I can open it! We don't need to worry about taking the glass out.'

He inserted his hand cautiously and lifted the locking bar, then jiggled it until the window began to move outwards. He pulled it towards himself as far as the hinges would allow, and considered what to do next.

'Not enough room for me,' he announced. 'But I reckon Stephen can get through.'

He jumped down and told Stephen to remove his coat, then he and Margaret lifted the younger boy and helped him to squirm into the gap. There was a groan of dismay when the edge of his trouser pocket caught on the window latch and held him fast, but he managed to ease it away and finally slithered through. He could not find a handhold anywhere and landed on the floor inside with a thump and a muffled protest.

'Are you all right?' called Margaret.

'Yeah.' Stephen picked himself up and rubbed his knees and his right arm.

'See if you can open the front door,' Robert directed. 'If not, come back and open the big window.'

Stephen walked through the room and into the hall. The front door was fastened only by a yale type lock at shoulder height, so that presented no difficulty.

'That wasn't hard, was it?' he boasted, inviting the others in with a flourish of both arms and a deep bow.

Margaret and Robert carried the luggage inside, closely followed by Pauline. She closed the door behind her, shutting out the daylight.

'Look for a light switch,' Margaret instructed. 'It'll be really dark soon.'

Stephen found a switch on the wall nearby, but when he pressed it down nothing happened.

'We'll have to turn the generator on,' he said.

'They don't have generators in England,' replied Robert. 'Don't you remember all those poles and wires in London? They've got them here, too, you know. Electricity comes from the town centre.'

'Do you think the bulb is bust?'

Margaret looked around the dim carpeted hall, her spirits sinking again as she realised what the reason for this problem might be.

'You'd better open the door again, Pauline. We have to be able to see what we're doing.'

Pauline reached up and fumbled with the lock, then pulled the door open. She was about to turn away when a movement outside caught her eye and she stiffened with alarm. A tall man in a navy-blue uniform and distinctive helmet was propping a bicycle against the gate post. He had opened the gate before she recovered sufficiently enough to warn the others.

'Margaret! Margaret!'

'What on earth's the matter?'

'There's a policeman coming up the front path!'

74

A dismayed silence followed her words and instinctively they all moved closer together.

'Someone must have seen us break in,' muttered Robert.

'Listen, whatever happens, we mustn't let him know we're here on our own,' said Margaret urgently. Memories of the discussion in the Matron's office were still preying on her mind. 'We wouldn't be allowed to stay.'

The policeman's arrival prevented any further discussion. He was so tall and broad he seemed to fill the porch and the interior of the house darkened as if the door had been closed again.

Robert stepped forward. 'Good evening,' he said with a touch of bravado.

'Good evening.' The policeman looked past him and saw three more children standing anxiously in the hall. Apart from the smaller boy they were all wearing outdoor clothes. 'Well, well. What are you all doing here?'

'We've come to stay with our aunt,' replied Margaret.

'Have you indeed?' The policeman stepped off the porch and looked at the small window, which was still wide open, then moved towards it. Robert followed and watched as the man switched on a torch. The beam instantly caught the glint of broken glass on the carpet inside the front room.

'I'm afraid I did that,' Robert admitted. 'Aunt Joan wasn't expecting us, you see, and we couldn't get in.'

Joan Wheatley was listed as the owner of the property, mused the officer. The boy had her first name correct.

'You'd better tell me all about it. Do you mind if I come inside?'

Robert went back to join the others and the policeman entered the hall. He looked at the cluster of frightened children, then at the suitcases near the foot of the stairs, all bearing airline baggage labels.

'That's our luggage,' said Margaret. 'We've just arrived.'

'You said you had come to stay with your aunt. How is it that she was not expecting you?'

Margaret explained about the outbreak of war and their hasty departure from home. 'I don't think Aunt Joan got our cable.'

'Have you got any proof that the person who owns this house is really your aunt, and that you have a right to be here?'

None of them spoke for a moment. The children looked doubtfully at each other and then Robert brightened.

'We've got a copy of the cable we sent.'

'I'm afraid that wouldn't do. Anybody

could send a cable.'

'I don't think there's anything else,' said Margaret glumly. 'We had to leave in such a hurry, you see. We've got our passports and birth certificates. But our names aren't the same as Aunt Joan's. Her name is Wheatley.' Her eyes brightened suddenly. 'Oh, I know! We've got a letter from Dad, giving Aunt Joan authority to withdraw money from his bank account.'

'That sounds more promising. Is it addressed to the bank?'

'No, it's in a blank envelope. I'm sure Aunt Joan won't mind if we open it.'

As Margaret lifted her shoulder bag off the floor the policeman looked along the hall.

'We could do with some light in here.'

'We were just wondering what to do about that when you came,' said Robert. 'The light's not working.'

'That's because the power has been turned off.'

'Could you help us to put it on please? We're used to a private generator, you see. We don't know how this works.'

'The main switch is probably under the stairs.' The policeman turned his torch on again and pointed to his right. 'There you are, you see. Behind that door there'll be a useful space that goes right under the stairs. I expect it's under there.' He showed them how to switch on the power and they all blinked at the sudden light that flooded the hall.

'That's better. Now let's look at this letter of yours.'

Margaret rummaged inside her bag, then tore open the thin white envelope and handed a folded page to him. He read the contents quickly and to her relief he nodded.

'Yes, that seems to be in order.' He smiled kindly at Pauline, who was keeping well in the background, and Stephen plucked up enough courage to ask a question.

'Did someone report us for breaking in?'

'No, when I arrived I was just making a routine check. Your aunt asked us to keep an eye on the house while she's away. That's why I had to make sure who you were.'

Margaret drew in her breath. 'Do you happen to know when she's coming back?'

'Not exactly. She left last week for South America. She said she expected to be away for about three months.'

'Three months!' gasped Margaret.

The policeman nodded. 'That's right. Obviously we can't get your aunt back, so that leaves us with another problem. Who's going to look after you for the next three months?'

Margaret stared at him in consternation,

not knowing how to answer, and Pauline raised one hand to her mouth, biting hard on a knuckle to prevent any sound from escaping. The threat of being taken away and placed in separate Children's Homes was looming larger than ever.

Stephen suddenly spoke up. 'Our big sister will look after us, of course.'

The policeman gave a strange backward jerk with his head, his relief clearly evident. 'Oh, you've got a big sister, have you?'

'Yes,' agreed Robert. 'She brought us all the way to England. She'll look after us. We don't need anybody else.'

'So you've got a big sister. That's good.' The policeman smiled, glad to hear that he could knock off promptly after all. Arranging for the family to be taken into care could have turned out to be a complicated business, especially at this time of the day. Council offices would be shut by now. 'I don't suppose your aunt will object to you all staying here, seeing as this situation is an emergency, but you'd better get your sister to tell the neighbours that you've moved in. Mrs Croft across the road will need to know. She's got a key, and she's supposed to look in every now and again to make sure everything is all right.'

He smiled again before departing, and

turned to wave as he retrieved his bicycle. Robert closed the door and patted Stephen on the back.

'Good for you, Stephen. I'm sure I wouldn't have thought of saying we had a big sister. I thought we were sunk.'

'We didn't tell him the truth,' said Margaret.

'Of course we did,' protested Stephen. 'You're my big sister, aren't you? You're Robert's big sister — and Pauline's. And you're looking after us.'

'But he didn't know you meant me. He thinks there is somebody else, someone older.'

'That's his fault, isn't it?' retorted Robert. 'We didn't tell any fibs. If he wanted to know more about our sister he should have asked.'

'Anyway, now we know what to say if any nosey-parkers come around here asking questions,' put in Stephen. 'As long as you keep quiet and let us say we have a big sister, nobody will try to send us away.'

Margaret was still wrestling with a guilty conscience, but Pauline said the one thing that was likely to change the subject.

'Let's explore.'

'Yes, let's,' urged Stephen. 'This is a really big house.'

They left their luggage where it was and

filed up the stairs, going first to the large room at the front.

'This must be Aunt Joan's room,' said Margaret. 'We won't use this one.'

Two other rooms held twin beds and looked exceptionally neat, while a fourth room at the back looked as if it were kept as a workroom and office. Margaret closed that door again and went back to check the beds in the adjoining room.

'They're not made up. We'll have to find the linen cupboard.'

There was a tiny room with a toilet, next to a large bathroom with a shower recess, a bath and a wash-basin. While the others were exclaiming over the decorative tiles and the etched design of fish around the edges of a huge mirror, Margaret opened a cupboard on the landing.

'I've found all the sheets and things,' she called.

'Don't start making beds right now,' yelled Stephen. 'I'm hungry. What are we going to have for tea?'

'We'll have to see if there's any food downstairs.'

They followed Margaret down to the hall and found that the rear door on the right led to a large kitchen with a fireplace and a well-scrubbed whitewood table. A huge old-fashioned dresser and a white enamelled cabinet stood opposite the window, beneath which they saw a white porcelain sink. The remaining space along the walls was taken up by cupboards and a gas stove.

'That's a refrigerator,' said Robert, pointing to the cabinet.

'It's not shut properly,' said Stephen, hurrying towards it. 'Oh, look, it's empty. Why's Aunt Joan left this piece of wood sticking out?'

'Obviously, it has to stay open,' replied Margaret. 'Leave it exactly as it was.'

She opened an inner door leading to a walk-in larder, and exclaimed with delight at the sight of so many shelves packed with tins, jars and packets.

'I can make a meal in no time,' she declared. 'There's soup and beans. Look, cracker biscuits. They'll do instead of bread.'

Robert went to inspect the cooker and turned one of the taps. As he half expected, there was no response.

'I'll go out and switch the gas on.' He went through the adjoining scullery and unbolted the back door to go outside, but moments later he returned, frowning and scratching his head. 'There's another toilet out there. But there's no gas tank.'

'I'll find it,' declared Stephen, but he came

back looking nonplussed. 'He's right. There's no tank.'

Margaret stared at them in bewilderment, then she suddenly laughed. 'I'd forgotten,' she chuckled. 'People don't have gas tanks in England. It's like the electricity. The power comes from a big tank in town. It's the same with the water.'

Stephen hurriedly turned on the nearest tap and they watched a few drops of water dribble into the sink.

'Everything has been turned off,' he said. 'How do we turn it all back on again?'

'I don't know,' admitted Margaret. 'But there must be switches somewhere. We'll have to ask someone to help. We don't know what to look for, and we can't go twiddling just any knobs in case we do something dangerous.'

Robert hesitated, unwilling to admit defeat, but then he nodded.

'I'll ask the people across the road. That policeman said we ought to tell them we're here, anyway.'

'I'll come with you,' said Stephen.

Robert nodded thankfully. He was doing his best to appear manly and full of confidence, but they knew nobody here and any scrap of support was welcome. When they crossed the road they found that they had to turn the corner to reach the front of the other house. A tall, plump middle-aged woman answered their knock. She raised her eyebrows at the sight of two strange young boys on her doorstep, but she gave them an encouraging smile and Robert launched into a brief explanation about how they came to be there. Neither he nor Stephen could remember the name the policeman had told them, but Mrs Croft quickly introduced herself.

'Goodness gracious me,' she exclaimed. 'What a shame. To think you have come all this way, only to find an empty house! You only missed your aunt by a couple of days, you know. Thank goodness you came to tell me you were here. I'd have had a fit otherwise when I saw the lights on.' She stepped out to the garden path so that she could see the house across the main road. 'Ah, yes. If we'd been in the dining-room we would have seen that light. We'd have sent for the police if you hadn't come to tell us you were there.'

'It was a policeman who switched the lights on for us,' said Stephen.

'So the police know you're here. That's good.' Mrs Croft rubbed her arms to warm them and moved back to the shelter of the doorway. 'It will take you a while to get yourselves organised, I expect. Do you need anything right now?'

'Actually, we need some help,' said Robert. 'The water and the gas have been turned off and we don't know how to turn them on again.'

'Oh dear. I'd better ask my husband to go across with you.'

Les Croft was a slight man, barely an inch taller than his wife. He came out without his jacket, and noticed the chill in the other house as soon as they entered.

'You'll have to put a radiator on,' he said. 'You won't want to start making a proper fire just now, but it's rather cold in here and I don't suppose you're used to our English weather.'

Pauline crept part way down the stairs to see the newcomer, but when he looked up at her she was overcome by shyness and fled back to the landing. Croft smiled to himself and led the way to the kitchen. He found an electric heater in the bottom of a tall cupboard and showed the boys how to plug it in and operate the controls.

'Be careful around this,' he warned. 'You'd better not move it away from the hearth here. Don't stand too close to it, and always make sure it's switched off before you go out. Now let's see about the gas and the water.'

He had brought a large flashlight with him and he showed the boys where the stopcock was and how to turn on the water supply, followed by the gas.

'Simple when you know how,' he remarked. 'Now then, is there anything else I can do?'

'No thank you,' replied Robert. 'Thank you very much for your help.'

Croft paused as they went through the kitchen again. 'You won't have had a meal yet. Shall I ask my wife to rustle something up?'

'No, thank you, we'll be all right,' answered Robert quickly. 'There's lots of food here. We're going to have soup and stuff like that tonight. Now the gas is working it won't take long to get things ready. And we'll be going to bed pretty soon.'

'I see.' Croft frowned as a sudden thought occurred to him. 'How did you get in?'

'I had to break a window,' said Robert. 'I'll fix it up tomorrow.'

'You'd better show me. We shouldn't leave anything insecure.'

Croft nodded thoughtfully when they took him to the front room. 'I'd better cover that hole. I've got some clear stuff at home, like perspex. It'll keep the draught out, and make the place safer.'

He spread his fingers and made a quick estimate of the window's dimensions, then went home again to collect the material. The boys watched with admiration as he attached it neatly to the frame.

'You're good at that sort of thing,' said Robert. 'Is that what your job is?'

'Not really, but I've done a lot of home repairs. If you ever need any help, just let me know. By the way, you'd better have this key. You don't want to have to break in again.' Croft felt in his pocket and handed a key ring to Robert. It had a leather tag and held only a single yale type key. 'If you can't find any others, we'd better get that one copied. We should hold a spare at our place in case you lock yourselves out by mistake.'

'Thank you,' said Robert gratefully. It sounded as though their neighbour was going to be a helpful person to know.

'I noticed a little girl on the stairs. Who's looking after you while your aunt's away?'

'Our big sister. She'll be upstairs right now.'

'She's making beds,' added Stephen.

'Oh, I see. Well, we won't interrupt the good work then. I expect you'll all be ready for an early night tonight, after that long journey.'

'Yes, we're just going to have supper and go to bed,' agreed Robert.

Margaret and Pauline came downstairs as soon as the front door had closed behind their neighbour, and they all hurried into the kitchen to warm themselves in front of the radiator. The rosy glow helped to increase the sense of victory, and Margaret's smile widened into a self-satisfied grin. After an unpromising start and an unnerving visit from the policeman, they had attained success. They had reached Aunt Joan's house safely and they were together.

More importantly, she was in complete charge.

6

It was after eight o'clock before the children began to stir the next morning. Stephen called out to Pauline, suggesting they start to explore their new surroundings, but she preferred to stay where she was, warm and snug. Margaret gave no sign that she was awake, but when silence fell again she turned onto her back and lay staring up at the ceiling, fretting about their dilemma. The glow of triumph had vanished, and gloom crept over her now as she considered her position as head of the family. As soon as they reached England she was supposed to hand over responsibility for them all, but now it seemed that her task had only just begun. The more she thought about likely consequences, the more alarming the future seemed to be. Problems were sure to crop up, and none would be easy to solve. She began to consider the kind of tasks that ought to be tackled on the first day, her despondency deepening as the mental list grew longer.

Some deep-seated courage suddenly came to her aid and she admonished herself. This was not a time for cowardice. She must stop merely thinking about their situation and start to do something worthwhile. Besides, any kind of action would be better than brooding.

'Come on, everybody,' she called, sitting upright and using what the others always referred to as her 'schoolmarm voice'. 'You've all got to get up. If you don't come down for breakfast as soon as I call, you won't get any.'

She plugged in the small electric heater in the kitchen and the others huddled around it while she read the directions on a packet from the larder and then made porridge. As they ate, she began to reveal her plans for the day.

'One of the first things we have to do is go to the bank. And I expect the Town Hall will be the best place to find out about schools and things like that.'

Stephen lifted his head, shocked into full attention. 'School?'

'That's right,' answered Margaret.

'You can't mean it. You're not expecting us to go to school,' complained Pauline. 'Not here.'

'Yes. Definitely.' Margaret gave her sister a severe look, determined to prove that she was in control and was going to remain so. 'You went to school every day at home. Surely you knew you would have to go while you were in England.'

Pauline stared at her, her face creasing with fright. 'I don't want to go to a strange school,' she wavered. 'I'll be scared. You can teach me at home.'

Margaret shook her head. 'I wouldn't be allowed to. All children have to go to school in England. It's the law. I know that much.'

'Let's wait until Aunt Joan gets back,' suggested Stephen. 'She can fix everything like that.'

'Aunt Joan won't be back for three months,' Robert reminded him. 'We can't wait that long. We'll be reported, and then we'll be taken away and put in Children's Homes.'

'That's right,' said Margaret. 'In this country, every child has to go to school every day. They even employ people to catch those who skip classes. So we've got to be careful. If we want to stay together and look after ourselves, we'll have to do everything just as though Aunt Joan were here looking after us. We mustn't give anybody any excuse to come snooping around.'

Her warning had the desired effect and the younger ones decided not to raise any more objections.

'There's a bus that goes past this house,' said Margaret. 'I expect it will go near to the Town Hall. That should be in the centre of town. We'll start off there. They should be able to tell us where all the important places are, and anything else we need to know. And then before we come back, we'll have to get fresh milk and eggs and things like that.'

She gathered up the empty plates and Robert carried their cups to the sink.

'Let's leave the washing up until we get back,' he suggested.

Margaret looked at the pile of dirty dishes from their meal the previous evening and felt tempted to leave everything until later, but good sense prevailed.

'No. We've just agreed to do everything as though Aunt Joan were here, and if we don't start off properly we'll never keep things straight. We must wash up after every meal, and we're not going out this morning until all the beds are made and all clothes are put away. So, you others, go up now and make sure everything is tidy.'

When they left the house they turned in the direction of the town, and found a bus-stop about seventy yards along the road. Only six minutes later a bus came along, and Stephen gleefully led the way to the upper deck. Pauline sat beside him on the front seat, her qualms temporarily forgotten in the excitement of the journey.

'It's lovely up here, isn't it?' she cried. 'I

wish we had buses like this at home.'

They soon realised that the district where their aunt lived was far more modern than other parts of town. As they neared the centre of Allingham the streets grew narrower and the houses were clearly much smaller, the majority tightly packed in terraces with the front doors opening directly onto the street.

'I'm glad we've got such a big house and a garden,' said Robert. 'I wouldn't want to be staying around here.'

'It must be a very old town,' answered Margaret. 'But you're right. We're lucky to have such a nice house and so much space.'

The conductor called the children down when they neared the Town Hall, and an employee in the information office there gave them a bus timetable and a street plan of Allingham. He also directed them to the Education Department around the corner.

'We'll go there first, seeing as we are so close,' said Margaret firmly.

The clerk in the education office frowned when four unaccompanied children entered. Margaret quickly explained the reason for their unexpected journey to England, and said she believed that her younger siblings would be obliged to attend school.

'Yes, that's right. I expect you will be here for quite some time, so school will be obligatory.' The man pushed his chair back and drummed his fingers on the desk, clearly irritated. 'Where are your parents? Why aren't they here with you?'

'They couldn't leave Africa. Our big sister is looking after us,' answered Robert hurriedly.

'I see. You'll have to give her some forms to fill in.' The man smiled at Stephen and Pauline in a belated attempt to make them feel at ease. 'So you are nine, young man, and you are seven, young lady. You will go to the same school. There's one quite close to where you're living.' He drew a red circle on a small map and turned his attention to Robert. 'Let me see now . . . How old are you?'

Robert drew himself up proudly. 'I'm fourteen.'

'We have to find a school for you as well.'

'Not for me!' protested Robert. 'I've already had my birthday and I've left school really. I was only helping out till the end of term.'

The man shook his head. 'I'm sorry. The school leaving age is fifteen here.'

Robert cast a despairing glance at Margaret. 'I shouldn't have to go to school. I should be starting a job.'

'We'll have to abide by the law,' answered Margaret, and the man nodded.

'That's right. Now then, let's see which one would be the best to suit you, young man. Have you done any classical studies?'

They all stared at him in bewilderment and he shrugged. 'No Latin, no Ancient Greek history? Ah, well . . . how about algebra? Geometry?'

'Measurements and angles and so on,' Margaret prompted.

'Oh, yes, I can measure and build things,' said Robert.

The man held back a sigh. This family looked extremely odd, and it was surprising that neither their aunt nor their sister had thought it necessary to come with them. The children's education had probably been rudimentary at best, and this boy's standard would be well below par.

'Allingham Modern is the one for you. They do more practical work there, and you can leave at fifteen. It's a new school, on the east side of town. You'll like it.' He drew another red circle, then wrote on three forms and handed them to Margaret, together with the map.

'Tell your sister to fill those forms in. As soon as she's done that she can make appointments to see the Principals. All three should be able to start next Monday. Tell your sister not to worry about uniform for young

Robert to begin with.'

'Uniform?' faltered Margaret.

'All the boys wear grey trousers, grey pullovers and blue shirts.' The man's eyes flickered over the group again, noting the ill-fitting clothes and the incongruous mix of overcoats worn with sandals. 'Don't worry about that for the moment. Obviously there will be a lot of adjustments to be made, and uniform won't be at the head of the list. Still, if the Principal insists on him wearing it, you can ask the Welfare Department to help out with the cost.'

'That won't be necessary,' said Margaret proudly. 'Our parents have a bank account in England. We shall have to buy some new clothes, anyway, to return these we borrowed, so we might as well get the right colour for Robert.'

'I see. Good. Well, I hope you all settle down very well and that you don't find our English climate too cold for you.'

Margaret folded the papers and placed them carefully in her shoulder bag, then she thanked him for the information and they filed out to the street.

'School!' grumbled Robert as soon as they were outdoors. 'I'm supposed to be the man of the family. It's not fair. If I was at home they couldn't force me to go.'

'We wouldn't have any of this trouble if we were at home.' Pauline's eyes filled with tears and Margaret put an arm around her shoulders.

'It won't be for long. You'll probably enjoy your new school once you've got started, and just think of all the new things we can do while we're in England. We can do lots of exciting things.'

'Yes, just look at those shops over there!' shouted Stephen. 'Come on, let's go and look at all those fantastic toys.'

They crossed the road and the two younger children exclaimed in wonder at the display of colourful models and toys, but Robert soon noticed that Margaret was looking into the neighbouring shop window and the expression on her face was one of dismay.

'What's the matter?' he asked.

'Just look at the price of shoes.' Margaret pointed to a pair that she thought would fit Pauline. 'Look, three pounds for those, and three pounds ten shillings for those others. One English pound is just about three of our bukas.'

'Hm. They do seem a bit expensive. If we want to buy some we might have to look for a cheaper shop.'

'We'll have to buy some,' responded Margaret. 'We'll need at least one pair each.

We can't walk around in rain wearing sandals. My feet are cold enough now, when the weather's dry. I hope there's plenty of money in Dad's account.'

'There's sure to be.'

'Well, before we do anything else we'd better go to the bank. Then we can start looking for some of the things we need.'

She pulled out the map that she had received at the Town Hall and they searched together for the position of the bank.

'There it is,' said Robert, pointing to a black dot. 'Number fifteen is the one we want.'

Margaret turned the map around to make sure they headed in the right direction, and called the others away from the toyshop window. They cut diagonally across the town square and into a crooked narrow street, Margaret noting that the library was conveniently located in an ornate building on a nearby corner. She led the way to the foreign currency counter in the bank and changed the American dollars, but she received only five pounds and a few shillings.

'We'll need more than that before we can start shopping,' she said. 'We'll have to withdraw some from the account.'

The teller directed them to a queue further along, and when their turn came Margaret presented the letter of authority.

'I want to withdraw twenty pounds, please,' she said.

The young female teller had never dealt with such a request. She gave a puzzled frown as she stared at the letter and the form attached to the back of it, and decided she needed advice.

'Just a minute,' she said. She walked to a desk behind the counter and spoke softly to a man who was sitting there. He looked up at the group of youngsters as he listened, then he rose to his feet and strode towards them.

'There seems to be a little misunderstanding here,' he said. 'Would you please tell me exactly what it is that you want to do?'

Margaret pointed to the letter in his hand. 'Our father has an account here and we want to withdraw twenty pounds,' she explained.

He quickly read the letter again. 'But you are not Miss Joan Wheatley,' he pointed out.

'No, she's our aunt.'

'Well, Miss Wheatley will have to come here herself. She is the only person who can make withdrawals from this account.'

'She's gone abroad,' said Robert. 'She won't be back for three months.'

'In that case, you'll have to send a cable to your father and ask him to send authority for someone else to make withdrawals from his account.'

Margaret sighed. 'We can't do that. There's a war on, and the last we heard all communications had been cut.'

'Hm. You are in a pickle, aren't you?'

Margaret nodded miserably. 'Can't you help us out, please? Dad didn't know Aunt Joan was away when he wrote that. Everything happened in such a rush.'

The man shook his head and pushed the letter back across the counter. 'I'm sorry. That authority is made out in Miss Wheatley's name, so she is the only person who can access the account. We know Miss Wheatley, and there would be a matching record of that authority here, but we can't let complete strangers come in and start using other people's accounts.'

'We can prove who we are,' exclaimed Margaret. 'We've got our passports here with us, and our birth certificates. Our father . . .'

'I'm sorry,' the man interrupted. 'Your identity doesn't matter in the least. The only person who has authority to withdraw money is Miss Wheatley. The regulations are made to protect people's money, you must understand that.' He thought for a moment and then continued, 'Supposing you had lost that letter on the way here and someone else tried to use it. You would have thought we were very stupid if we allowed that person to have the money.'

'Yes,' agreed Margaret. 'I see what you mean.'

Her eyes watered as she thought of the small amount of cash they had. They needed so many things, yet they could afford so little. Unless they obtained some money soon she would stand no chance of keeping the family together and independent.

The man leaned forward, realising that he must show some kindness and understanding. 'Don't take it too much to heart. Look, I assume you're staying with other relatives in the meantime. If they're short of money, they should go to the Welfare Department. That Department is there to deal with such problems, and they will help out with everything until Miss Wheatley gets back.'

Margaret mumbled thanks and led the way back to the street.

'Aren't we going to get any money at all?' enquired Pauline as they gathered in a small group at the corner.

'Shush!' said Robert sharply. 'Just stand still for a minute and keep quiet while we think.'

Stephen opened his mouth to express his opinion, but quickly thought better of it and remained silent.

'Well?' asked Robert after a long pause.

'Everybody wants to send us to the Welfare Department,' Margaret exploded angrily. 'We can't go anywhere near there. They are the people we've been trying to keep away from. They're the ones who'll take us away. As soon as they find out we have no adults with us, they'll pounce.'

'That's probably what will happen in the end,' murmured Robert. 'How much money have we got? About thirty English pounds altogether? That won't last long between four of us.'

Margaret stared into the distance, biting her lower lip. She had no idea how they might survive without help, but a glimpse of Pauline's woebegone face forced her to rally.

'We'll go back to the house,' she announced. 'We can't make proper plans while we're standing here. It will be warmer in the house and we need time to think.' She produced a smile and gave Pauline a light hug. 'Don't look so worried. We're not absolutely poverty stricken, you know. We've got a larder full of food, and thirty pounds will buy a lot if we're careful.'

They found their way to the correct bus-stop and returned to their aunt's house in a subdued and gloomy mood.

'How are we going to keep those two occupied for a while?' asked Margaret as she watched the younger children scurry ahead along the garden path.

'Television,' answered Robert promptly.

'We don't know how it works.'

'It should be simple enough. It's electric, isn't it? It must be like switching on anything else. All I have to do is make sure it's plugged in, then try all the dials and buttons — like a radio set or something.'

'Mind you don't break it.'

'Trust me — I'm Mr Fix-it, remember. It can't be that hard. But if I can't do it, I'll go across and ask Mrs Croft to help.'

'We don't want either of them coming in poking around all the time. Not if we want to stay independent.'

Robert laid his hand gently on her shoulder. 'It will be all right. Don't worry. We'll work things out.'

His confidence in his own expertise proved to be correct and he managed to obtain a clear picture on the television screen within a few moments. Pauline and Stephen settled down to watch a children's educational programme, their current concerns swept aside by the thrill of the new experience. The older pair went into the kitchen and Margaret examined the papers she had received that morning.

'I think we're beaten,' she said regretfully.

'If you three don't go to school we'll be reported. But to get to school, an adult has to sign these forms and go for an interview.'

'Let's see.' Robert made a grab for one of the forms and read the instructions. 'It doesn't say anything about adults. Look, parent or guardian. You're our guardian. You sign them.'

'That wouldn't be honest.'

'Of course it would. You're our guardian. Mum and Dad put you in charge.' Robert tipped his chair back and studied her thoughtfully. 'If we get into school, what then?'

'I'll have to get a job. We need money.'

'Right.' Robert let the chair legs down with a crash. 'Don't worry, we'll manage. Come on, Margaret. There's a telephone in the hall. You'd better call those schools right now and get the interviews fixed up.'

The directory was conveniently placed on a ledge below the telephone and Margaret wrote down the numbers she needed. She called the junior school first and the secretary made an appointment for ten o'clock the following morning. The headmaster of the senior school spoke to her personally and he also suggested the next morning for an interview, but when Margaret explained that she had another appointment he agreed to

104

see her in the afternoon.

'There you are,' said Robert as she replaced the receiver. 'That wasn't difficult, was it?'

'They won't be so pleased when they meet me tomorrow,' replied Margaret dubiously.

'You're our guardian. They can't argue about that. Now let's find out how we get to those schools.'

'You can do that while I find something for lunch. I know there's rice in there, and some tins of meat.'

Margaret was struggling with a tin opener when Robert brought the map over to her.

'That school is a long way off,' he said.

'Which one? Yours?'

'Yes.' Robert pointed to the map. 'Look, we're about here. I'd have to go right down this road to there, then turn up that way and then down there.'

Margaret stared at the red circle and then searched for a shorter route, but there was no escaping the fact that Robert would have a long distance to travel.

'We'll have to find out about buses,' she said at last. 'You couldn't possibly walk all that way every day. It must be two miles at least, probably more.'

'Bus fares cost money.'

'You needn't remind me. Everything I think of costs money,' sighed Margaret.

'Perhaps they'll let me change to a different school. There must be one nearer than that.'

'Yes, where you're supposed to know Latin and stuff like that. Besides, if we say we can't afford the bus fares . . . '

'Don't say it.'

Margaret picked up the tin opener again, then gave up and dropped it onto the table. 'I can't even open a tin. How could I ever believe that we'd manage by ourselves?' She turned to face Robert, fighting back tears, and took a deep breath. 'Perhaps we ought to do the right thing and go to the Welfare Department now, before we get in too much of a mess. The Children's Homes won't be anything like that place where we stayed in London. It will only be for a few weeks, anyway. It won't be permanent.'

'Just imagine Pauline going to a strange place without you. It's bad enough sending her to a new school, and Stephen will be going to the same one.'

'I know. But if we can't manage . . . '

Robert picked up the tin opener and examined it. 'Look, that has to be the cutting edge. And that little wheel will have to run on the tin somehow. Let's try it again.'

Margaret pushed the tin towards him and he experimented with the gadget.

'There you are!' he exclaimed suddenly.

'Look, the wheel goes on the side, not the top.' He turned the handle of the opener triumphantly, and when the lid came smoothly away from the tin he held it out to her. 'There you are, you see. I told you I was Mr Fix-it.'

'Clever, aren't you?'

'You're not so bad yourself in some ways. Look, Margaret, if we help each other we'll get by. Between us we'll manage.'

She smiled, pretending to regain her confidence. 'We'll do our best. Those interviews tomorrow might put an end to it all, but if we get through them successfully it will be a good sign. Once I've got a job we won't have to worry any more about money.'

7

After lunch, Stephen and Pauline consented to help with the washing up, but their hopes of watching television again immediately afterwards were soon dashed. Margaret shook her head, impervious to their pleas.

'Looking at that too much could be bad for your eyesight. Besides, we have more important things to do.'

'Like what?' demanded Pauline.

'For a start, we ought to look for some spare keys. And we have to find out where everything is kept, like brooms and mops and so on.' Margaret had already decided that her own first task must be to check the larder and try to estimate how long the stock of food was likely to last. They had already used a fair amount of rice, oats and dried milk.

Stephen and Pauline were glad of an excuse to poke about in drawers and cupboards, but their enthusiasm did not last and after a few minutes they sidled outside to explore the garden. They rushed back into the kitchen with a whoop of glee, just after Robert had discovered two bunches of keys under a pile of tea towels in a kitchen drawer.

'We've found two bikes,' shouted Stephen. 'In the shed in the garden. You can see them through the window.'

'Let's get them out.' Pauline jigged up and down excitedly. 'I've never been on a bike and I'm dying to try it.'

'Two bikes!' exclaimed Robert. 'Isn't that a bit of luck? Now I can ride to school and save all those bus fares.'

'But they're not ours,' Margaret demurred. 'And none of us can ride a bike properly. We might damage them.'

'They're old!' cried Stephen. 'I bet they haven't been used for years and years. Aunt Joan wouldn't mind if we used them.'

'We could buy her a new one when she gets back,' said Robert. 'When we can use Dad's account we'll have lots of money.'

'Have you found any keys?' asked Pauline. 'The shed's locked.'

Robert held up the two bunches and they all went out to watch him tackle the lock on the shed.

'Easy!' he boasted. 'It has to be this long thin key.'

One bicycle had a crossbar, while the other was a lady's model, and both were strung to the roof of the shed with ropes. As Stephen had said, neither looked as though they had been ridden for years. The frames were encrusted with dirt and all the chrome fittings were scarred by rust.

'Aunt Joan will be pleased to see them cleaned up,' declared Robert. 'I hope there's some oil somewhere. They'll need oiling.'

'I hope you don't hurt yourself,' responded Margaret. 'You'll have to practise riding in the garden. Don't you dare go near the road.'

'I tried a bike on holiday last year, remember,' said Robert. 'It's not that difficult. Even little kids can ride bikes.'

Margaret returned to the kitchen, determined to continue with the project she had set for herself, but the others devoted all their attention to the bicycles. Robert soon found everything he needed to start renovations, and he quickly commandeered the man's machine for himself.

'You two clean that other one properly,' he instructed.

When Margaret looked out to check their behaviour she realised that the new activity would keep them occupied for a considerable length of time, so she took the opportunity to walk to a shop she had spied from the top of the bus that morning.

'I would like a local newspaper please.'

'Today's edition isn't out yet,' said the newsagent. 'I can let you have a spare one from yesterday if you like.'

'Thank you. Yes, I will take that.'

'On the house,' he said, waving aside the shilling she offered. 'Come back after half past four if you still want today's.'

Margaret gasped with shock when she caught sight of the headline and photograph on the front page. She folded the newspaper quickly and hurried out of the shop, forgetting her parents' insistence that she must always be courteous when departing. All she wanted to do was race back to the house where she could read the news in private. Her hands were shaking so much she had to lay the paper down on the kitchen table, and she moaned with despair at the horror that was revealed. Her own problems had overwhelmed any thoughts of the situation they had left behind, but now she saw that the fighting had developed into a maelstrom of cruelty and savage revenge. Whole villages had been ransacked and burned, old men, women and even babies hacked to death with axes and machetes.

Robert came into the house while she was still staring down at the front page, trying to decipher words blurred by tears. At the sound of the door opening, she stiffened with alarm and hastily turned the page.

111

Robert came to a sudden halt, his triumphant announcement squelched. 'What's the matter?' he asked.

'Nothing much.' Margaret turned away and tried to wipe her eyes surreptitiously. 'I went out to get a paper. For the advertisements.'

'You're not fooling me. What's happened?'

Margaret drew a deep breath, then met his gaze. It was useless trying to withhold the information, she decided. Even if she hid the newspaper, he was sure to see one before long.

'It's Gnujeemia,' she said, turning the page back to reveal the dreadful truth. 'It's just terrible what's happening over there.'

Robert read the first few paragraphs, his expression strained and anxious. 'What about our village? Does it say anything about Jambuki?'

Margaret shook her head. 'I don't think so. I couldn't read it all — it went all blurry — but it looks as if they haven't gone up past the port.' She looked around before she continued, to make sure the younger children had not followed him indoors. 'The North is fighting back much harder than anyone expected. They've organised an army and got supplies of arms from somewhere.'

'So they might have been planning something after all,' murmured Robert. 'The

112

Southerners said there was a plot. They said the North intended to invade and take over the whole country.'

'I don't suppose it matters now which side started it,' said Margaret. 'But we mustn't let the others see this.'

'No. Let me have these pages. I'll tuck them away under my pillow or somewhere.'

Robert went upstairs and read the first part of the account again, then folded the pages and hid them under his mattress, determined to read them thoroughly when he was alone. He returned to the kitchen to find Margaret looking more dejected than ever.

'No likely jobs?' he guessed.

Margaret gave a deep sigh and jabbed her finger onto the list of advertisements. 'We couldn't possibly live on my wages. Just look. Junior, two pounds a week. School leaver, two pounds, five shillings. It would take weeks just to earn enough to buy shoes, and we need heaps of other things.'

'You're not a junior, or a school leaver. You've been to work before.'

'Only in our village, not in a big town like this. Besides, I think it's your age they go by.'

'Who's to know? Tell them you're eighteen or twenty or something.'

'I mustn't try to get a job by telling lies.' Margaret glanced at the printed columns again. 'If only I didn't look so young. It would be good if I could apply for a senior job and just not tell them my age. You're not supposed to ask a lady how old she is.'

Robert eyed her pale, thin face. Her hair was parted in the centre and was held back over each ear by a tortoiseshell hair slide.

'You do look young,' he agreed. 'I suppose we ought to do something about that before we go to those schools tomorrow.'

'I can't look older just by wishing.'

'No, but you could do something about it.' Robert paused to consider a thought that had occurred to him while he was oiling the bicycles. 'Look at film stars. They can start off looking young and then get older and older as the film goes on. It's all done with make-up.'

'But I haven't got any make-up, and we can't afford to buy any.'

'I bet Aunt Joan has lots of it in her room. She wouldn't mind if you used it. After all, it's urgent, and we could always . . . '

'Buy her some more when she gets back,' finished Margaret with a little chuckle. 'You're always saying that.' She hesitated a moment longer then gave a little shrug. 'You're right, I suppose. I'll have to do something. Let's try it and see how it looks.'

Robert peeped outside to see if Pauline and Stephen were still fully occupied and saw they were already heading back to the house, bored with their cleaning tasks. He switched on the television for them and beckoned to Margaret.

'Come on, let's try the make-up. They won't interrupt.'

Lipsticks, eyebrow pencils and various pots, bottles and tubes were all neatly arranged in a special partitioned tray in the top right hand drawer of their aunt's dressing-table. Margaret sat down on the padded stool and stared at the collection.

'It seems awful, coming into someone's bedroom and using their personal things without asking,' she muttered guiltily.

'Well, this is an emergency, so get on with it,' urged Robert. He picked up one of the larger containers and read the label. 'Vanishing cream. What's that? They surely don't expect you to vanish.'

Margaret shrugged, not bothering to respond. She had never used anything but sun cream for her complexion, but she had watched hcr mother getting ready for special occasions on their rare visits to the city. She found some moisturiser and smeared it sparingly over her face, then applied liquid foundation from a small bottle.

'That's terrible,' exclaimed Robert. 'What an awful colour! Here, is that what vanishing cream is for? To get it off?'

Margaret stared into the mirror, willing herself to remain strong and not give way to tears. She needed a much lighter shade, she realised, but if she were lucky there would be something suitable. She had never expected to find such a large array of cosmetics in one person's drawer.

'Cold cream gets stuff off,' she said. 'Look, there's a big pot on the top here.'

She tried three foundations before finding one that was more satisfactory. A light touch of rouge made her look healthier, and lipstick was easy to apply. However, she spoiled the effect when she added mascara and then tried an eyebrow pencil.

'That's no good. It looks better without that,' she murmured, reaching for the cold cream again.

'You'll just have to keep practising, that's all,' advised Robert. 'Have another go.'

A sudden shriek and a plaintive yell from downstairs intervened.

'Margaret! Come quick! Robert! Quick!'

Margaret dropped the wad of cotton wool and followed Robert in a rush down the stairs.

'What's the matter?'

'Look, quick! On the television!' shouted Stephen.

They dashed into the front room and stopped short at their first glimpse of the scene displayed on the screen. Through billows of smoke they could discern men running from buildings, spraying the road with bullets from machine guns. Suddenly a missile hurtled through the air and a building exploded in a mass of flames and debris.

'It's Gnujeemia,' whispered Pauline fearfully.

Margaret stared at the film, knowing she should turn the set off, but somehow unable to move forward to do so. As she stayed motionless in the doorway, biting her thumb in agitation, the scene changed from the thunderous noise of battle in a town to the eerie silence of a small village, where smoke was rising from the smouldering remnants of wooden houses. A cluster of survivors slumped forlornly under a tree, all suffering from severe wounds. The commentator reported that refugees were fleeing from both towns and villages, and that organisations such as the Red Cross were unable to reach any of the affected areas. The scene faded as he stopped speaking, and the programme continued with news of the Middle East. At last Margaret felt able to control her limbs and she walked quickly across the room. She did not know how to switch off the television, but Robert came to her aid and pushed the correct button.

'That was Gnujeemia,' cried Pauline again, tears streaming down her face.

'Yes, it was.' Margaret held out her arms and Pauline rushed to be comforted, immediately joined by Stephen.

'What about Mum and Dad?' he demanded. 'What's happened to them?'

'They'll be all right,' said Margaret, choking back her own sobs. 'We've seen the newspaper. The fighting isn't near our village. It's all much further south.'

Robert cleared his throat, doing his best to maintain a manly appearance. 'That war is even worse than I thought.'

Margaret nodded. 'I never thought of it coming on the television.' She glanced down at the two younger children, then shook her head as a warning to Robert to keep quiet about the subject in their presence. 'It will be all right. It will all end soon. Come on, let's go and see what we should have for tea today.'

They were all subdued when they sat down for the evening meal and nobody enjoyed the tinned meat, tinned peas and dried potatoes. For the first time Pauline and Stephen were suffering the full pangs of fear and homesickness, while Robert was brooding over the terrible scenes shown in the newsreel. Now he understood why their parents had sent them all to England in such a rush. Mum and Dad must be in great danger. If the fighting spread further north, how could Mum and Dad be saved? Would their whole village be burned down, like those others?

Eventually Stephen noticed Margaret's face. 'What's the matter with your eyes?' he asked. 'Have you been crying, too?'

'No.' Margaret's hand went up automatically and she felt the grease around her eyes. 'Oh, I was trying out some make-up. I was just wiping it off when you called me. I'd forgotten about that.'

'You don't look very glamorous. It's all smudgy,' said Robert, doing his best to lighten the atmosphere. 'Why don't you start again and show us how you're going to look tomorrow?'

They all trailed upstairs and the other three lounged on the bed while Margaret cleaned her face and applied fresh make-up.

'You look like a real lady,' said Pauline. 'Are you going to put your hair up as well?'

A crystal dish on the dressing-table held a good supply of hairpins, but Margaret soon found that pinning her hair up was far more difficult than she had imagined. Unhelpful comments from her brothers only made her feel more inadequate and she wished they would go away. She was close to losing her temper when the front doorbell rang.

'Go down and see who that is,' she instructed. 'I can't go. I'm not tidy enough to see anybody.'

Robert opened the door and found Mrs Croft waiting on the doorstep, a large covered plate in her hands.

'Hello, dear,' she said. 'I've made some biscuits and I thought you'd all like some.' She peered past him and saw two smaller children in the background. 'Hello, everybody. I just came across to see how you were getting along.'

'We're getting on very well, thank you,' replied Robert. He paused, wishing he could just take the biscuits and send Mrs Croft away; but that would surely be bad-mannered and ungrateful. 'Er — would you like to come in? Show Mrs Croft to the front room, Stephen.'

Mrs Croft handed the plate to Robert and he took it quickly to the kitchen. He then hurried to the front room, where he switched on a radiator that was standing on the tiled hearth and joined the other children on the sofa.

Mrs Croft settled herself more comfortably in her armchair. 'I was watching the news on television,' she began, and knew by their reaction that they had also seen the film about the war. 'I thought you might be feeling rather depressed, and I wondered if I could help at all. You must be feeling a bit lost, all alone in a strange country.'

'We're managing all right,' answered Robert.

'Yes, well, there must be a lot of things you're not used to. Have you been out today?'

'We went on a bus,' said Pauline timidly.

'Oh, I'm glad to hear you found the stop and everything all right. What's your name, dear?'

Robert made awkward introductions and Mrs Croft looked around, wondering how to encourage them to say more. It was difficult to hold a conversation with children who were so shy. 'Where's your big sister? I haven't met her yet.'

'She's upstairs,' replied Robert. 'I don't think she'll be coming down.'

'She's been trying to do her hair and it looks a mess,' said Stephen in a sudden rush of frankness.

Mrs Croft gave a nod of sympathy and understanding. 'Oh dear. Is she having that trouble? I expect the English climate has affected it. Would you nip up and ask her if she would like me to give her a hand?'

Margaret's immediate response was to

reject the offer, but a moment later she changed her mind. If Mrs Croft guessed she was too young to be left in charge, it would only prove that everybody else would do the same. Besides, she needed advice. She had to do her best to look mature and sensible.

'Bring her up,' she said.

When Mrs Croft entered the room, Margaret was resting both elbows on the dressing-table, staring at herself in despair. Her limp blond hair was already slipping down from numerous pins.

'The climate has got at you, that's for sure,' said Mrs Croft, coming to stand behind her and looking into the mirror.

'What am I going to do with it?' Margaret had to fight back sobs. 'It won't stay up, but when I leave it down it makes me look like a little kid.'

'I can imagine that.' Mrs Croft tilted her head to one side as she studied the image in the glass. The girl was just a slip of a thing, and no stylist had touched that hair. 'Let me see what I can do.'

She pulled out the pins and ran her fingers through the hair at the back. It scarcely reached the girl's shoulders, not long enough to plait or tie into a safe knot.

'I don't think you'll pin this up successfully. It's too fine.'

'I'll have to do *something* with it.'

'If you want my advice, you'll have it cut. A really short modern cut would suit you very well.'

Margaret's shoulders sagged, and Mrs Croft immediately guessed that cost might be a factor.

'Look, I'll do it for you if you like,' she offered. 'I wanted to be a hairdresser once, but I got married instead. I used to do my daughter's hair though, so I've had plenty of practice. And I still cut my husband's hair. I'll make a good job of it, I promise.'

'That would be very good of you,' said Margaret shyly.

'I'll just nip back across the road and get my scissors and things. You find yourself a cloth to put around your shoulders. I'll be back in a minute.'

The other children were intrigued by her departure and swift return. Robert thought of following her up the stairs, but she waved him away with a peremptory gesture.

'This is women's business. You look after the others downstairs.'

She stood quietly for two or three minutes, considering her approach, then she began to snip. Margaret watched in the mirror, her eyes widening in dismay as the long strands began to fall away. It was too late to change her mind now. Still, the woman could hardly make things much worse. That was one consolation.

Mrs Croft continued working until the hair was extremely short, lying smoothly across the crown of the girl's head and framing her face with sharp peaks.

'How's that?' she asked proudly, stepping back to admire the effect. 'I think that's more sophisticated.'

Margaret gazed in wonder. 'It looks absolutely different,' she exclaimed. 'People won't think I'm just a young kid now, will they?'

'You do look a little older,' replied Mrs Croft, wondering what the girl's real age might be. She could hardly ask about that just now, but presumably the girl was older than she looked. 'If you don't mind me saying so, you should extend your rouge just a little further towards the cheek bones. Let's see . . . not too far . . . yes, that's better. You do the other side. Yes. Now, just a touch of eye shadow, very faint. Is there a brown pencil? Your eyebrows are very fair.'

When they went downstairs, the other three were astonished by the change. They praised Mrs Croft for her cleverness and she glowed with pleasure.

'I'm glad you all like it,' she said. 'Now

don't forget, if you ever need anything, or if we can help in any way at all, we're just across the road.'

She declined to stay for a cup of tea, and Margaret thanked her again as she escorted her to the front door.

'I don't know what I would have done without you. When I get my new clothes I'll look much better.'

'You'll be a real picture,' Mrs Croft assured her. She raised her voice to call to the others. 'Good night, everybody. Keep yourselves warm, and sleep well.'

The two younger children were tired and they made little fuss when Margaret told them to go to bed, but they were both sobbing when she went upstairs again only a few minutes later.

'Don't cry,' said Margaret. 'You're safe here.'

She lifted Pauline up and carried her into the other room, where she sat on the edge of Stephen's bed. Holding Pauline on her lap and patting Stephen's shoulder with her free hand, she did her best to comfort the pair.

'I want Mummy. And I want Daddy,' wailed Pauline, clutching her sister tightly.

'I want them, too,' cried Stephen. 'I don't want them to be left behind with all that fighting and bombing and everything.'

'They'll be all right,' said Margaret staunchly. 'There's no fighting around our village.'

'We might never see them again,' sobbed Pauline.

'Of course we will. But they're going to be very busy for a while. The Red Cross will probably open a hospital there, and Mum will be a nurse again.'

Stephen scrambled out from under the bedclothes and Margaret held both children in her arms, talking continually in a soft and soothing tone. She dared not think what might happen to their parents if the fighting continued. She could only repeat assurances that all would end well, and cling to the hope that her words would come true.

8

Margaret borrowed an alarm clock from Aunt Joan's bedroom, and set it for half past six to ensure that she allowed herself plenty of time to get ready for the difficult day ahead, but she awoke long before it rang the next morning. Her interviews at the schools were the first real tests she had to face in her new role as guardian, and she was beginning to think it was hopeless to tackle such a challenge.

None of the children had slept well, and they felt too short-tempered and edgy to take much interest in breakfast. Pauline was tearful, persistently clinging to her big sister and demanding attention, but Margaret shooed her away before attempting her make-up. She was determined to be free of spectators.

'There's washing up to be done,' she ordered. 'And none of you are to come into this room. I'll be too busy to bother with any of you.'

Her hands trembled a little as she worked, but she followed Mrs Croft's advice and decided she had achieved a fairly good effect.

No skill was needed to comb through the new hairstyle, and Stephen greeted her with a cheer when she went downstairs.

'Not bad,' said Robert. 'I almost wish I was coming with you so that I can see what happens.'

The junior school was only three blocks away, but Margaret insisted on setting off early, which meant they had to make a detour to fill in time. The size of the building was overwhelming, and Pauline almost panicked as they entered the playground. Margaret gripped her hand tightly to prevent her from running away.

'Don't be frightened,' she said. 'I know it's a big place, but it's only a school. I expect everybody will be very nice.'

The headmistress, Miss Chapman, was a very tall, well-built woman, whose dark hair was coiled high on her head, making her look even taller. The two younger children stared up at her with mounting apprehension and Margaret swallowed nervously. She felt small and insignificant beside the imposing figure, and feared this first interview would prove to be her undoing.

'So you have come from Gnujeemia,' said Miss Chapman when they had completed the introductions. 'That's a sorry state of affairs over there.'

The warm tone gave Margaret some confidence and she drew herself up more resolutely. 'Yes. We are hoping things will improve soon.'

'Have you got relatives here in Allingham?'

'Yes, our aunt lives here. We are staying at her house,' replied Margaret.

Thank goodness for that, thought the headmistress. Uprooting young children in such a fashion and sending them off to a different country without their parents could lead to all sorts of complications and trauma. Their sister did not look competent enough to deal with consequences of that nature, and it was a relief to know that a mature woman could be called upon to help if problems developed. She gave a friendly smile to conceal her opinion, and turned her attention to Pauline and Stephen.

'Have you ever been to school before?'

They only nodded silently and Margaret felt obliged to explain.

'Our school was tiny. Pauline and Stephen were both in my class. They're not used to any other teachers.'

'Oh, so you taught in the school!' Miss Chapman could not hide her surprise, but she felt another surge of relief. The young guardian was clearly unsophisticated, but perhaps she was older and more experienced than she appeared to be at first sight.

'They can both read and write well,' Margaret continued. 'They know basic arithmetic, too, but they don't know much about the way of life over here. Everything is new and strange.'

Miss Chapman smiled at the nervous young pair. 'You'll soon settle in,' she said. 'The classrooms and the playground might seem very large at first, but you'll get used to them very quickly.'

She went on to describe a typical school day and the more important rules. 'We don't want anybody to have an accident. That's the main reason why we have rules. And, of course, we expect everybody to help in keeping the school tidy. Is there anything you want to ask me?'

They shook their heads silently and Miss Chapman suggested that Monday would be a good day to start.

'She was nice, wasn't she?' said Margaret as they walked back towards the gate.

The others nodded reluctantly, still feeling too shaky to talk, but after they had turned the first corner they began to chatter and when they reached the house they were able to give the impression that they had acted bravely. Stephen told Robert that going to school might not be so bad after all, and he shifted uneasily in the armchair where he had been trying to distract himself with a magazine.

'I wish I could go to that school, too,' he muttered. 'I've still got to find out what mine will be like.'

'You'll be all right,' answered Margaret firmly. She was feeling more sure of herself now that the first interview had been accomplished. 'You're not shy. We'll go into town now and find out which bus we have to catch this afternoon. And we'll buy some shoes. We can't leave that job any longer in case it rains.'

When they had obtained information and another bus timetable in the same office as before, they walked to the shops in High Street. Margaret bought a suspender belt and a pair of cheap nylon stockings for herself in an old-fashioned department store, and asked for directions to the ladies' room. While she was struggling into the new garments the others waited near a busy counter, enthralled by the unusual sight of containers zipping across overhead, carrying payments and change.

Shortly afterwards, Margaret led them into a shop that seemed to have a good selection of inexpensive shoes. An assistant came forward at once and invited them to sit down.

'Who is going to have new shoes today?'

'We all are,' replied Margaret. 'I don't know what size, but we all need something strong and weatherproof — and not too dear, please.'

'This won't leave much money,' whispered Robert as the assistant went away to fetch some boxes.

'We need them. It might rain. Besides, I have to look respectable when I apply for a job.'

They all wore their new shoes when they left the shop, Pauline looking down at her feet every few yards.

'They feel heavy, but they look nice,' she said.

'My feet are much warmer already,' said Robert. 'Don't go kicking stones or anything around, Stephen. These have to be for best as well as everything else, and they have to last a long time.'

They decided it would be cheaper to go back and make their own lunch at the house rather than visit a snack bar. Pauline and Stephen should then stay there together while the other two went to the senior school. At the last minute, Margaret began to worry about what might go wrong while the younger ones were left unsupervised.

'We'll be as quick as we can,' she said. 'If

you get tired of television you can look at the pictures in those encyclopaedias. Now behave yourselves. No arguing, no lighting matches. Don't touch the television set, and don't switch on anything else. And don't answer the door to *anybody*.'

'Come on,' urged Robert.

She took a last look at her reflection and touched up her lipstick, then followed Robert out to the street. A bus approached before they reached the stop and they both groaned with disappointment, but the driver pulled up and waited for them.

'Thank goodness for that,' murmured Margaret as they took the nearest seats on the lower deck. 'It's hard to run in these shoes. It's the heels.'

'It's a good job you didn't get any of those really high ones,' chuckled Robert.

A second bus carried them almost to the front gate of the senior school. It was larger and much more imposing than they had expected, but Robert was pleased to see the expanse of sports fields.

'Look, they've got a real football pitch! I'll be able to play proper football.'

Margaret merely nodded in reply. It was all very well for him, she thought enviously. It would not matter how he behaved or how childish he seemed to be — whereas she had to pretend to be grown up and capable of looking after them all.

Signs directed them to a receptionist, who invited them to sit down. Moments later they were ushered towards the principal's office and Margaret took a deep breath, striving to look calm and competent when they entered.

Mr Redhead came around his desk to greet them, struggling to mask his first reaction. Some of his students looked older than this girl when they dressed themselves up for Saturday outings.

'So you are Robert's guardian, Miss Barlow? Good afternoon.'

'Good afternoon. Yes, I am looking after the family until we can rejoin our parents.' Margaret carefully phrased her next remarks. 'Our aunt lives in Allingham. We are staying at her house for the time being.' He gave a nod, indicating that such arrangements sounded satisfactory, and she continued, 'Robert is fourteen. He was expecting to leave school within a few weeks.'

'And the regulations here have put a stop to that, eh? How are you, Robert?'

'Very well, thank you.'

Mr Redhead invited them to sit down, and went back to his chair behind the desk. 'I will take you on a brief tour in a moment. But first we have to decide which form will be the most suitable for you. What are your strong points, Robert?'

The boy gulped. 'I like reading. And fixing things.'

'What kind of things? For example, have you done any woodwork?'

'I can work with wood *and* metal,' responded Robert. 'I help Dad quite a lot.'

'I see. Have you learned any languages?'

'Gnujeemian,' was the automatic response.

Mr Redhead gave a thin smile. 'I'm afraid that would serve no purpose here. We offer German and French.'

'Oh well, I speak French,' Robert answered off-handedly.

Mr Redhead raised his eyebrows. '*Parles-tu bien le français?*'

'*Assez bien. Quelquefois nous parlons tout le jour en français.*'

Mr Redhead quickly reverted to English in case he ran into difficulties. 'You seem to be quite fluent. How is it that you speak French so well?'

'We all do.' Robert lifted one shoulder in a nonchalant shrug, then realised this was an ideal opportunity to impress someone who held an important position — to make him see just how capable his big sister was.

'Margaret teaches French,' he announced.

'Indeed?' The headmaster looked at her

135

with more interest. Perhaps she was not as childlike as she appeared to be. The boy did not look as if he could be fourteen, either, so it could be a family trait. 'Tell me more. Is French useful in Gnujeemia?'

'Very useful,' replied Margaret. 'French is the official language of neighbouring countries. It is useful for trade and for dealing with migrant workers.'

'Margaret teaches English as well,' said Robert, determined to emphasise his sister's qualities and ability. 'And all the other subjects, of course, like reading and writing.'

'So you're a school teacher, Miss Barlow?'

'Yes. I have been teaching for three years now.' Margaret hid her right hand under her shoulder bag and crossed her fingers, telling herself there was no need to explain that the school was a primitive one-roomed establishment that suffered from a shortage of supplies and expertise.

'That's very interesting. We must talk more about it one day.' Mr Redhead rose to his feet. 'I expect you will be keen to see the facilities we have here. Would you both like to come with me now?'

As soon as they had left the school buildings behind and they were safe from observation, Margaret and Robert shed their restraint and hugged each other with triumph.

'You did it!' shouted Robert jubilantly. 'You convinced him that you are our proper guardian.'

'You helped a lot,' said Margaret. 'I just hope they never ask what our school was like at home.'

'Never mind about all that. We know what to say to people now.' Robert clapped her heartily on the back. 'We're saved. All you have to do now is get a job.'

They made their way back by bus, alighting one stop before reaching the house so as to buy a newspaper at the corner shop.

'Hello,' said the newsagent, grinning at Margaret. 'So you're here again. Have you moved into these parts?'

'We are staying at our aunt's house,' said Margaret cautiously. 'I don't know how long we will be here.'

'I hope you like it, anyway. Do you need anything else, or just the paper?'

'Today's newspaper, please. Nothing else.'

Margaret paid him, reminding herself not to glance at the news until she was outside and safe from onlookers. To her relief, the doorbell jangled and the newsagent instantly switched his attention to a new customer. Robert followed Margaret quickly out of the shop and by tacit agreement they looked for a quiet spot where they could read about the war in Gnujeemia. The complete lack of such news on the front page came as a surprise. How could local council affairs take precedence over a serious matter like that? Margaret clicked her teeth and frowned with disapproval, then turned to the inner pages. The report about the war was shorter than she had expected, and gave no new information.

'Well, things don't seem to have changed much over there,' Margaret murmured. 'I suppose that could mean it's no worse. Perhaps we should be thankful for that.'

'What do we tell the others?'

'Just that our village is safe. We mustn't let them see anything about it on television, though.'

Stephen and Pauline greeted them with exclamations of joy and relief, glad they were all together again. They jumped about with excitement when they heard how well the second interview had gone.

'No one can take us away now,' yelled Pauline thankfully.

'I've still got to get a job,' Margaret reminded her. 'Let's see what we can find in the paper.'

Wednesday seemed to be a good day for advertisements of all kinds. Margaret and Robert separated two pages and searched for likely jobs, while the younger children watched and listened hopefully. Robert called out whenever he found something attractive, but Margaret lacked training so she rejected all his suggestions. Her gloom deepened as she ran her finger down the small items on the page she held. It seemed that she had no hope of gaining any worthwhile job until she had previous experience. But how did one obtain that experience in the first place if nobody would employ you?

She pushed the newspaper away with a dejected sigh, and then drew it back again and stared at the head of the page. Spread across three columns was a large notice in bold print, separated from other advertisements by space and an ornate border. Robert leaned towards her, intrigued by her sudden stillness.

'What have you found?'

Margaret pointed to the advertisement. 'It's so big I didn't even read it at first. They wouldn't want anyone like me, though.'

'Tell us,' urged Stephen.

'It's a job at this same newspaper. They want someone who can look after correspondence, do general office work and assist the editor.'

'That's just what you did for Dad!' exclaimed Robert. 'Wow! That's exactly right.

139

How much do they pay?'

'Eight pounds.' Margaret shook her head despondently. 'That's more than most people are offering. They want someone especially good.'

'You are especially good,' cried Pauline. 'Dad was always saying he didn't know what he'd do without you.'

Margaret smiled. 'Dad didn't run a big newspaper like this. And he didn't have many letters to write, either.'

'You were doing all that teaching as well,' Robert pointed out. 'You'll have all day to write letters at this place. How are you supposed to apply for the job?'

Margaret looked again. 'Phone for an interview,' she read aloud.

'Go on then. I bet they're still open. The phone's in the hall. Ring right now.'

'I'd better see what else there is first.'

'No, do that right now. You might get in first.'

Margaret still hesitated, but she knew the others would give her no peace until she complied. More importantly, she must not forget their desperate need for funds. Eager nods by all the children boosted her courage, and finally she pushed her chair back from the table.

'All right, I'll do it. But don't expect miracles.'

She closed the kitchen door firmly behind her as a warning that she would not accept eavesdroppers in the hall, and took a deep breath before lifting the telephone receiver. Her fingers became clumsy with nerves as she dialed the number, but the woman who answered sounded pleasant and Margaret was able to speak to her clearly and calmly.

The others gathered around excitedly when she returned to the kitchen, demanding that she tell them everything that had happened.

'I have to go for an interview at half past nine in the morning. Thank goodness Mrs Croft cut my hair for me last night.'

'Everything is working out beautifully,' said Stephen. 'I don't know why you were so worried.'

Margaret and Robert exchanged meaningful glances. They both knew the result could be disappointing; but the possibility of success had raised their siblings' spirits and, until they could no longer avoid it, neither of them would say anything to dampen the buoyant mood.

9

Margaret awoke early again the next day, and again she instructed the others to do the washing up while she applied make-up. She twirled in front of a long mirror afterwards, assuring herself that the stockings and new Cuban-heeled shoes made her look taller and far more refined. Even the borrowed clothes seemed to fit better now that she was well shod. The others made flattering remarks when she paraded for inspection, and she was still glowing with satisfaction when she entered the front door of the *Daily Tribune*, six minutes before the appointed time.

The receptionist asked for her name and invited her to sit on a nearby chair. She did so, reminding herself to sit with her back straight and her knees together. She must look like a lady, she told herself fiercely. People were not supposed to ask a lady her age. She had watched the Ambassador's wife at a formal function. If she acted like her, considering her posture at all times, and if she remembered to think carefully before speaking, she could make a good impression. There was only a remote chance of being chosen for this job, but at least she had not been asked to wait in a long line of applicants, and she could always look upon the coming interview as a good practice run for whatever else might follow.

The minute hand of the huge clock on the far wall showed almost exactly the appointed time when the receptionist said that Mr Anderson was ready to meet her, and escorted her to the editor's office. Margaret thanked her serenely and stepped through the doorway with a show of confidence, but her courage ebbed as a huge man rose to greet her.

'Good morning, Miss Barlow,' he boomed.

'Good morning,' she answered faintly, watching his massive hand close over hers in a brief handshake. His head towered at least twelve inches above her head and his shoulders suggested that he might have been a heavyweight boxer or a wrestler. Beside him she felt small, insignificant and very young.

'Would you like to take your coat off?' He held his hands out ready, as though she had no choice in the matter, and she hastily unfastened the buttons. He took the coat from her and inclined his head in the direction of a chair. 'Please take a seat.'

Anderson watched her sink gracefully onto the padded leather seat as he hung the coat on an old-fashioned hatstand in the corner. She carried herself well, he decided — not like some of the young people he saw slouching about the streets these days. Still, that was no qualification for the job on offer here. It was highly unlikely that this applicant would meet the requirements, but there was something about her that intrigued him and he would not rush her away.

When he sat down behind the desk his bulky frame became less obvious and Margaret was able to meet his eyes with poise.

'Now then, I understand that you've had experience in a newspaper office,' he prompted.

'Yes.' Margaret paused to consider her words. Had she exaggerated her experience too much when she telephoned the office yesterday? Almost instantly she reminded herself that the family was relying on her to get a good job. She must speak up for herself and try to convince him that she could handle the work.

'My father runs the newspaper,' she continued. 'When I was at home I typed items for him, and I typed letters and things like that.'

'That's promising. Was that a daily paper?'

'No, it only came out once a week. But we had two editions; one in English and the other in the local language.'

'Ah hah.' That explained the accent. She had not said much as yet, but he had already picked up the faint difference in speech. 'What language would that be?'

'Gnujeemian.'

His shoulders stiffened and his eyes gleamed with a sudden avid interest. 'Does that mean you have been living in Gnujeemia? When did you leave?'

Margaret explained how she and her younger siblings had been evacuated barely a week before, and he covered his mouth with his hand to conceal his immense glee. There was a great opportunity here, he told himself, and he must take advantage of it. He had a nose for news and this girl could provide him with the story of the year, if not a lifetime. She might not be the person he was looking for as an assistant, but perhaps he could find some place for her while he dug deeper for an unusual story.

'Tell me more about the newspaper.'

'Some of our news came from neighbouring countries. We translated it from French.'

'So you speak French as well.'

'Yes.' Margaret hoped he would not question her too closely about the newspaper. He would not be impressed if she explained that some editions consisted merely of a single sheet. At times the power plant failed and they had to print copies by hand. She looked down at her hands and noticed that they were clenched tightly together in her lap, an obvious sign of tension. She willed herself to relax and spent a moment smoothing her skirt over her knees. Anderson watched, thinking her behaviour revealed a remarkable mix of immaturity and sophistication.

'What speed is your shorthand?'

Margaret's head jerked up and she stared at him in consternation. 'I can't write shorthand.'

'Do you mean to say your father wrote all his letters in longhand?'

'No. He just told me what he wanted to say and I wrote the letters myself.'

'Did you now? That's interesting.' Anderson picked up a pencil and twirled it in his fingers. The girl sounded less and less suitable for work in his office, but he wanted to learn a great deal more about her before he lost contact. 'Have you had any other experience, such as another job — apart from working with your father?'

'I was a teacher. I had been teaching in the local school for three years.'

'A teacher, eh?' He leaned back in his chair and gazed at her thoughtfully. She was a slight little thing and she was certainly uneasy, but she was doing a good job of controlling her nerves. 'Have you thought of applying for a job as a teacher over here?'

'No, I haven't got the right qualifications for teaching in an English school.' Margaret tilted her chin, hoping he would not ask what qualifications she did have. She had never had any formal training at all, and the village school consisted of just one room, crammed with nearly a hundred children.

Anderson clasped his hands behind his head and leaned back further, causing his chair to creak loudly. For several moments he studied her in silence, pursing his lips and watching her slender fingers intertwine and tighten again. She didn't look old enough to have done all the things she had told him about.

'How old are you?'

The sudden question startled her. 'How old am I?' she gasped.

He nodded slowly without changing his position, and Margaret sought for a satisfactory answer.

'Well, I'm not twenty-one yet.'

'I didn't think you were. In fact, I'm thinking you're probably a good deal less than that.'

Margaret bit her lip, but she refused to be drawn. The editor watched her expression for several more seconds, then he shifted his weight forward and rested his forearms on the desk.

'You interest me,' he said. 'I'm not going to insist on knowing your real age, but I do want to know why you are so keen to get this job. Do you fancy yourself as an ace reporter? Someone who's going to produce a tremendous scoop? Is that why you want to work for our newspaper?'

Margaret shook her head, unwilling to go into details about herself, but he was an experienced journalist. Within minutes he learned that she had become responsible for the upkeep of the family and she needed a good wage to pay for food and more warm clothing. His friendly smiles and nods persuaded her to reveal more than she had intended, but she stopped abruptly when she realised she had let her guard slip.

Anderson smiled again, deciding this was not the time to press her. 'Well, you've certainly taken on a big task, looking after the other children like that. I should think you could fit into some company over here and become a very useful employee. You've had more worldly experience than a great many people who are much older than you.'

Margaret's shoulders sagged as the meaning of his words struck home. He was telling her in a roundabout fashion that he was not going to employ her himself.

'I have to say that I had an older person in mind,' he went on. He paused, keenly aware that he should probe deeper. The girl had not told him everything. She was holding back something important, and if he let her slip through his fingers he would never find out what that something was.

'You said you wrote letters for your father. Do you mean you actually composed them yourself?'

'Dad told me what he wanted to say, and then I put that in polite terms for him.'

Anderson hid a smile at the hint of censorship. 'I'd like to see one of your letters. Look, I'll tell you what I'll do. I'll give you a fortnight's trial if you can write a letter that satisfies me. I couldn't be fairer than that now, could I?'

Margaret's hopes soared. 'What kind of letter would you like me to write?'

'Write to a Mr David White and tell him we apologise for putting his wedding announcement in the wrong section yesterday. Make up an address for him. Use your own if you like. You can type it on that machine over there.' Anderson waved one hand in the direction of a lower desk beside the wall. 'You'll find plenty of paper in the top drawer. Practise on the machine first and then have a go at the letter. I'll leave you to it for a while. I'm always being told that people can't type if I stand over them.'

He lumbered to his feet and gave a jaunty salute, then strode towards an inner door and disappeared into an adjoining office. Left alone, Margaret walked hesitantly to the low desk and removed the cover from the typewriter. In contrast to the battered machine at home, this one looked new. She sat down and ran her fingers lightly across the keys, then found a sheet of paper and inserted it into the roller, her hands quivering from a mixture of excitement and dread.

She was still trying to accustom herself to the typewriter when the receptionist sauntered into the office and regarded her with curiosity.

'Mr Anderson thought you might need a cup of tea.'

Margaret blushed. 'Thank you. I would like one.'

'With milk and sugar?' The receptionist returned almost immediately with a cup and saucer and set them down on the desk.

'How are you getting on?' she enquired.

Margaret looked up shyly and decided the woman was friendly. 'I'm not,' she confessed. 'I've been trying to set the margin, but I can't find out how it works. I'm used to a very old machine.'

'Oh, this is one of those new-fangled things. The first time I tried it I got the whole carriage jammed. Look, it's got keys on the front here. That key operates the left side, and that one operates the other.' She nodded approvingly as Margaret followed her instructions. 'That's right. As they always say, easy when you know how. I'd better get back and keep an eye on things. Take your time. Mr Anderson is having a cup of tea and then he's got lots of other things to keep him busy.'

'Would you please tell me how the editor signs his name?'

'Oh, yes. E.W.Anderson, Editor. Don't let your tea get cold now.'

Margaret made a rough draft of her letter without any further difficulty, and the finished product was well spaced with no typing errors. She sat quietly staring at it. Should she find the receptionist and tell her she had finished, or wait until the editor returned? The answer came before she could make up her mind. A member of staff, who had been listening for the sound of clacking keys to stop, had passed a message to Anderson.

'Finished, have you?' he boomed as he strode in. 'Let's see.'

Margaret handed the letter to him and watched his face as he studied it, but his expression gave nothing away.

'Hm,' he murmured at last. 'Not bad. Not bad at all. In fact it's pretty good. Nobody could take offence at that and I rather like the style. More natural than the usual type of business letter and sounding as though we really mean what we say. Yes, we'll use that. We really did make a hash of someone's announcement, you know.' He looked at her and chuckled. 'Well, you certainly passed the first test. No wonder your father left the letter writing to you. Come over here and we'll discuss this business a bit further.'

Margaret was unable to hide her elation as she went back to the chair by the large desk, but he pretended not to notice. He pulled out a bottom drawer on his side of the desk to use as a footstool, then settled himself comfortably and told her about the aims and policy of his newspaper.

'That's about all you need to know just now,' he ended. 'You'll find us a friendly crowd. We don't stand on ceremony and no one pulls rank, so long as the work gets done. How do you think you'd like a trial period with us?'

'I'd love it!'

'Good. Now let's see . . . today's Thursday . . . but you've hardly had time to get over the change in time zones yet. Could you start on Monday?'

'Yes,' replied Margaret, but her eager smile vanished as she remembered Pauline and Stephen.

'What's the matter?'

Margaret bit her lip, wondering how understanding he really was, then decided she must explain her hesitation.

'I was thinking about my little brother and sister. They're starting school on Monday and they're both scared.'

'I see.' Anderson swung his chair slightly and put both feet on the floor, considering the best procedure. A slight delay shouldn't make too much difference. On the other hand, it wouldn't do for his rivals to find out about her. She was no ordinary evacuee; there was an unusual story behind this one's arrival in his office, he was convinced of that. He must keep track of her. More importantly, he must keep her out of reach of that other mob.

'Let's see . . . I wouldn't want you sitting here worrying yourself to death all day. How would it be if you took the kids to school first, then came along here afterwards? You could nip back at lunch-time to see how they're getting on, and leave in time to meet them when they come out in the afternoon.'

'That would be very good,' said Margaret gratefully. 'Are you sure that wouldn't cause too much inconvenience?'

He laughed. 'Having you here for part of the day would be better than not at all. I hope you'll be able to manage full days after that?'

'Oh, yes. Once they've got through the first day they should be all right, but starting is going to be a real challenge. Everything is so strange to them yet.'

'Of course. You must keep a journal, you know. Start it now. Write down everything that has happened in the past couple of weeks, and keep doing it every day. Once everything becomes commonplace you'll forget interesting little incidents, like your first reactions to English habits. Now then, I don't suppose you've got your cards yet?'

Her puzzled look gave him an answer and he explained about Income Tax and National Insurance cards.

'You'd better get all that organised today,' he told her. 'They'll be closed over the weekend. Apply for Family Allowance, too, if you're the children's guardian. You're going to need it if you're the only wage earner in the family.'

Moments later he helped her into her coat and she left the building, scarcely able to resist the urge to skip along the pavement.

Anderson watched from the receptionist's window until she was out of sight, then he returned to his office and sat thoughtfully at his desk. His temporary employee certainly had an intriguing background. The mixture of childish and adult mannerisms had attracted him from the start, and her recent exploits promised a story that would appeal to all his readers. Within a few days he must break down her reserve and find out exactly what that story was.

10

Margaret's euphoria carried her along in a bubble of joy until she reached the main square, but once she had paused there to take stock of her surroundings, her natural caution began to make itself felt. It had been a strange experience, she reflected. She moved close to the wall of a nearby office building to avoid a crowd of bustling pedestrians, and lingered there, mulling over the details of her meeting with Mr Anderson. A vague sense of unease quickly grew into anxiety.

Things could not be as rosy as they might seem, she thought. The whole business seemed odd now that she had time to consider. For a start, Mr Anderson was nothing like her mental picture of an editor. And how could it be that the procedure had gone so easily in her favour? Surely she could not be the only applicant for the job? And surely Mr Anderson could not be so desperate for help in the office that he would have taken the first person to come along? Besides, the place had seemed unusually quiet. She had always imagined a large newspaper office to be buzzing with activity.

Had the previous employee left unexpectedly? And if so, why? Perhaps the trial period meant nothing. He could have offered that just to give himself more time to find somebody else. Still, even if it did not last, at least she would earn money for two weeks. It would be a good idea to keep an eye on advertisements, ready to apply for another job immediately afterwards.

She pulled the town map out of her bag and looked for the street where the editor had told her she would find the offices she needed. If she didn't get all the required forms, she could not be employed anywhere. It would save bus fares if she collected the papers now while she was in the town centre, rather than coming back again later.

The younger children had taken it for granted that Margaret's interview would be successful and they welcomed her back with only a few questions, impatient to impart news of their own.

'You'll never guess what's in the garage,' said Stephen.

'It doesn't sound as though a car would be the right answer.'

'No! Come and look.'

Robert had discovered another bunch of keys on a hook behind the larder door, and had spent time that morning finding a lock to match each key. Margaret was bewildered by the unexpected darkness when he opened a door at the side of the garage, but Robert quickly switched on a light to reveal benches of equipment. The windows were blacked out by heavy curtains and she quickly noticed red bulbs in nearby lamp sockets.

'It's a darkroom!' she exclaimed.

'I bet Aunt Joan has gone to South America to take photographs,' said Stephen.

'Ah, yes! She's a professional photographer. I'd forgotten until I saw all this.' Margaret shook her head and spoke sharply as she realised why Robert was so tense with excitement. 'Don't think you can come in and use any of this equipment, because you can't. None of you must touch anything in here.'

'It seems a pity just to leave it sitting here doing nothing,' muttered Robert, but he decided not to argue the point for the time being. He cast another wistful look at the enticing equipment, then he locked the door again and returned the key to its place behind the larder door.

Margaret was determined to fill in the application forms before doing anything else, and he sat down beside her at the kitchen table to offer help.

'This looks good, a Guardian's Allowance,' he said, picking up a leaflet.

'We can't apply for that,' replied Margaret at once. 'I read it on the bus. It's for orphans really, and they ask all sorts of questions that we don't want to answer. They'd be sure to check properly before they paid any money, so we can't risk it.'

'No, better to manage without,' agreed Robert. 'We don't want any nosey-parkers coming here and interfering. When are you going to hand these in?'

'I thought this afternoon would be best, while the weather is nice and dry. We'll all go. We haven't seen much of Allingham yet, and we must do some shopping.'

Submitting the documents did not take as long as Margaret had feared, and an unexpected spell of sunshine encouraged the children to explore further afield. Not far from the Town Hall they found an older and smaller open space, in the centre of which stood an ancient market building. Soon they discovered an historic church and signs near there directed them to a river. A humped bridge with decorative stonework crossed the water, but it was too narrow and flimsy for modern traffic so a new bridge had been built about two hundred yards downstream.

They walked half way across the old bridge and leaned on the stone wall, watching a group of white birds with long graceful necks,

159

floating on the water below.

'Those are swans,' said Margaret. 'Lovely, aren't they?'

'I'd rather see my picture of Swan Lake in my bedroom,' said Pauline regretfully. 'When do you think we'll be able to go home to Mum and Dad?'

'We can't go for a while. But we'll find lots of interesting things to do while we're here. It's quite a picturesque town, isn't it?'

'Mm. Lots to photograph,' responded Robert pointedly, but Margaret ignored that remark.

They walked back towards the shopping centre by a different road and found a cinema, where they stopped to look at posters and photographs. No one was willing to say so, but they were all longing to go inside and wishing they could afford tickets. Margaret urged the others to move on, but as they were about to turn the corner she came to an abrupt stop.

'Look at this. It's exactly what we need.'

'What we need?' echoed Robert, staring into the shop window. A miscellany of clothes, ornaments and kitchen implements had been arranged around a hand-painted sign. 'All proceeds donated to cancer research,' he read aloud.

'We'll never find anywhere cheaper than

here,' declared Margaret. 'Look at that nice coat. Only one pound, and that skirt for half a crown.'

'We don't need to buy clothes,' said Stephen.

'Of course we do. You can't keep wearing those same things for ever. We need things to change into while the others are washed.'

'But those aren't new,' Pauline objected. 'They're all second-hand.'

'So are those you're wearing now.'

'Well, that's different. We didn't have to buy them.'

'No, and it's time we sent them back. I said we would.'

'We could keep them until you've earned some money,' said Stephen. 'Then we could buy new clothes.'

Margaret shook her head. 'No, we must return them before anybody starts making enquiries.'

'You're always getting into a panic about the people at that hostel,' complained Robert. 'They must have a lot more to do than worry about what happens to all their stray visitors after they've left there.'

'I've read stories about Children's Officers and people like that,' said Margaret. 'Once they start writing case reports they don't put them away until they're quite certain that the children are properly supervised.'

'You shouldn't believe everything you read in stories. Besides, we don't know that anybody started writing anything.'

'We can't risk it. Anyway, we need more warm clothes and we can't put off buying them any longer. Come on.'

The others reluctantly followed Margaret into the shop. They had never been short of money before and never expected to have to face the prospect of buying second-hand goods. An elderly woman came to greet them as they sidled past the crowded racks just inside the door.

'Good afternoon,' she said briskly. 'What can I do for you?'

Her forthright manner restored a little of their morale and their spirits lifted.

'We need complete outfits for everybody,' replied Margaret. 'That is, if we have enough money at the moment,' she amended.

'We'll see. Now then, I suggest that you just browse to begin with and choose the most important items first. Coats are all over there, dresses are on that side, gents' things over there and separates down here. If you can't find everything you want today, you could drop in again. We're getting new supplies all the time.'

The woman eyed them all to judge their

sizes, and as the youngsters headed towards the coats, she sorted through the rack of children's dresses.

'This should be about the right size for the little girl,' she said, bringing a green dress to them. 'I take it you don't want heavy clothes now that summer is so close.'

'Yes, it's warm clothes we're looking for,' answered Margaret. 'We've been living in the tropics and we find it cold here.'

'Oh, in that case you're very lucky. People are beginning to buy their spring and summer outfits now, so the winter things are much cheaper.' The woman fumbled amongst the dresses again and pulled out a bright blue woollen one. 'How about this? Only four shillings and it's in extremely good condition. Never even had the hem let down.'

They were all thoroughly satisfied with their purchases when they left the shop. They each had a respectable coat that was the right size, and two outfits to wear beneath. One of Margaret's skirts needed shortening, but no other alterations were necessary and they had managed to find grey trousers and a grey jumper for Robert.

'I'm glad we got school things for you,' said Margaret. 'You don't want to look too conspicuous when you start on Monday.'

Even Pauline was pleased with her clothes

and she tried on the red tartan skirt again as soon as they reached the house.

'I like this,' she said. 'It's just like a real Scottish kilt.'

'I like it, too,' agreed Margaret. 'Now then, everybody change so that I can wash those jumpers.'

By now she felt less inhibited about opening drawers and cupboards and using their aunt's supplies. Aunt Joan was a well-organised person who kept her goods and utensils neatly placed. Not only that, she had exceptionally large stores. It seemed that no matter what the product, she kept at least one new package handy as a spare. The tiled scullery next to the kitchen served as a laundry, and in the cupboard there Margaret had found a liquid which claimed to be specially designed for woollen goods. Following the directions, she washed the borrowed jumpers, rolled them in towels to soak up excess water and draped them over a clothes-horse to dry.

She was arranging the last garment when the front doorbell sounded, and moments later Stephen brought Mrs Croft through to the laundry.

'Thank you, dear,' she said gaily. 'Hello, Margaret. I hope I'm not interrupting anything important, but I made some scones today and I thought you might like to try some.'

'Oh, thank you.' Margaret looped a sleeve over a bar of the clothes-horse and turned to accept a large plate covered with a tea towel.

'I see you've been busy,' said Mrs Croft, looking at the array of wet woollens. 'Have you got a lot more to do?'

'Not just now,' answered Margaret. 'I'm only doing the jumpers today.'

'I'm glad I didn't arrive when you were in the middle of the job.' Mrs Croft looked around with keen interest. 'That's a good machine there. Have you ever used a washing machine?'

'Oh, no.' Margaret looked at the big white contraption. 'No, I'm not going to touch that.'

'You can't possibly do all the laundry by hand. Especially when there's four of you.' Mrs Croft nodded decisively. 'Don't worry about it. When you decide to do the washing, just let me know and I'll come over to give you a hand. It's quite easy to use that thing, once you know how.'

'Thank you,' said Margaret. That response did not seem sufficient and after a moment she added, 'Would you like a cup of tea?'

Mrs Croft eyed her for a moment, longing to find out more about the family, but the girl looked extremely tired.

'No, I won't stop, thank you, not today. You must have had a very hectic time recently. We'll have a cup of tea and a chat some other time.'

As they walked along the hall, Pauline happened to emerge from the front room and Mrs Croft paused to speak to her.

'Hello, dear. What have you been doing with yourselves today?'

Pauline edged away. 'We went shopping.'

'That's nice. I hope you are all settling in all right.'

Stephen hastened to join his sister in the doorway. 'We're doing fine,' he declared, determined to prove they were capable of caring for themselves. 'We're going to school on Monday. And Margaret got a job today.'

'My goodness, you have been busy.' Mrs Croft turned to give Margaret a look of admiration. 'What kind of job did you get, dear?'

'I'll be working in the office at the *Daily Tribune*.'

'My goodness!' Mrs Croft stared in surprise. 'How did you manage to land a job like that?'

'Margaret worked on the newspaper at home,' said Stephen. '*And* she was a teacher.'

'Goodness gracious me.' Mrs Croft shook

her head, scarcely able to believe that she had heard correctly. She almost blurted out that Margaret did not look old enough to have been employed anywhere, but she restrained herself in time. The girl would feel insulted, and justifiably so. Wait till Les heard this titbit of news. They'd been trying to guess how old the girl might be, but it seemed they had been far wide of the mark.

'I must get on my way,' she said. 'I'm pleased to hear you are settling in so well. But don't forget — if you do need anything, we're just across the road.'

The children were weary after their recent experiences and the long walk that afternoon, so they made no protest about going to bed early. Margaret longed for sleep, too, but she forced herself to start a letter to the Matron at the hostel. It would only take a few minutes, she promised herself. She would merely say that they had reached their aunt's house safely, that she already had a job and the others were about to start school.

The jumpers were still damp the next morning, but she decided that the heater would dry them off during the day if she moved them into the kitchen. She told the other children to sign the letter of thanks, and only then realised that she would need strong wrapping paper for such a large package.

Brown paper was an item she had not seen anywhere.

'We could ask Mrs Croft if she's got any,' suggested Robert.

'We'll need a big piece. Oh, look, there's an empty box. If we use that we won't need any paper. String will hold it together and there's plenty of that.'

On Saturday morning she managed to squeeze all the borrowed clothes into the cardboard box and the four children walked to the local Post Office, not far beyond the newsagent's shop. Margaret almost gasped aloud when she found out the cost of postage, but she was determined not to take the parcel back again.

'Yes, we'll send it,' she said, overriding Robert's objections. 'We want it to get there as soon as possible.'

Robert was frowning with anxiety when they left the Post Office, but Margaret gave a little skip of jubilation.

'We are really organized now,' she announced with a smug smile. 'We're wearing our own clothes and we don't owe anybody anything at all. That means we are safe. No one can say we can't look after ourselves.'

11

Monday morning was grey, windy and wet. None of the children wanted to leave the warm comfort of bed, but Margaret finally did so and insisted that the others must get up and dress. The chilly air encouraged them to move faster than usual, but when they reached the kitchen, all they wanted to do was huddle around the electric radiator.

'What horrible weather,' grumbled Stephen.

'It's awfully cold,' complained Pauline. 'Do we really have to go today?'

Margaret drew herself up, determined to set a good example. 'We'll get used to cold weather when we've been here a bit longer. Now you'll all have to be careful with your new shoes. Try to keep them as dry as you can.'

'That will be just about impossible,' retorted Robert. 'What a day to start school and everything.'

Their slow start resulted in a rushed breakfast and a scramble to be ready in time, leaving the beds unmade and the dishes unwashed in the sink. Robert departed first to catch his bus, and Margaret told the others to clean their teeth while she applied her make-up.

'It's a good job we had these raincoats,' she said as she helped the two youngsters to pull plastic coats over their other clothes. 'And there's no need to make such a fuss about rain. We've been in much heavier rain than this.'

'At least it wasn't cold at the same time,' grumbled Pauline.

She and Stephen hung back nervously when they reached the school gate, but Margaret urged them on across the playground and into the office where Miss Chapman was waiting to take them under her wing.

'There's no need for you to wait,' she declared, indicating with a twitch of her head that Margaret should leave at once. 'I'll take them to meet their teachers.'

Margaret gave each child a brief comforting hug, then hurried out to the main road to catch a bus to town. When she reached the newspaper premises, the receptionist greeted her with a friendly smile and Anderson welcomed her in a hearty manner.

'Children safely ensconced at school? Good. Come with me.'

He led her to a room next to his office and directed her to hang her wet outer clothing on a peg near the door.

'Right. Now you'll be working in here for a start.' He slapped the top of a metal cabinet. 'Filing system. Usual sort of arrangement. Alphabetical order. Letters here, newspaper clippings here, all the odd junk down there.' He kicked the bottom drawer to explain his next words. 'That's the stuff that's going to give you the biggest headache. If you have any spare time later you'd better see what's down there. If you ask me, it's a collection of all the bits and pieces your predecessor didn't know what to do with. Right, now come with me.'

Margaret followed him to a large workroom where he introduced her to other staff members. She smiled and uttered polite phrases, wondering how she could be expected to remember all the names and the position each person held.

'You'll soon sort everybody out,' said Anderson, noting her confusion. 'The important thing is for them to know who you are. You know Miss Dale, don't you?'

The receptionist gave an acknowledging wave. 'Call me Sue,' she said. 'Everybody else does, unless we have visitors.'

The staff drifted away to their own jobs in various parts of the building and Anderson escorted Margaret back to her office.

'Now, these are the letters I want you to

look at first,' he instructed, waving one large hand in the direction of an overflowing wire basket. 'After today your first job will be opening all the mail that comes in.'

Margaret started by sorting letters from members of the public, separating them into groups according to subjects and opposing points of view. Time passed quickly while she was typing and it did not seem long before Sue came in to suggest that she leave.

'You want to get there before the bell goes,' she said. 'Especially on the children's first day. Leave everything just as it is. No one will move anything.'

Margaret reached the front entrance of the school several minutes before the bell rang and she went into the foyer, where a cluster of women waited.

'You're a new face,' said one woman, and all the others turned to inspect the new arrival. 'Doing a favour for a friend, are you?'

'I've come for my brother and sister.'

'Ah, I see. Didn't think you looked old enough to have kids of your own at school. Glad about that. If other mothers start looking that much younger than me, I'd have to admit I'm getting a bit long in the tooth.'

The other women smiled at the comment and then, to Margaret's relief, they resumed their previous conversations. She would not be subjected to any searching questions on this occasion.

Moments after the bell sounded the first children began to dash out of the building, scarcely pausing to don their raincoats. Others took time to dress properly for outdoors, a few walking sedately across the yard, the majority larking about. The number of waiting parents dwindled until Margaret was the only person left, but still Stephen and Pauline did not appear. Margaret began to fidget, wondering what had caused the delay. Surely all had gone well. What would she do if Pauline made a scene and refused to come back this afternoon?

Eventually, a woman came into sight, Stephen sauntering on her left, affecting a casual manner, Pauline holding her hand on her right.

'Good afternoon,' said the woman as they drew closer. 'You must be Miss Barlow. I'm Miss Weston, Pauline's teacher.'

'How do you do,' said Margaret.

'Pauline has done very well this morning. Everything is different for her, of course, but she'll soon find her way around and make friends. She won't have any trouble keeping up with the lessons. She can read very well, and she can spell well, too.'

'I'm glad to hear it,' said Margaret.

'I'm sure they'll both get on very well. You'll come for Pauline again this afternoon, won't you, Stephen? In a day or two you will both know your way about the school, but for a start I think she would like you to come to the classroom for her.'

Rain was still falling heavily and the three youngsters walked home with their heads down, almost in silence. Concern over the younger children's welfare and the strain of learning so many new tasks had tired Margaret, and the others were feeling despondent.

'I hate English weather,' said Pauline as they hung their dripping raincoats over the bath.

'We're having hot soup. That will make us all feel better,' said Margaret briskly. 'Now, we haven't much time, so don't mess about.'

'They don't even know how to do arithmetic at that school,' exclaimed Stephen as they settled at the kitchen table. 'They play with counters and coloured blocks, and they draw things instead of doing sums. The teacher said I'd have to learn to do it that way. Why should I have to mess about with bits of wood when I can work out sums without them?'

Margaret chuckled. 'It should be easier. I

174

wonder how Robert is getting on?'

'I don't like that teacher,' murmured Pauline.

'She seemed very nice to me. She sounds kind and she has a nice smile.'

'It's all right for you. You don't have to be with her all day.'

Anderson had stayed away from his young employee since introducing her to the staff, thinking she would settle in better if she did not feel pressurised, but he was keen to find out as much as he could about her demeanour and her abilities. On the way back from his lunch break he stopped by Sue's desk.

'How's that new lass doing?'

'She's very nervous. But she's doing her best. She seems willing.'

'Mm. She's got her mind on those little kids right now. Let's hope they settle in at school.' Anderson started to walk away, then changed his mind and turned back. 'Talk to her, Sue. She'll probably open up to you more easily. You know — young women together. I want to find out all about her. There's a big story there, I just know it.'

'Well, I'll do my best.'

'Don't be too insistent. Just be chatty, okay? And this afternoon find an easy typing job or something for her. She won't be here

175

long enough to finish a big job, anyway.'

The rain stopped for a while during the afternoon, but it was beating down again when school ended for the day. Margaret arrived in time to meet her brother and sister, and they trudged home as silently as before.

'I hate this country,' Pauline grumbled as the front door closed behind them.

'The weather's not like this all the time,' answered Margaret soothingly. 'Put your sandals on and some dry socks.'

She filled the kettle and lit the gas ring and they all stood close to the heater, rubbing their hands as they waited for the water to boil.

'I hate that school, too.' Pauline was in one of her rebellious moods. 'They don't do anything the way we used to.'

'You'll soon start to like it,' Margaret responded.

'How was your job?' asked Stephen.

'Not bad. It's all new, of course, but I think I'll be able to manage.' Margaret decided it would be unwise to express any doubts about her status. She had to gain approval if she were to stand any hope of keeping the job, but with all the travelling to and fro that day there had been little opportunity to prove her worth.

'I don't like the children either.' Pauline

was looking for any reason to criticise the school.

'You'll get used to them.'

'The boys laughed at me because I felt cold,' Stephen complained. 'They said I wasn't tough like them.'

'You'll soon show them whether you're tough or not.' Margaret gave an encouraging smile. 'The water's boiling. Let's have a nice cup of cocoa.'

Robert returned about half an hour later, far more enthusiastic about his experiences.

'We had woodwork this afternoon,' he told them. 'They've got a terrific workshop, absolutely crammed with tools.'

'What did you make?' asked Stephen.

'Well, nothing yet, but I will soon. I had to show the teacher that I know how to use the saw and drills and things.' Robert grinned proudly. 'He was surprised how well I could do it, so I told him I helped to build the church at home.'

'What are the boys and girls like?' asked Pauline.

'All right. The form master told them I'd come from Africa, so they kept asking me about lions and things all day.'

Stephen's face brightened. 'I'll tell them about lions at my school. They won't say I'm soft then.'

'That's right,' agreed Robert. 'I bet none of them have been camping in the bush.'

'I'll tell them about elephants and snakes and crocodiles.'

Margaret turned away to hide her amusement. She could imagine the exaggerated tales that Stephen was likely to tell if the other boys continued to tease him, but it was a relief to know that her brothers were settling down. Pauline was always shy with strangers, so it was no surprise that she had not enjoyed her first day at school.

Mrs Croft called in again that evening and found Margaret battling with a loaf of bread.

'Getting lunches ready for tomorrow are you? Good idea. You'd have a job trying to get all that done in the morning. And they won't go stale in the fridge overnight.'

Margaret gazed ruefully at the crooked remains of the loaf. 'I'm hopeless at this. I just can't cut it straight. And the slices are so thick I know they're all going to complain.'

'Let them do their own if they're not satisfied.' Mrs Croft smiled gently. 'I'll do a couple for you if you need some more — not that I'm much of an expert, but I've had more practice.'

'Oh, thank you. Just three more please.'

Mrs Croft produced three neat slices and helped to fill sandwiches with corned beef.

'You know, dear, you can buy bread that's already sliced. It would save you an awful lot of time, and it would please everybody because the bread would be thinner.'

'Oh. Where could I get that?'

'Right there at the local baker's, my dear. It's wrapped up, so you probably didn't know what was inside. Just ask for a sliced loaf. It costs about a penny more, but it will probably go further. Thinner slices and no wastage, you see. It keeps fresh longer when it's wrapped up, too. It's waxed paper, you see.'

Mrs Croft turned to the refrigerator and her eyes widened.

'Oh, you haven't got this switched on.'

'We haven't used it,' said Margaret. 'We've never had one, so we don't know how it works.'

'Goodness me, you must make use of this, dear. Look, I'll show you everything you need to know.'

Mrs Croft switched on the refrigerator, set the regulator and then filled an ice cube tray with water.

'Next time I come I'll show you how to get the ice out of this. Now then, you'll see the fridge has a separate compartment up here. Inside this is where you keep frozen things.' She placed the cube tray inside and closed the door. 'If you buy a lot of meat you can freeze some of it in there — keeps fresh for weeks that way. When you want to use it you just take it out and defrost it.'

'Thank you, Mrs Croft. I'm so glad you help me with all these things.'

'Well, what are neighbours for? I know it must be difficult for you with everything being so different. If I went to Africa I'd need you to help me.' Mrs Croft turned back as she was leaving. 'By the way, Les hasn't forgotten about that window. He's got the glass and he'll help you to put it in on Saturday afternoon, if that will be convenient for you.'

'That would be very good of him,' said Margaret. 'Thank you. Yes, we will be here on Saturday afternoon.'

The following day seemed to drag for Margaret and it was difficult to concentrate when she was worrying about the two younger children going home from school alone. Would they do anything silly when they were there by themselves — break something, or lose the key? When she arrived home, the sight of Pauline's tear-streaked face only confirmed her fears.

'What's the matter? What's happened?'

'She's just being a baby,' said Stephen disparagingly.

'I'm not going to that awful school any

more,' Pauline mumbled.

'What happened today?'

'Nothing.'

'Something has upset you. What is it?'

Eventually, Pauline revealed that she would have to take something to show the class. Each pupil had a set time during the week, and Pauline had learned that her turn would come on Thursday.

'It's called Show and Tell. I haven't got anything to show. We haven't got any of our things here. So I'm not going.'

'You can make something before Thursday. Just think of all the toys the children used to make in the village.'

'I've got nothing to make with.'

Margaret thought rapidly. 'You could make a whirly disc. I bet the other children have never seen one. They'd love to have one, and you could show them how to do it. There's plenty of cardboard around, and string.'

The suggestion had an immediate effect. 'Yes. That would be good. Can we use those coloured pencils?'

'Yes. We might find some paints, too.' By now Margaret had accepted that Robert's attitude was more practical; they could use anything they needed and replace it when Aunt Joan returned.

Making the simple toys raised Pauline's

spirits and she looked forward to her chance of showing something new to the class, but they were all beginning to realise that looking after themselves was not going to be as easy as they had believed. Their beds were not made properly and the washing up never seemed to be finished. More and more tasks cropped up unexpectedly, and regular chores had no appeal. The person who was supposed to be watching the grill tended to lose patience, so toast always seemed to be either burnt or underdone; Stephen and Pauline grumbled about the detour they had to make to buy bread and milk on the way home from school, while Robert fumed when he was asked to peel potatoes.

'Why don't we just have rice? That's much easier.'

'Because we have to eat plenty of vegetables. We need the vitamins. You know that.'

Sliced bread helped Margaret to pack lunches more easily, but that job was tiresome because everybody pestered her for different fillings.

'I wish we could all go out and order a nice meal instead,' she sighed as she wrapped yet another packet of sandwiches.

Mornings tended to be chaotic no matter how she planned ahead, and breakfast time always seemed to end in a desperate rush. She dared not skimp her make-up, and she felt impelled to give detailed instructions to Pauline and Stephen before sending them off to school.

'Remember, when you come home you must be very careful. Don't switch on any heater except this one in the kitchen. And don't put anything near it. Don't switch it on at lunch-time. Keep your coats on instead. And be very careful crossing the road.'

By Friday evening they were all feeling disgruntled. Margaret had received her first pay packet, which eased her worries about buying fresh food, but she had not allowed for Income Tax and National Insurance deductions, so her total wage was less than she had anticipated. She cooked a simple meal of sausages and rice for tea, and sat down to eat with little appetite. She was missing her parents more than ever before, and she lost her temper when the two younger children began to bicker about washing the dishes.

'Stop arguing,' she shouted. 'You'll all do what you're told, *when* you're told, and I don't want to hear another word about it.'

A sulky silence followed, but as Robert gathered up the greasy plates, Pauline began to grumble again.

'I hate it here. Everybody keeps bossing me about. And I'm not going to that awful school any more.'

Margaret looked up, her cheeks reddening with anger. 'Please yourself,' she snapped. 'It doesn't matter to the rest of us. You can go to a Children's Home instead, and that will make life easier for me.'

She jerked her chair back from the table and rose quickly to her feet, then stalked out to the hall, slamming the door behind her.

'Now you've done it,' whispered Stephen after an uneasy pause.

'Well, I don't like that school,' muttered Pauline defiantly.

'Better to go there than live in a strange place with none of us anywhere near you,' said Robert.

The outburst made them stop and think, and they looked at each other with mounting guilt. They had relied on Margaret to care for them and take the place of their parents, often complaining or criticising, but never pausing to consider that she must have been feeling unhappy too. Compared with all the cooking and washing that she had done, their chores seemed small.

'We've been selfish,' said Robert. 'We ought to do more to help.'

'Let's have a really good clean up now and

put everything away,' suggested Stephen.

'Yes, and let's do it every day without waiting for Margaret to start yelling,' said Pauline.

Soon afterwards she went in search of Margaret and found her sitting in darkness in the back room.

'I'm sorry,' sobbed Pauline. She ran across the room and leaned against her sister's knees, flinging her arms around her neck. 'I'm sorry. I won't say nasty things about that school any more. Don't send me away.'

Margaret hugged her closely, tears streaming down her cheeks.

'I won't send any of you away. Everybody's tired and cross today and none of us meant what we said. It's going to be hard, living by ourselves until Aunt Joan gets back, but we'll manage somehow.'

She wiped her eyes with a crumpled handkerchief and hugged Pauline again.

'Come on. We've all been longing to experiment with the coal in that brass box. Let's see if we can light a fire in here, and then we'll play some kind of game before bedtime.'

12

It was easier to carry out good intentions on a Saturday, when none of them had to go to school. The calm atmosphere gave Margaret greater confidence, and she smiled and waved jauntily to the other children when she set off for her half day at work. They had already made a start on the washing up, and they had promised to help each other to change the sheets on all the beds.

'Right,' said Robert as he closed the front door. 'Now let's get the whole place clean and tidy before she gets back.'

Mrs Croft had been keeping an eye on their house from across the road, and she saw them go in a group to the local baker's shop. They were such a nice family, she thought. So close. It was lovely to see how they co-operated and cared for each other.

Her husband grinned when she called him into the dining-room for lunch.

'What's going on over there today?' he asked.

'I don't know what you mean.'

'Come on now, you can't kid me. A quick snack in the kitchen is more usual for Saturdays.'

Mrs Croft laughed. 'I'm watching for

Margaret. If she has a half day off today it would be an ideal time to do the laundry.'

'She might be planning to take the others out somewhere.'

'If she is, that's all right with me. Though she did say they'd be there. You said you'd fix that window today.'

'That job won't take long.'

Mrs Croft shrugged, then her chin lifted with sudden interest. 'Look, here comes the bus now. Yes, there she is.' She nodded with satisfaction. 'I'll give her time for lunch, then go over and see what's what. It would be silly for her to do the whole wash by hand when she has a perfectly good machine sitting there waiting to do the job.'

Margaret answered the ring on the front doorbell and she greeted her neighbour with genuine pleasure. It was such a relief to know that she lived close by and was continuing to be so helpful.

'I just wondered when you'd thought of tackling the laundry,' said Mrs Croft. 'If you want to make a start now I can stay and help. Otherwise, I'll just explain and you can do it by yourself when you feel inclined.'

'Oh, no, I'd much rather you were here,' said Margaret fervently. 'We've never even seen a machine like that. I'd love it if you could stay.'

'It's not difficult, once you know how.' Mrs Croft followed the girl through to the laundry. 'Les will be here in a few minutes. He's got the glass for that broken window.'

Once the machine had started, Mrs Croft said they could all relax and leave it to do its work. The family had never seen washing accomplished with such little effort and they were highly impressed, but Margaret still felt impelled to supervise. She kept going back to make sure the machine was operating smoothly, but the others found it more interesting to watch Robert and Mr Croft replace the broken pane in the front room.

'I can't believe this could all be done so quickly,' said Margaret, as she and Mrs Croft pegged sheets onto the line in the back garden. The machine was already dealing with a second load. 'The women in our village would be astounded, and very envious. They have to carry all their laundry down to the river. They beat the dirt out with stones.'

'Did your mother have to do that too?'

Margaret chuckled. 'No, she hired a washerwoman.'

Mrs Croft vaguely recalled stories of European women in India, who seemed to recline for most of the day, prostrated by the heat.

'Did you have a lot of servants?'

'No. Someone helped with the ironing, but that's all. Mum did all the cooking and everything.'

'What kind of iron did you have?'

'An old-fashioned one. You had to heat it over a fire.' Margaret smiled reminiscently, thinking of the plump woman who came regularly to do that job. High temperatures never seemed to affect her, even on the hottest days. 'It's much easier to do everything in this country — once you know how things work.'

'You seem to have settled in very quickly.'

'Thank you. But it is much easier here. Take supplies, for example. You don't have to think days or weeks ahead. If you need something you can just go to a shop.'

'Huh! It wasn't always like that. Rationing hasn't been over for long, you know. Just be glad you don't have to bother with ration books and all those points and things.'

Trying to obtain ration books would have been the biggest hurdle for them, thought Margaret, but she merely nodded and Mrs Croft began the first of several stories about wartime shortages.

The next morning Robert spent most of his time tinkering with the man's bicycle. He then set up an obstacle course for himself on the back lawn and rode in and out between the tins and plant pots, gradually improving his balance. Soon after lunch he announced that he was going out to cycle properly.

'It's too dangerous,' snapped Margaret at once.

'No, it's safe enough over here. The roads are smooth and there aren't any rough edges. People stick to the rules, too.'

'There's too much traffic.'

'I'm going to school by bike tomorrow, no matter what you say. The streets are quiet today, so it's better to try it now.'

'No, it's too dangerous.'

'All the other lads do it.' Robert began to stride out of the kitchen, brushing aside her objections. 'Anyway, you can't stop me. I'm the man of the house. In Gnujeemia I'd be the boss, not you.'

'We're not in . . . ' Margaret gave up as the door slammed behind him. As he had said, there was no way to stop him, and before long they might find far more important issues to argue about.

Les Croft was working in his garden, clipping the hedge that ran along the inside of the low brick wall. He gave a friendly wave when Robert wheeled the bicycle out to the road and Robert waved back, hoping he would be able to mount and steer with expertise whilst being watched.

'I see you've got yourself some transport,' Croft called. 'Where are you off to?'

Robert braked and stopped near him, resting one foot on the kerb. 'I'm going to ride to school and find out how long it takes.'

'Hm.' A frown flickered across the man's face. 'What did Margaret say about that?'

'She knows.'

Robert coloured slightly and Croft guessed there had been a dispute. 'I suppose she's not keen on the idea.'

Robert nodded and Croft frowned again. The boy claimed to be fourteen years old, but he looked as if he might only be twelve. Still, the whole family looked remarkably young. Perhaps they'd all inherited a childish appearance.

'I can understand why Margaret feels uneasy,' he said. 'You haven't had much experience with our traffic, and you probably don't know all the rules.' He came to a quick decision. 'How would you like me to come with you, just for this first time? I could show you the best way. You know, so as to avoid main roads.'

Robert barely hesitated. Despite putting on a brave front for Margaret's benefit, the journey had loomed as a formidable trial. It would be good to have a companion, someone to watch out for cars while he found his way. 'I would like that. Thank you very much.'

'Nip over and tell Margaret while I get my bike out. She'll feel more comfortable if she knows you're not out alone.'

The two riders travelled safely to and from the school, taking a quiet route along back roads, and the next morning Robert set off in high spirits. Margaret waved farewell from the doorstep, wishing she felt so confident about her own prospects. Starting a new week seemed almost as great a step as starting the job in the first place.

Sue Dale greeted her in her usual chatty manner.

'Good day off yesterday?' she asked. 'Did you do anything special?'

'Not really. There were too many jobs to be done.'

'Yes, well I suppose it will take a week or two to get yourself properly organised.'

Margaret nodded in agreement and edged away towards her own office without saying more. No doubt the receptionist was only trying to be friendly, but she tended to ask personal questions and it was too risky to let anyone know too much about family affairs. Moreover, the comparison between them was so great. She always felt awkward and inexperienced beside the older, more professional member of staff. For one thing, she could never forget that she was wearing second-hand clothes, while Sue was always impeccably dressed, appearing in a different outfit each day. Sue probably felt great disdain for her regular two garment change.

Sue was determined to break down the newcomer's reserve, so she went into the office on the slightest pretext, staying to gossip for several minutes each time. She told herself that Margaret was beginning to act more naturally and it would not be long before she opened up. One great point in her favour was that she had the sense to ask for help before starting on a new task, rather than guess and make a hash of it.

It was late morning before the editor sent for Margaret. She took in the letters that she had already typed and he accepted them with a nod and a smile before handing her another page.

'No rush for this,' he said. 'Finish everything else first. How was your weekend?'

'Very nice, thank you.'

'How are you managing with your money?'

Margaret took a deep breath. 'Very well, thank you.' He must not suspect that she could foresee financial difficulties ahead. She had hoped to buy extra clothes for them all this week, but the groceries had cost more than she had expected on Saturday afternoon. The shelves in the larder were still well stocked, but she could not depend on tinned goods. She had to buy fresh food to keep the family healthy. After putting aside enough to pay for bus fares, bread, milk and eggs, there was not much left over.

Anderson studied her face and gave a grunt. 'Hm. I presume you don't have to pay rent. You said your aunt owns the house, didn't you?'

'Yes.' Margaret looked down at the paper in her hand, wishing he would stop asking such intrusive questions.

'Would you please tell me why I always seem to scare you so much?' he demanded suddenly. 'I'm not such a fierce old bear, am I?'

Margaret smiled faintly. 'I'm not scared of you.' She looked up quickly to prove her words. She would have to find some reason to explain her reticence. 'It's just that I'm not used to meeting many people. We lived in a rather isolated place, you see.'

'That didn't seem to inhibit you when you first applied for the job.'

Margaret blushed and he continued more gently. 'Look, if you're worried about getting the push at the end of the week, forget it. I know I said a fortnight's trial, but I've definitely made up my mind to keep you. That is, if you want to stay, of course.'

'Yes, please.'

'Good. Now then, I do wish you would relax a bit more. I want to feel that I can lean back and think aloud and get some suggestions from you as we go along.'

'Suggestions from me?' exclaimed Margaret, startled out of her usual reserve.

'Why not? Your father ran a newspaper, didn't he? You must have some ideas of your own and I'd like to hear them.'

Margaret blushed again. It seemed that her eager claims were about to cause trouble and it would be better to own up now rather than try to bluff her way through the consequences.

'Oh, I don't think I know enough about . . .'

He interrupted with a wave of his hand. 'I don't mean I want you to rack your brains trying to think of ways to improve this place. I just want your honest opinion when I ask for it.'

He said nothing more along those lines that day, but the following afternoon he called her into his office and invited her to sit at the small desk where she had typed her trial letter.

'This might interest you,' he said, dropping a typed manuscript down in front of her. 'Just

195

read it through, would you?'

He strolled to his own desk, pulled out the bottom drawer to rest his feet and opened a large national newspaper so that Margaret would not feel as if she were under observation. From behind the broadsheet pages he watched her reading the manuscript, and was pleased to see the sudden frown and a flush of irritation. He pretended to study his newspaper for two or three minutes after she had laid the report down, then he casually folded the pages.

'Finished that? What are your reactions?'

Margaret felt sure of her ground and for once she did not hesitate to speak.

'Whoever wrote that doesn't know what he's talking about. All that piffle about religious persecution, for instance. It's not religion that causes trouble, it's tribalism. If the smaller tribes had worked together instead of squabbling about trivial issues, the two largest tribes wouldn't have gained such importance in the first place. Now the minor tribes are trapped in the middle. They have to agree with whichever side has the most power in their district.'

'I see. What are those two large tribes fighting about?'

'Wealth and power.' Margaret cast her mind back to her father's explanations.

'Mineral deposits are in the north — copper mostly — which is how the north became wealthy. But oil has been discovered in the south, and oil could prove to be far more important.'

'How come that's not generally known in the outside world?'

'The tests are not complete.'

'Ah-hah. Is your father in the oil business?'

'No, he's a surveyor mainly. They were planning a new railway to the port.'

Anderson nodded thoughtfully. 'No doubt a railway would be vital to a new oil industry. But let's get back to that report. What about the tribal customs?'

'A lot of nonsense. Most of the people are Christian.'

'Witch doctors still exist, don't they? That surely proves that primitive beliefs haven't died out.'

Margaret paused to gather her thoughts. Her mother was a fully trained nurse and this was a subject that her parents had discussed frequently.

'It's the ritual that's important,' she said quietly. 'All nationalities and religions have rituals that mean something to the people who take part. In western medicine we have the placebo, don't we? The doctor sometimes gives a fake pill. The patient believes it will do him good, and so when he recovers he thinks the pill has cured him, even though there was no drug involved whatsoever.'

Anderson nodded again, a glow of excitement rapidly expanding within him. His hunch had been right. No matter what her personal story turned out to be, this girl was going to be extremely useful.

'I really believe we are lucky having you with us just now when this war is headline news,' he said. 'You can give us the true background. You actually lived there and taught local children, so you can make our stories more authentic.'

'I don't know anything about the war,' protested Margaret. 'Only what I read in your paper. I don't even watch the news on television, because I daren't let my young brother and sister see it.'

'You know what the people are really like.' Anderson rubbed his hands together and gave a little clap. 'In fact I'd like you to write an article for us. Tell us what it was like to grow up in a small African village.'

'Well, I'll try,' faltered Margaret.

'Good. Make a start on it this evening and see how it goes. We'll pay you freelance rates if we can use it.'

He suddenly stood up, swept a bundle of papers off his desk and strode away, leaving

Margaret to wonder how to approach the task, and how much the freelance rates would be if she were successful.

⋆ ⋆ ⋆

Robert pedalled to a shop he had noticed on the way to school that morning, hoping that no other boy would arrive there before him. He heaved a sigh of relief when he saw the sign was still fixed to the front window.

BOY REQUIRED
FOR NEWSPAPER ROUND
Must have own bicycle

Carl Perkins smiled as the flushed youngster entered the shop.

'You're in a hurry. What can I do for you?'

'I've come about the job — delivering papers.'

Robert had asked one of his classmates what the job would entail, and learned that several boys had tried newspaper rounds for varying lengths of time when they had felt the need for money. The main reason for giving up was the early start in the mornings. It was hard to get out of bed so early, especially in the winter.

Perkins smiled again and shook his head.

'I'm sorry. You've got to be fourteen. That's the law.'

'I am fourteen!' protested Robert.

The shopkeeper eyed him doubtfully and Robert drew himself up, warning himself to maintain dignity and make sure he did not lose his temper.

'I assure you that I am fourteen,' he said in his most formal manner. 'I can bring in my birth certificate and my passport.'

'A passport, eh?' Perkins studied the boy more carefully. He certainly looked younger than he claimed to be, but not many boys of that age had a passport. 'You're not from around here, are you?'

'I live quite close,' replied Robert. 'I pass here on the way to school.'

Perkins nodded. 'Allingham Modern. What makes you think you would like this job?'

'I need the money,' said Robert frankly. 'If we hadn't come to this country I wouldn't have to go to school. I could have left and got a full-time job.'

'That must be frustrating. Where have you come from?'

Robert went through the interrogation that always followed when people learned that he had been in Gnujeemia when the war had broken out, and then they returned to the subject of delivering papers. Robert claimed that he was used to rising early in the morning and Perkins decided that he liked the lad. He looked immature, but he seemed to have a good head on his shoulders and he certainly sounded keen to get the job. Besides, nobody else had applied and he needed someone. His wife had enough to do with a new baby, without having to mind the shop while he did the paper round himself.

'I'll tell you what I'll do,' he said. 'If your parents will give permission for you to work, I'll give you a trial run.'

'Our parents aren't here,' replied Robert. 'Our big sister is our guardian for the time being.'

'I see.' Perkins reached for the batch of forms waiting on a ledge below the counter. 'If your guardian is willing to sign this, and if you bring proof of your age tomorrow afternoon, I'll take you in the van to show you the round. If you still want to do it after that, you can start the next morning.'

Robert rode home, puffed with pride and whistling cheerfully. The two younger children completed their chores with only mild grumbles and he hugged his news to himself, waiting for Margaret to arrive. The announcement would cause a sensation, he was quite sure about that, and he wanted to enjoy his special moment to the full. He was concentrating so hard on his own affairs, trying to decide on the best time to disclose his secret, he failed to notice how distracted Margaret seemed to be. She usually listened attentively to the younger ones' prattle, trying to behave as if she were truly interested in their school activities because their mother would have done so; today, however, her mind was occupied by thoughts of the task set by her editor. It was a challenge, she decided. He wanted to test her. She should not have exaggerated her experience and accomplishments so much. Yet he had already said she could keep her job. Perhaps there was no need to worry so much about failing.

Robert restrained himself until they were all sitting down to their meal, then he announced with a casual air, 'I got a job today.'

'That's nice,' murmured Margaret.

'A job!' exclaimed Stephen.

Margaret looked up, the words suddenly making an impact. She stared at Robert, noting his excited expression, and laid her loaded fork down. 'Did you say a job?'

'That's right.'

'You can't. You have to stay at school, that's the law.'

Robert shook his head and a tantalising

pause followed while he took a mouthful of rice, but he was unable to keep them in suspense for long.

'I'm going to deliver newspapers for a shop down that way.' He waved one hand to indicate the direction. 'All you need is a bike. I'll get two pounds a week. How about that? We'll be able to buy all sorts of things. Like coal. You said that would only last a few more days. We can get some more shoes, too, and stop all that nagging about wet feet. And get some chocolate for a treat. Or ice cream. It'll be marvellous.'

'Just a minute,' Margaret interrupted. 'Forget what we could do if we had money. Tell us more about the job.'

'I told you. I'm going to deliver newspapers.'

'When?'

'In the afternoons.' Robert flushed slightly and then stared at her defiantly. 'In the mornings, too. That's why I'll get so much money.'

'What time in the mornings?'

'Quarter past six. I won't need to get up till six o'clock. I've only got to go two streets away.'

'I don't think that's a very good idea.'

Robert scowled. 'Why not?' he protested. 'When we were at home we got up at six o'clock. Even before that sometimes.'

'That was different. It was hot there so we had to start early. Besides, we rested in the afternoons.'

'Not always.' Robert decided he must not allow himself to be sidetracked into an argument. He was the man of the family, perfectly capable of making important decisions on his own initiative. 'Anyway, I've told them I'll take the job, so they're relying on me to turn up.'

'Not tomorrow morning!' gasped Margaret.

'No, but I've promised to be there in the afternoon. The boss is going to show me round.'

'What's wrong with the idea?' asked Stephen. 'I think it's terrific. I wish I could get a job like that.'

Margaret smothered a sigh. 'For a start, I want to know who's supposed to get him there on time. You know what it's like getting out of bed in the cold.'

'I'll get myself up,' declared Robert. 'There's no point in rushing out of bed just to go to school, but it'll be worth it when I'm earning money.'

Margaret could think of numerous reasons why he should not accept such a job.

'You'll get soaked if it rains. You can't go to school all wet.'

'There's a stack of yellow gear in the shed. It's waterproof, specially made for bike riders.'

'What about Pauline and Stephen? They'll be alone every afternoon.'

Pauline stared at them, her lips parting in dismay, but Stephen's pride immediately surfaced and he sat up straighter.

'We can manage perfectly well by ourselves. We don't need a nanny.'

'We need the money,' said Robert. 'So you might as well stop making all this fuss.'

'Yes, I suppose you're right.' Margaret realised he should be rewarded for his good intentions and she managed to smile. 'Try it for a week, anyway, and see how you get on.'

Robert grinned triumphantly, holding back an important piece of information until the table had been cleared.

'You have to sign that,' he said, pulling a folded piece of paper out of his back trouser pocket and flicking it towards her.

'What is it?'

'It's a form to say that I'm fourteen and you give me permission to work.'

Margaret sighed as he handed her a fountain pen. 'I don't know if this is legal — me signing these sorts of things.'

'You're my legal guardian. Dad said you were in charge. By the way, I have to take proof of my age, so I'll need my birth certificate and everything as well.'

Margaret hesitated a moment longer then gave in. Signing this form could hardly matter after the other more official ones she had signed. 'I hope you don't find this all too much for you. You'll have to go on Sunday mornings as well, you know.'

'I know.' Robert folded the completed form and put it back into his pocket.

'And what about homework? Have you got any today?'

'That's finished. All done in the lunch break.' Robert shrugged nonchalantly. No need to explain that another boy had drawn the maps for him in exchange for a French translation. 'How was your job today?'

'Mr Anderson wants me to write an article about our village.'

'That's terrific.'

'I don't even know how to start.' Margaret shook her head. 'I shouldn't have made out that I know so much about running a newspaper.'

'What's so hard about writing an article?' demanded Robert. 'It's only another name for an essay, isn't it? We have to write essays all the time for school.'

The other children also thought the task should be easy.

'I reckon that's a great idea,' exclaimed Stephen. 'Something to show the kids at school. Will it have your name on?'

'They might not print it,' laughed Margaret. 'Even if I manage to write it.'

'It won't take long,' said Pauline complacently. 'We'll all help you.'

13

Rain was falling heavily again the next morning.

'You're surely not going on your bike today,' objected Margaret, as Robert struggled into the yellow leggings and cape.

'Of course I am. I couldn't possibly get wet underneath all this. Besides, I'll be riding my bike this afternoon when I start my job.'

'I don't think you'll last long at that job if this weather keeps up.'

Her words only served to increase Robert's determination. 'Stop fussing. I'm the one who's doing it, not you. Think about something useful instead, like that article of yours.'

Margaret had stayed up late the previous night working on the article. She had carried their aunt's typewriter down to the kitchen, telling herself that she should adopt Robert's attitude. Surely he had the right idea; if a teacher had asked for an essay, she would have just got on with the task without worrying about it. After several false starts she had decided to imagine she was writing a letter to a new penfriend. She would confine herself to a description of their house and a few other buildings in the village, and then relate how generators and gas cylinders had helped to provide modern comforts in a remote area. She would make no mention of the school. Too many people were aware that she had claimed to be a teacher, and she did not want to explain the strange circumstances that had brought about that situation. It would not do to reveal her complete lack of training.

Anderson was impatient to see what his protégée had produced, so he sent for her immediately after she arrived for work.

'Did you make a start on an article for me?'

'Yes, but . . . ' Margaret had been tempted to leave it at home, not wanting to let anyone see it before she had time to make improvements; but she had finally decided it was better to take proof that she really had written something.

'Good. Bring it in here and we'll have a cup of tea while I have a quick gander.'

'It's not ready for . . . '

'I'm not expecting perfection. I just want to see what you've done so far.'

His expression gave no indication of his thoughts as he read quickly through the manuscript, but inwardly he was exultant. He was going to learn a great deal more about his young employee within a very short time. Margaret watched him turn back to the front page, and her spirits sagged as he reached for a blue pencil and crossed out the first two paragraphs.

'I want you to start here, right in the village itself. Don't bother with explanations. We'll make a short introduction at the head of the piece.' He looked up and gave an encouraging smile. 'Yes, I like it. I think our readers will like the style, too.'

'Thank you.'

'I notice that you haven't mentioned the school yet.'

Margaret blushed. It seemed that she would have to include it after all; but if she did that, it might be impossible to hide her age and true work experience.

'Which is good,' he went on. 'We can make a special little feature of that later. Something for our readers to look forward to. So leave this as it is. But this evening I'd like you to write about the school. Tell us how big it is, what is taught there, and what kind of facilities the teachers have.' He finished his tea in one long gulp and heaved himself to his feet. 'We're having a full staff meeting at eleven o'clock. Be there.'

Margaret slipped self-consciously into the room where the meeting was to be held, a few moments before Anderson entered. He looked around to make sure everybody was present, then drew his chair closer to the table.

'Right, we don't want to waste any time, so let's get started straight away. Margaret, you keep a few notes.'

The discussions began and Margaret was surprised to learn that the business was in decline. More customers were buying the *Daily Chronicle*, which was published in a nearby city and, as a result, sales of the local paper had diminished. Several local firms had already transferred their advertising accounts to the rival newspaper, and the woman who had previously held Margaret's job had gone to work there.

'We can hold on a bit longer,' said the accountant, 'but we'll have to change things around pretty soon. Time is short, remember that. Once that new road is put through and the industrial estate gets going, the situation will only get worse. More workers will be travelling out of Allingham then, and thcy'll buy the city paper.'

'So we have to find ways to prevent that,' responded Anderson. 'We get news just as fast as they do. What we have to do is concentrate on reader appeal. Presentation is the key. Any ideas?'

The meeting continued with suggestions and arguments from all sides of the table. Margaret was the only one who remained silent, but she almost plucked up enough courage to speak when a middle-aged man raised the subject of Children's Corner. As soon as the meeting had ended, Anderson beckoned her into his office.

'Now then,' he said as she shut the door behind them. 'What did you want to say about Children's Corner?'

Margaret reddened. 'Well, I — er — '

'Come on, out with it. I told you I wanted honest opinions. What about Children's Corner?'

'Well,' she began hesitantly. 'I was just thinking that if children were really interested in the paper they would ask their parents to buy it. You could have a bigger section for them, and perhaps one more often instead of just at weekends.'

'We could do things,' he corrected. 'Don't forget you're a part of this set-up. Now then, what kind of items do you suggest?'

Margaret thought quickly. 'You could — I mean we could — have something different for competitions. Children don't want to colour a picture every week. And we could have little stories; maybe a serial.'

'Do you think you could produce enough

items to keep that section going for a reasonable length of time?'

Margaret gulped. 'Me? Do you mean you want me to do some of it?'

'Why not? You're the one with all the experience with children. And you've worked on a newspaper before. It's no secret that the children's section is useless, but nobody else seems eager to put their mind to it and help with improvements. I've thought of ditching it altogether often enough.' Anderson rubbed his hands together with an air of satisfaction and gave a little clap. 'See if you can organise a new competition for this coming Saturday. I'm sure you'll manage to do that at home. The overtime pay will come in handy.'

He went out for an early lunch and Margaret looked down at the notes she had scribbled during the meeting. Why couldn't she have hidden her feelings when the subject was raised, and why did Mr Anderson have to be so observant? Anyway, he surely didn't think she was capable of doing so much. Writing one or two articles about the village at home was one thing, but providing material for Children's Corner every week, perhaps even more often, was quite another. If only she had been honest at the start and given a real description of her father's newspaper; but she could not find the

213

courage to do so now.

She managed to hide her anxiety long enough to allow Robert to give an enthusiastic account of his new job experience, but soon afterwards she mentioned the challenge that she was facing. As before, her brothers and sister could see no difficulty.

'That will be fun,' said Pauline. 'We'll all make puzzles and things.'

'That's right,' agreed Stephen. 'We'll think of puzzles for juniors. You and Robert can think of some for seniors.'

'It's an easy way to make money,' exclaimed Robert.

Margaret smiled. 'If it were so easy, the problem wouldn't have arisen. It's true that Children's Corner is dull at the moment. None of you were impressed when I brought those pages home.'

'It'll be different when you do it,' replied Stephen. 'You can use the puzzles you made up for school, and all those stories you used to tell.'

'You can tell them how to make a whirly disc,' said Pauline. 'They loved that in my class. Oh, and I need something to show them this week, too.'

'Let's have trick photographs for the first competition,' suggested Robert. 'You know, a close-up of the end of a pencil or something, or a tiny part of a building. There are lots of funny looking buildings in this town.'

'We haven't got a camera.'

'Aunt Joan has.'

'We can't use that!' gasped Margaret. 'Aunt Joan is a professional photographer. Her cameras will be very valuable.'

'I wouldn't hurt it. Dad always lets me use his. Besides, if anything did happen to it, we could buy her another when she comes back.'

'You'll be able to print the photos here, too,' said Pauline.

'We are not going to use Aunt Joan's darkroom,' said Margaret firmly. 'We haven't got time to do anything like that for this week, anyway.' She thought for a moment then added, 'But perhaps we could use her camera later. Aunt Joan must have taken her best one with her, so if anything did happen to the one she left here it wouldn't be too much of a disaster. We definitely can't take the chance of spoiling her other equipment, though. We don't know enough about it.'

Robert resented the last remark, but he decided it would be wiser to ignore it for the time being. Margaret was gradually settling in, treating the house more as if they had a right to be there and not worrying so much about using their aunt's belongings. It would not be long before he had access to the darkroom.

The next day he awoke before the alarm clock sounded and he began dressing at once. He moved about as quietly as he could, but the floor boards near his bed squeaked and the bedroom door tended to stick and then open with a rasping noise. The electric light switch on the landing gave a loud ping when he pressed it down, and just as he reached the kitchen door he heard the clock ringing in the bedroom. He raced back upstairs, telling himself he was stupid to forget to switch the alarm off and hoping that nobody else had heard it. Margaret lay in bed listening to his activities. He had insisted that she leave him to get ready by himself instead of treating him like a baby, but she felt guilty. Mum would have got up and made a hot drink for him before he went out, but if she tried to do the same thing they would probably start arguing all over again.

Robert returned with a good appetite for breakfast and the cheerful announcement that no problems had arisen.

'So you can stop making such a fuss. I told you it would be all right.'

For the first competition in the newspaper they had all agreed that Margaret should write the beginning of an exciting story and the prize-winners would be those who sent in the best endings. Anderson nodded approval when she told him.

'Yes, far more interesting than the stuff we've had before. We'll run a promo in today's edition, telling kids to look out for a new competition. You carry on. And I like the thought of trick photographs. If you decide to go ahead with that idea, bring the film in here. The pictures will be developed the same day.'

He swept sheets of paper off his desk with his usual exuberance and marched towards the door, pausing there to make his parting shot.

'You'll be kept pretty busy after this if things go well — judging the entries. I suppose you realised that.'

Margaret stared after him, her eyes widening with dismay, but soon after she had returned to her desk her spirits rose again. She had achieved a great deal, both at home and in the office. If only her parents could see how well she was coping. She gave a little sigh at the thought, wondering what was happening in the village and hoping that everybody there was still safe. Working in a newspaper office meant that she had access to all the national daily publications, but no news from their home area had reached the outside world. So far, however, it seemed that most of the fighting was still taking place further south. She would start another letter tonight and hope it would be delivered eventually. She could give positive news without telling any untruths or leaving out too many details. It was better not to mention Aunt Joan at all. It would only worry Mum and Dad if they knew she was not there.

Margaret leaned back, thinking about the housekeeping arrangements and congratulating herself for organising everything so well. Who would have dreamed that things would be running so smoothly without Aunt Joan's help? She could even smile now over some of the mistakes and mishaps. Mrs Croft had been effusive with apologies when she heard that the lamb chops had frozen into a solid mass, stuck to the bottom of the freezer compartment.

'Oh, I'm sorry, dear. I should have told you — but I never thought. You have to wrap everything before you put it in. I should have remembered to tell you that. I did the same thing with a big fish when I first started.'

She showed Margaret how to defrost the refrigerator, and then explained that each item should be individually wrapped before freezing.

'You can't separate them otherwise. I broke

a knife once, trying to separate some cutlets.'

Mrs Croft had proved to be a great boon, popping in almost daily with cheerful words and little baked treats, as if to make sure that the younger ones had returned safely from school. She had introduced them to the pop-up toaster, so breakfast was easier and, better still, she had shown them how to use the vacuum cleaner. Everybody had wanted to experiment with that the first time, but the novelty was wearing off now.

She could not claim all the credit for success, Margaret reminded herself ruefully. If their neighbour had not visited so often, there would have been far more disputes over chores. Still, everything was working out well. Stephen and Pauline rarely woke in the night now and, so far as she knew, neither of them had wept during the past few days. She was also sleeping better herself.

That evening Margaret decided to cook mashed potatoes for a change, and was so intent on her task she did not notice how the others were suppressing excitement. When everybody had been served she went to her place, to find two large silver coins resting in the centre of her table mat. She stopped short in surprise, then picked up the money and set her plate down.

'Where did this come from?'

'I earned it,' Stephen declared proudly. 'I did some weeding for Mrs Summers.'

'Who's that?'

'She's the lady who lives two houses away. That way.' Stephen jerked his thumb towards his right.

'Five shillings? That's a lot of money for weeding.'

'It took me two days,' retorted Stephen huffily. 'She hadn't done anything for ages and the weeds were as high as this.'

He held out his hand to demonstrate their height and Pauline gave a little giggle.

'I hope you didn't pull all her good plants out as well.'

'Of course I didn't. Anyway, she said it didn't matter much if I made a mistake. I told her I didn't know English flowers, so she showed me her special ones.'

'Fancy being able to keep it a secret until you were paid,' exclaimed Margaret. 'That's wonderful.'

'She asked me to do some digging next week, so I'll earn some more money then.'

'Good! With Robert's money and yours, and my extra, we'll be able to do a lot of shopping on Saturday afternoon.'

'Your extra?' cried Robert. 'Does that mean they're going to print your article?'

'That's right. Two of them. They'll pay a

guinea for each article. That's one pound and one shilling. Next week I'll be doing Children's Corner again.'

'Yippee!' shouted Stephen. 'You're going to be famous and we'll be rich as well. When are you going to write some more articles?'

'I don't know that I'll have time,' she laughed. 'I only found out this morning that organising a competition means marking the results as well.'

'It's only like marking the lessons at school,' said Robert off-handedly. 'Anyway, we'll help.'

14

On Saturday morning Margaret repeated her usual instructions and warnings about behaviour.

'I'll be back in time for lunch. Now remember — no arguments. And be sensible. Don't do anything silly.'

The others solemnly agreed, but not long after she had set off to work the boys decided it would be an ideal time to experiment with Aunt Joan's camera.

'Outside,' said Robert. 'It's a really fine day and we shouldn't waste that good light.'

'Let's go to that funny little street where we bought the clothes,' Stephen suggested. 'Some of those buildings have weird carvings on them.'

'We can't go that far. There's the bus fare to think about.'

'We've got two bikes. I've been practising. We could get there and back pretty quick.'

'You can't even reach the saddle.'

'You don't need a saddle. I stand up.'

'Oh, I dunno . . . ' Robert knew that Margaret would have forbidden such an outing, but the temptation was too great and before long he had succumbed. 'Go on, then. You get the bikes out while I put a film in the camera.'

Pauline was half way up the stairs when they shouted to tell her they were going out. She raced after them as they headed for the front gate.

'What about me?' she grumbled.

'You can't come,' said Stephen. 'We've only got two bikes. Besides, you can't ride well enough to go in traffic.'

'You've got jobs to do, anyway,' added Robert. 'You haven't made your bed yet and you've got to do that errand.'

The boys gave flippant waves as they mounted their bicycles, then pedalled away, leaving Pauline staring after them with an angry scowl. They spent almost an hour photographing quaint features from various angles, and returned home full of enthusiasm after using up the whole film.

Pauline did not answer Robert's call when he opened the front door and he felt a rush of concern.

'Where do you think she'll be?'

Stephen shrugged. 'She's sulking.'

'Very likely.' Robert dashed upstairs, hoping to placate her before Margaret came back. They had been selfish to go out without her, he knew that well enough, and now they had to make amends.

He soon found that Pauline was not in the house, nor in the back garden, and he clutched his stomach to quell a sudden lurching sensation.

'Do you think she's over the road at Mrs Croft's?'

'Bound to be. I bet she told her a big story.' Stephen was more interested in putting the bikes away. He would not admit to feeling tired, but he needed a few minutes of privacy in which to rub his aching legs. 'Don't worry. Mrs Croft will send her back now we're here.'

Pauline had not returned by the time he came back from the shed, and soon he began to share Robert's unease.

'She'll have gone for the bread,' he said, hoping that might be true. 'I bet she left that job to the very last minute.'

They fidgeted and pottered about nervously until Robert decided he would go out to search for her.

'You stay here,' he said. 'I'll go over the road.'

No one answered at the Crofts' house, so Robert hurried to the baker's shop. Mrs Talbot remembered the small blonde girl.

'The little girl who usually comes in with her brother after school? Yes, dear, I think she came in for a loaf this morning. About half past nine, I'd say. Is everything all right?'

'Yes, thank you, it's all right,' mumbled Robert, edging away quickly to deflect any awkward questions. 'If she got the bread, I don't have to.'

He could think of no other place to look. What were they going to say when Margaret came home?

Margaret was surprised when her little sister did not rush to greet her as usual.

'Where's Pauline?' she asked immediately.

The boys glanced sheepishly at each other. They had been dreading this moment.

'We don't know,' said Stephen. 'We haven't seen her since we went out.'

'She can't have got lost just going as far as the baker's shop,' said Robert defensively. 'She must have found someone to play with.'

Stephen tried to change the subject, explaining that they had been working and they had made a good start on the new competition, but Margaret cut him short with an exasperated sigh.

'Fancy not taking Pauline with you. You should have waited until she was ready.'

'We couldn't. We've only got two bikes.'

'Do you mean to say you've been out on those bikes? I can't trust you to be sensible, can I?' Margaret glared accusingly at Robert. 'It's far too dangerous, you know that. Fancy taking Stephen out on the roads! Besides, that wasn't fair, going out without Pauline.'

'I suppose she's sulking now,' muttered Stephen.

'Well, if she is, it would hardly be surprising. She was bound to feel left out of things, all on her own here. If you want to take photographs you'll have to wait until we can all go together.'

Fifteen more minutes passed before Pauline let herself in, using the key she kept on a string around her neck.

'Where have you been?' demanded Robert.

Pauline sidled past him hanging her head. 'I've been shopping.' She went into the kitchen and put her canvas bag down on a nearby chair, eyeing Margaret in a furtive manner. 'Sorry I'm late.'

Margaret frowned. Her little sister looked more nervous than she should for merely being late, and her eyes were brimming with tears.

'What happened?' she asked gently, going to her and placing an arm around her shoulders.

Pauline glanced up at her, then took a deep breath. 'I went shopping.'

'What happened after you got there?'

'Nothing.' A tense silence followed, during which Pauline flicked the corner of the mat up and down with one foot, then she continued, 'It's the money.'

Margaret clasped her hands together, striving to be patient. 'What was the matter with the money? You had a half crown. You should have got change.'

Pauline nodded miserably. 'I lost it.'

'You lost it?' shouted Robert. 'How much?'

'All of it, except this.' Pauline fumbled in her pocket then handed a threepenny bit to Margaret and burst into tears. 'I'm sorry.'

'We'll have to go and look for it,' said Robert. 'Where did you lose it?'

'I . . . I don't know. Along the road. I've been looking. We'll never find it now.'

'Trust you to do a thing like that,' grumbled Stephen.

'Margaret made that special purse on a string for you. Why didn't you put the money in that, like you were told?' scolded Robert. 'We didn't earn all that extra money just so that you could lose it.'

'She didn't do it on purpose,' Margaret interrupted. 'You two go back along the pavement and see if you can find it. Ask in the shop as well, just in case she dropped it there.'

She did not expect them to find any coins, but she wanted them to be occupied and out of the way while she comforted Pauline. By the time the boys returned, disgruntled and empty-handed, Pauline had calmed down and Margaret had decided how to handle the matter.

'Pauline is very sorry and she'll be more careful in future,' she said before the boys could speak. 'Now, we don't want to hear any more about it. Weekends are too short for squabbling.' The little girl looked down at her feet, too ashamed to face any of them, and Margaret hurried on with plans for the afternoon. 'We'll go back to that same shop and buy some extra clothes. And while we're in town we'll choose something nice for tea.'

As soon as Pauline had left the kitchen after lunch, Stephen complained that he had worked hard to earn money and he had a right to say what he thought about her carelessness with it.

Margaret paused in the midst of folding the tablecloth. 'Pauline hasn't had your experience, so you will have to help her. Leaving her alone this morning was not a good idea.'

'We've only got two bikes.'

'So you shouldn't have gone.' Margaret hurried on as he opened his mouth to protest. 'You mustn't leave her alone. She can't think properly if she's upset. She's only young, and she didn't do it on purpose.'

'Still . . . she should be more careful. She

knows we're short of money.'

Margaret tried to imagine how her parents might have dealt with the situation, and finally remembered how Mr Askejinaki used to deal with miscreants in his class at school. He always appealed to the pride of the bigger boys.

'Look, Stephen, Dad said that Robert is the man of the family now, didn't he? Well, when Robert isn't here you will have to take his place. That means that when Robert is not here, you are the man of the family. So every afternoon, while Robert is out doing his job, I want to be sure that you are looking after Pauline properly.'

Stephen straightened up and puffed out his chest. 'Yes. Right. You can depend on me.'

Although nobody mentioned the incident again, Pauline was obviously brooding about it and Margaret took great care not to pass comment about the cost of anything that afternoon. They called at the charity shop first and found that fresh supplies had come in, as the assistant had foretold on their previous visit. When clothing had been chosen for the younger children, she pro-duced a bottle-green matching jacket and skirt that fitted Margaret beautifully.

'That costume's new, you know,' the assistant confided. 'I was hoping you would come back before someone else bought it.'

'How is it that something as good as this came to be here?' Margaret turned around again, admiring her reflection in the long mirror. She would feel really smart when she arrived in the office on Monday.

'It's got the wrong label in. It's much too small for a fourteen. We often get new garments, you know, especially at the end of a season, but more often than not it's because of a mistake.'

'Well, I have to admit I'm glad they made a mistake,' said Margaret. 'This is ideal. Absolutely ideal.'

They went to the public library next, where Margaret was able to prove her identity and address with her wage packet from the *Daily Tribune*. She signed as Legal Guardian for the family, accepting responsibility for any books that her brothers and sister borrowed, and they were all allowed to choose books that afternoon.

'Just look at all those books!' exclaimed Stephen, staring around at the crowded shelves. 'There's thousands of them.'

'It's marvellous,' agreed Margaret. 'You won't be able to say you've got nothing to read now. We'll never manage to read everything here.'

She read a story to the younger children

that evening and gave Pauline an extra hug before tucking her into bed, but when she went up again minutes later she found Pauline weeping.

'What's the matter?' she asked, sitting down beside her. 'Surely you're not still worrying about that money? We can manage without it, and you'll be very careful another time, I know you will.'

Pauline raised her head slightly, then turned away and pressed her face into the pillow, gulping and gasping.

'Come on,' coaxed Margaret. 'Stop crying. You couldn't help it. Everybody loses something sometimes.'

Pauline suddenly twisted around then jerked upwards and flung herself into her sister's arms. She hid her face, shaking with sobs, and muttered a few indistinguishable words.

'Don't cry,' said Margaret again. 'You couldn't help losing it.'

Pauline lifted her head then drew herself back slightly and took a deep breath.

'I didn't lose it,' she wailed. She lifted the bottom of Margaret's cardigan and buried her face under it, her body quivering with emotion. Margaret clasped her tightly, unable to think of anything to say.

At last Pauline began to recover and she

drew away from her sister again, rubbing her eyes with the backs of her hands.

'What did you say?' asked Margaret. 'I couldn't hear you.'

'I said I didn't lose it.' Pauline's eyes filled with tears again and she bit her lip, fighting to prevent the tears from spilling over.

'What happened then?'

'I spent it.'

Margaret stared in disbelief. 'You spent it?' she whispered.

Pauline nodded dismally. She looked up at Margaret's expression and again her tears began to flow. She gave a loud sniff and wiped her eyes with her pyjama sleeves, but this time she did not hide in Margaret's arms. She was determined to complete her confession.

'What did you spend it on?' asked Margaret at last.

'I went to the pictures.' Pauline looked away and gulped, then flung herself down on the bed again. Margaret said nothing as she struggled to regain her own composure, stroking her sister's hair with one hand. She could not imagine Pauline doing such a thing when they were being so careful to eke out their money. How she wished their parents were there to help. What would Mum do in a case like this? Of course, if Mum were here the situation would not have arisen. She continued to stroke Pauline's hair, feeling compelled to do something to fill in time. The silence was becoming so drawn out it would be hard to break it.

Pauline moved her head away and sat up. 'I'm sorry,' she sniffled.

'You'd better tell me all about it,' said Margaret. 'What made you do it?'

'I was fed-up!' Pauline exploded. She glared defiantly for a moment, then slumped into a tearful huddle again. Margaret drew her closer and held her in her arms.

'Tell me about it.'

'I'm always left out of everything,' mumbled Pauline. 'You got that lovely job. And then Robert got his job, and then Stephen got a job and now he goes out in the afternoon and leaves me all on my own. I have to do all the dull things like sweeping up and I can't earn money like everybody else. All the girls at school say I haven't got anything new and I never go anywhere and I never go to the tuckshop and I never go to the pictures on Saturday like they do, and I had all that money this morning and I wanted to show them we do have lots of money and I can go to places, so I got on the bus with them and I went to the pictures.' She paused to take a breath and added, 'I'm sorry, really I am.'

'I know it's hard for you, not being able to go anywhere when we're living in such an exciting place,' said Margaret softly.

'But you all earned money, and I haven't, and I'm the one who stole it.' Pauline began to sob again and Margaret hugged her more closely.

'Ssh! You made a mistake, but it's over now.'

'I'm the only one who isn't helpful.'

'Of course you're helpful,' said Margaret with as much emphasis as she could muster. 'How do you think we'd manage if you didn't do your jobs? They're not as exciting as Robert's newspaper job, or the one that Stephen did this week, but they're just as important. If I had to start cleaning and making beds and everything when I got home we wouldn't have tea until ever so late. And I wouldn't have time to do any writing. You've been helping with the writing, and you've been thinking of all the puzzles and stories we know.'

Pauline quietened as Margaret listed all the useful duties she had carried out, but she suddenly began to shiver with cold.

'Get into bed with me,' she urged. 'We can huddle together and make each other warm.'

She felt much better when the bed became cosy. 'I'm sorry,' she repeated. 'I'll never do it again.'

She lay silently for a few moments, then Margaret felt her stiffen.

'What about Robert and Stephen?' she asked. 'Are you going to tell them?'

Margaret briefly considered the outcome. 'No,' she decided. 'It wouldn't do any good. We'll just let the matter rest.'

Pauline gave her a quick kiss and apologized again. Margaret studied her repentant face and gave a little smile. 'You didn't tell me anything about the picture,' she said. 'Did you enjoy it?'

'No. I felt terrible all the time I was there, and all the way home I was frightened of what everybody would say.'

Margaret gave her another hug. It seemed that Pauline had learned an important lesson.

'Well, that's your punishment,' she declared. 'Now let's forget all about it. It's time you were asleep.'

15

'My, you're looking smart today,' said Sue when she caught sight of Margaret's new costume. 'You must have been shopping.'

A blush rose quickly from the girl's neck and up through her entire face. How was she supposed to respond to a comment like that? It was all very well to receive compliments from Mum or Dad, telling her how pretty she was, or how clever she was, but people outside the family didn't usually say things like that to her. Still, it was gratifying to know that the change in her appearance was so noticeable. By now she was more adept at applying her make-up, and yesterday evening Mrs Croft had trimmed her hair again. She had set out this morning feeling sophisticated and mature, sure she could meet any challenge that might arise.

'It really suits you,' Sue continued. 'Have you seen Mr Anderson yet? Well, he's delighted with the number of competition entries that have come in.'

The editor strode into Margaret's office just after the second post had arrived, bringing with it another batch of letters and stories from children.

'Congratulations,' he said. 'You were right when you said the kids would like to do something different. We wouldn't have had this many coloured pictures sent in, especially so early in the week.' He wafted one hand towards the piles of competition entries on her desk. 'Pick out a few good ones and we'll start printing them today. That will encourage more kids to take notice. What do you think you'll do for next Saturday? Did you give any more thought to the idea of photographs?'

'The boys tried out the camera this weekend. They took a whole roll of film.'

Anderson rubbed his hands together then gave the customary clap, a habit that Margaret had come to recognise as a sign of enthusiasm.

'Have you got it with you? Good. Let's send it down straight away.' He picked up the telephone receiver on her desk and made a call to the basement. 'That you, Tony? Come up to Margaret's office to collect a roll of film. And let me know as soon as the pictures are dry.'

He turned to Margaret again and his eyebrows rose in admiration as he took in the full effect of her attire.

'A new outfit, eh? Did you splurge your whole pay packet?'

'No!' Margaret reddened and sought quickly for an explanation. She must not give the impression that she had been throwing her money about wastefully, but on the other hand she did not want everybody to know that her clothes had come from a charity shop.

'I didn't pay the full price,' she said lamely. 'I just happened to be lucky.'

'End of Season Sale, eh? Well, I reckon you got a bargain there. Now then, you concentrate on the competition today. Someone else will deal with the other stuff.' He moved towards his office, pausing in the doorway as if another thought had just occurred to him. 'I like that article about the village school. Very modest, to leave yourself out of it like that, but it works well. Write one about local people now. Tell us how an ordinary village woman would spend her day.'

He had scarcely left the room before Tony came in by the other door. He checked for a moment, staring in surprise at the young girl behind the desk, and then smiled winningly at her. The new employee had definitely settled in. When she was introduced on her first morning, and again at the meeting last week, she had seemed gauche and insignificant, not worthy of his attention; but now it seemed that first impressions could be way off target. She had suddenly blossomed into a very attractive young woman, and if she had only just arrived in the country there would be no competition as yet for her favours.

'Hi, Margaret. I don't suppose you remember my name, but I'm Tony Forrest.'

She looked up at him and her cheeks grew pink as she gave an answering smile. He was a handsome man about twenty years old, with dark brown wavy hair and twinkling brown eyes.

'Hello, Tony. Have you come for the film?'

'That's right. But no rush. How are you settling in?'

'Very well, thank you. Mr Anderson seems satisfied.'

'And so he should be.' Tony watched her open her handbag and take out the roll of film. 'What's on there that's so important?'

'Only pictures of Allingham, but they might be used for the children's segment this week.'

'I'd heard you'd taken that over. Good luck with it.' She had lowered her gaze as if she did not expect him to linger, so Tony cast around for a means to continue the conversation. 'Are you keen on photography?'

'Not really. My father and my brothers are more interested in cameras than I am.'

Good manners forced Margaret to look up at him as she spoke, but she quickly turned back to the pages on her desk to discourage him from pursuing the subject. Once people started asking questions like that you could never tell what it might lead to, and she might let something slip if she were not careful. Tony watched as she marked a faint pencilled cross at the top of the page in front of her to signify that it would not be amongst those in the running for a prize. She placed it on a pile at the left side of her desk and picked up another sheet of paper covered with large neat handwriting. Her attention seemed to be fixed on the task and he decided this was not the best moment to exert his charm upon her.

'I'd like to stay and chat, but there's a heap of stuff waiting for my expert attention downstairs so I'd better keep moving. It looks as if you're pretty busy, too. See you later.'

Margaret read all the children's efforts and sorted them by age and likely prospects, then typed a few letters for Anderson. She had started work on her new article when the editor strolled in again, about half an hour before she was due to leave that afternoon.

'Have you had any other ideas for children, apart from photographs?' he asked. 'For a competition, that is. Something that would be simple to set up this week?'

'We could ask the children to send in

jokes.' Margaret smiled reminiscently, recalling the fun that her young pupils used to find in simple quips and rhymes. Humour had often helped to relieve the stress when frustration or anxiety threatened to overwhelm her in a busy day. 'Children love telling jokes, and that would help to fill the column later.'

'There's a newspaper mind at work,' teased Anderson. 'Okay. Now then, how about some more pieces about life in your village? With personal details this time. Our readers are going to want to know more about you. How did your family come to be living in a place like that, anyway?'

Margaret hesitated. She would have to be very careful. How much private information did he expect her to reveal?

'Why weren't you in a big town, or the capital city?' he probed.

'The village was about half way between two important sites. It meant that Dad could come home every day, no matter which project he was working on.'

'I see.' Anderson nodded. 'Right, then. Tell us what happened the day you left. What was it like, suddenly coming from there to England? What did you find that was different, and how did you all react to the change?'

'Oh, no.' Margaret looked down and her hands gripped each other tightly in her lap.

Anderson watched intently. She seemed to have reverted to her previous state — to being nothing more than a timid young girl. She had looked just like that when he asked for details at their first meeting. Obviously he was close to learning vital information. Whatever it was that she was so anxious to hide, he was going to unearth it pretty soon. During the past week she had acquired a veneer of sophistication, but it was paper thin and she was showing now just how vulnerable she was. She was clamming up now, though. He would have to tread cautiously.

'What's the matter?' he asked in a softer tone. 'Did you witness some of the brutality?'

'No, it's not that. There was no fighting around our village.' Margaret was afraid to look up, wondering how much she could write about personal experiences without giving away her true age. Silence would be the safest strategy just now, but early training was compelling her to make a full response. Her parents had always insisted on courtesy to others, which meant she would have to say something to explain her withdrawal and reluctance to cooperate.

'I don't want the young ones to hear too much about the war,' she said at last. 'If I write about the family, more people are going to find out where we've come from. They'll start asking questions and talk about what's happening there.'

'I see.' Anderson nodded as if convinced. Some disturbing incident lay behind her refusal to talk, he decided. Some drastic experience. He was getting closer to finding out, but it was better not to pursue it any further just now. Better to change the subject.

'Today's edition,' he said casually, handing her a copy of the newspaper. 'Some of your stuff's in there. If you want any extra copies, pick them up at the front desk.'

'Thank you,' murmured Margaret, embarrassment causing her to redden yet again. She wished she could overcome that problem. She felt sure that flushing so readily made her look more childish than she actually was.

As soon as she was alone again she looked for news of Gnujeemia. The item took up less space than yesterday's report and was printed below local news, but at least it was on the front page. According to the new account, the situation between the warring factions had not changed and she told herself she should take comfort from that. If the fighting had not spread further north, their parents should be safe. She could say that to the little ones truthfully enough. But an actual attack was not the only problem for the village; she had begun to realise that a few days ago. How long would supplies last? Mum and Dad had always been careful to keep a reserve stock of essential items, but food was not the only consideration. Generators and trucks needed gasoline, and how could that be delivered? How long would medical supplies last? Then there was the question of clean water. The new pumps would stop if the village ran out of fuel, and then everybody would have to carry water from the river. What about the purification plant? They'd have to start boiling every drop of water again. Margaret closed her eyes for a moment, willing herself to believe that the fighting would soon end and all would be well.

When she felt ready to read on, she found a footnote announcing that a special series about life in Gnujeemia was starting that day on page four. She hastily turned to that page and stared down at the first article she had written about the village. A paragraph in a different font at the head of her work introduced her as a new journalist, and promised exclusive stories about the war zone which would provide a true and authentic background.

'Oh dear,' she said aloud and quickly clasped a hand to her mouth. What had she started here? She could write about a villager's lifestyle safely enough, and perhaps she could follow that with a piece about the capital city. But how long would it be before Mr Anderson became far more insistent and demanded the personal accounts he was so keen to acquire?

She was still pondering over that dilemma as she walked to the bus-stop, and was only vaguely aware that somcone had called her name.

'Hey, Margaret!' The man's voice came again, sounding louder and more imperative, and she turned to see a red car drawn up beside the kerb. She was about to turn away, thinking the summons could have nothing to do with her, when the driver's door opened and Tony Forrest's head appeared above the roof of the car.

'Get in quick,' he ordered. 'I'm not supposed to stop here.'

Another car pulled up behind, the driver tooting his horn impatiently. Tony gave an apologetic wave then re-entcred his car and leaned across to open the passenger door. Not knowing what else to do in such a rushed situation, Margaret climbed in beside him. He grinned at her and drove on almost before the door had closed.

'I'm going your way,' he said blandly. 'I'll

give you a lift right to your doorstep.'

'Oh. Thank you. That will be nice.' Margaret had planned to make some purchases before catching her bus, but it seemed churlish to say so and to decline the offer. Her coat was bunched up uncomfortably beneath her, but she decided to sit still rather than wriggle about trying to straighten it. She did not want to advertise the fact that she had no idea how to enter a car gracefully.

Tony concentrated on driving as he negotiated traffic in the congested central streets, but when they reached the outskirts of town he glanced at his passenger.

'Had a good day?'

'Yes, thank you.'

'Have you seen those photographs yet?'

'No, not yet.' Margaret had forgotten that the film should have been developed by now. It was strange that Mr Anderson had said nothing about it. Perhaps that meant all the photographs had been flops.

'Well, they're good. Take it from me, they're better than I expected. You can tell that brother of yours that he did a good job.'

'I'm relieved to hear it.'

Tony was pleased to see that she was smiling at last. She would succumb to his advances, no doubt about that, but he would have to take things slowly. She was obviously

246

a truly reserved girl and if he rushed his approach she would shy away.

'I should be able to give you a lift on most days,' he said. 'How about tomorrow? If you come out the back way I could meet you in the yard. Much easier and safer than picking you up along the road.'

'Are you sure that wouldn't be taking you out of your way?'

'Quite sure.'

'Well, thank you. That would be very nice.' Margaret decided instantly that she would accept a lift whenever he offered to drive her. She would not only reach home sooner than by bus, she would also save the cost of the fare.

'You live on Ridgeway Drive, I believe. We're almost there. What number?'

'Number one four nine. It's on the right hand side beyond the shops.'

'I know where you mean.'

Tony drew to a smooth halt opposite the house, climbed out quickly and reached the passenger door while Margaret was still fumbling for the handle. He opened the door with a flourish and offered his hand to help her out. Margaret felt flattered by the attention, but she remembered to look back to make sure she had left nothing behind. Tony seemed to hold her hand slightly longer than necessary, but she told herself he was only being friendly and did not try to pull away. When he finally released his hold she smoothed down the skirts of her coat and then met his gaze again. He certainly was a handsome man. He must have lots of lady friends.

'Thank you very much,' she said.

'Think nothing of it. It was a pleasure to have your company.' Tony escorted her across the road and smiled down at her, his brown eyes sparkling attractively. 'Tomorrow then? The back yard straight after work?'

'Thank you. That will be very nice.'

He was tempted to try a quick kiss, but commonsense suggested a more formal approach so he held out his right hand instead. When Margaret responded, expecting an impersonal and brief handshake, Tony suddenly thought of a new tactic and raised her hand to his lips. He gave a lingering kiss to the back of her hand and pressed her fingers gently before releasing her.

'Until tomorrow,' he murmured, then he returned to his car, gave a cheerful wave to the blushing girl and drove away.

Margaret opened the garden gate and walked slowly along the path, reliving every detail of that fleeting episode. It was the first kiss she had ever received from a man, other than a relative, and the fact that he had kissed her hand seemed tremendously romantic. She could have been a titled lady being courted by a knight or a squire in days gone by.

She was still smiling at the idea as she unlocked the front door, but the sudden crash from within, followed by angry voices, swept away the sense of euphoria. Clearly Stephen and Pauline were engaged in another argument. As she stepped into the hall she heard Stephen shout: 'That's more money you've wasted.'

'I couldn't help it,' yelled Pauline.

'If you can't do things right you should leave them alone. We can't afford to waste stuff like that.'

Margaret hurried to the kitchen. 'What's happened?'

Pauline turned towards the doorway with a look of anguish, then burst into noisy tears. Stephen was standing on the other side of the room, legs wide apart, his hands on his hips, mouth agape at Margaret's unexpected arrival.

'You're early,' he said.

'Somebody brought me home in a car.' Margaret looked at the pool of milk spreading across the linoleum. 'I suppose that's the reason for all the fuss. What happened?'

'I couldn't help it,' sobbed Pauline. 'I was

getting everything ready for tea. I was trying to be helpful.'

'It was a whole new bottle,' scolded Stephen.

Margaret decided to ignore that remark. Blaming Pauline for the accident was not going to ease the situation. The best policy would be to stay calm and soothe the feelings of both.

'I suppose your fingers were cold,' she suggested.

'Yes.' Pauline quickly grasped that excuse. 'It slipped right out of my hand. I didn't do it on purpose.'

'Of course you didn't. But we'll have to move that mat in case it gets wet. Thank goodness there's no carpet in here. Get an old newspaper please, Stephen. That will help to mop it up, then we can wash the floor properly.'

Mrs Croft called while they were putting the dishes away after the evening meal.

'We saw your article in the paper, Margaret. My, we didn't realise we had such famous new neighbours.'

Margaret gave a little nervous giggle. 'Hardly famous.'

'Well, you certainly seem to have made a hit with our local editor. He's lucky to have found you.'

Mrs Croft glanced around the kitchen. It looked as if the family was managing everything much better now. They had seemed to be floundering at first, always in a bit of a muddle, but apparently Margaret was not as young and inexperienced as she had appeared to be. Perhaps it was no wonder they'd been struggling at first. They'd had a very long journey to get here, so they would have been feeling tired. On top of that, it must have been really confusing, trying to deal with different systems and all the strange equipment in a foreign country.

'You have all settled in very nicely,' she said. 'Have you had any problems?'

'Nothing serious,' answered Margaret quickly before Stephen could announce news of the mishap. 'A bottle of milk got spilt today.'

'Well, if that's the worst thing that happens, there's nothing much to worry about.' Mrs Croft smiled at them all and began to edge towards the door. 'Well, I won't hold you up. I know you must have a lot to do on a work day. Don't forget, mind — if we can be of any help, just let us know.'

Just before six o'clock the next morning Margaret heard the clanging of the alarm clock in Robert's room. Seconds later came the clatter of something falling, followed by a muffled expletive. Margaret sighed and pulled the bedclothes more snugly around her neck. No doubt the glow of achievement had dimmed and now Robert was finding the early morning delivery to be a chore that gave more pain than satisfaction. Pride would not allow him to admit such thoughts as yet. He was determined to prove his manhood. How long would it be before he could allow himself to give up the job?

When he returned home, Robert gave no indication that he had any such thoughts.

'It's going to be a nice day today,' he said. 'No rain clouds and no wind. Is breakfast ready?'

'Yes. Tell the others to hurry up if they want any.'

Stephen decided he wanted jam rather than honey and fetched it from the larder, but on his way back to the table he stumbled and dropped the jar. It struck the edge of the steel fender around the fireplace and the glass shattered.

'Oh, no!' he cried.

'That was a whole new jar!' shouted Pauline at once, anxious to point out that she was not the only clumsy one in the family.

Robert grabbed a spoon and moved forward to salvage some of the contents.

'Leave it,' said Margaret sharply.

'The floor's clean. It was washed last night,

remember. And this part's not on the floor, anyway. It won't be dirty.'

'There might be slivers of glass in it. We can't take the chance.'

'It seems an awful shame to waste all that.'

'You must remember Mum telling us how dangerous glass is. Even the tiniest bit does lots of harm to your insides. Mum always said if we broke a jar or a bottle we'd have to throw it all away.'

'I'm sorry,' said Stephen. 'Can't we rescue any of it?'

'No. And let me clear it up. You have to be very careful with glass.'

'Stephen hasn't tied his laces,' said Pauline.

Margaret intervened swiftly to prevent any further bickering between the two younger ones.

'That's how accidents happen, so both of you watch that in future. If your laces won't stay fastened you'll have to tie a double knot.'

She dealt with the mess as quickly as possible and urged them all to get ready for school as soon as they had finished eating, but Robert lingered for some reason. He usually left for school before the others, but today he seemed to be waiting for the younger ones to depart.

'What's the matter?' Margaret prompted. Perhaps he was about to announce that he could no longer face the early rising and had already quit his job.

Robert shuffled his feet and kept his eyes down. 'I had a mishap this morning. It seems to be catching.'

'I heard something drop. What was it?'

'The clock.' Robert looked up at last. 'It broke. I'm sorry. That means we'll have to buy a new one.' He bit his lip and added, 'I'll get paid on Friday.'

Margaret took a deep breath and managed to hold back a scathing remark. 'We'll think about it later. We've both got to hurry right now.'

She had to run for a bus but, by catching it and then walking as quickly as she could from the stop in town, she managed to reach the front door of the office with two minutes to spare before she was due to start work. She hastened past Sue's desk with only a brief greeting and quickly hung her coat on the peg in her office. Even before she could check her appearance in the small mirror on the wall, Anderson called for her.

Margaret stopped short just inside his door, disconcerted by the sight of a middle-aged woman who was sitting near the desk, a shorthand pad and a pencil held ready to take down any words that had to be recorded. It seemed that her boss had found the assistant he had desired when he placed the advertisement. How secure was her job now? Margaret's new-found confidence fled. Perhaps she would have to search for another job after all. But where would she find one that would bring in such a good pay packet? And why did this have to happen just when they were having such a run of bad luck with breakages and extra expense?

16

Anderson was leaning over his desk, his widespread beefy arms supporting his weight. He glanced casually over his shoulder, then frowned and stood upright. His young employee had never looked so upset. For some reason she was well and truly harassed, but she would clam up if he tried to delve too deeply. Again, he would have to go gently.

'You're looking a bit flustered this morning,' he said as he turned to face her. 'What's the problem?'

'Oh, er — nothing too serious.' Margaret struggled to produce a smile as she sought for a satisfactory answer. 'We were running late. I had to rush.'

Anderson rested his rump on the edge of the desk, folded his arms and stared thoughtfully at her. 'If you ask me, it's more a case of being down in the dumps. Come on now, what's brought this on? Some problem with the kids' school?'

Margaret shook her head. 'No, they all seem to be getting on well at school now.'

'So?'

She hit upon a troubling thought she could

share without risk of disclosing too much. 'Robert broke the alarm clock. He knocked it down in the dark.'

'Ah-ha. Hence the rush this morning. And I suppose you're wondering how you're all going to wake up in time every day now,' Anderson suggested. She nodded agreement and he shrugged. 'Well, that can be fixed easily enough. There must be lots of clocks around this place somewhere.' He stretched out one hand and lifted the telephone. 'Ah, Sue. Find me an alarm clock, will you? Try the basement first, but tell them I want a proper clock, not one of those timer things.'

He replaced the receiver then jerked his head sideways by way of invitation. 'Come over here, Margaret, and have a look at these.'

As she stepped closer Margaret saw that the usual clutter had been cleared away and the surface of his desk was covered with glossy black and white photographs.

'The film you brought in,' he explained.

All problems were swept from her mind and her cheeks glowed with pride as she stared down at the pictures. She had never expected Robert to produce such magnificent results. The focus on each photograph looked sharp, and only one suffered from slight under-exposure.

'That's good photography,' said Anderson.

Margaret's usual modesty surfaced. 'It would be a very good camera. It belongs to our aunt.'

'What make is it?'

She had to admit that she had no idea, but when she mentioned that Aunt Joan was a professional photographer the editor straightened up and his eyes glistened with excitement.

'What's her name?'

Margaret hesitated, wondering if she were about to give too much away; but she quickly realised that he would be able to find out if he really wanted to know. Besides, their aunt's background was entirely different from their own. Revealing her name should do no harm.

'Joan Wheatley.'

'Ah!' Anderson slapped his hands together. 'I know her. She's done work for us. You're right — it would be a good camera. But some people couldn't take pictures like that with the best camera on the market.'

He swung around, suddenly remembering the presence of another person in the room. 'By the way, meet Doris. She's our temp.' He rubbed his hands as the two females exchanged greetings. 'Doris has been hired as a temporary secretary for the time being. You're going to be too busy to deal with the more usual run of things, so Doris will take care of all that.'

'Oh.' Relief brought an added flush to Margaret's face. It seemed that she was not about to be sent away after all.

'First off, let's consider these photographs.'

Margaret looked at the pictures again. Each print consisted of a close-up study of some quaint item. She identified an ornate lamp, part of a monument, a weather-vane and an owl made of straw.

'Do you know where all of these were taken?'

She shook her head. 'No. The boys went out on Saturday morning. I wasn't with them.'

'Well, I hope they can find all those things again. We're going to need answers.' Anderson took a step backwards and went through the customary ritual with his hands. 'You and your brothers have started something here. We're going to make a whole new series out of this. And not for Children's Corner either.'

Margaret gazed blankly at him, wondering why the photographs had stirred such a reaction, and he chuckled.

'Do you realise you've had everybody on the staff wondering where the dickens some of these pictures were taken? It's going to be the same with our readers.' He grinned at her bewilderment. 'When people live in a place too long they take everything for granted and don't notice unusual nooks and crannies. Some folk never look up and see what's above their heads. This is an historical town, but everybody seems to have forgotten it. We're going to instil a bit of civic pride, and you are going to do most of it. If you need any help with the writing you'll get it, but you and your brother will take the pictures.'

He gathered the photographs into a neat pile and pushed them into a large stiff envelope.

'You'll have to take these. Let your brother see how well he was coping with the camera, and ask him if he knows where he took all the shots. We'll need a picture of the building or whatever to show where those details can be found. And then we could do with a whole heap more. Now then, I believe you said your brother is still at school.'

'Yes,' answered Margaret. 'He's only fourteen.'

'Well then, that means we'll have to wait till the weekend. Pity, but still . . . ' Anderson rubbed his hands and clapped them again. 'Anyway, I'll give you some films to be going on with.' He reached for a small canvas bag and handed it to her. 'You and your brother might like to experiment with the camera a bit more in the next couple of days. Try some of those trick shots you mentioned before, and bring the films in here to be developed. Now, on Saturday morning I don't want to see you in here. Go out with your brothers and get some interesting shots for us.'

'Thank you.' Margaret hovered by the desk, wondering what he was expecting her to do in the meantime, and unsure whether to ask or wait for him to explain.

Anderson smiled at her uncertainty. 'Start off by thinking about Children's Corner today. Write a letter to the children, and then jot some ideas down so that you've got material to work on for the next few weeks.'

Margaret felt shaky with nerves. How could she write a letter to hundreds of children she had never met? She was sitting at her desk, staring at a blank sheet of paper, when Sue came in.

'Hi,' said Sue cheerfully. She perched herself on the corner of the desk and settled down for a chat. 'You've caused a bit of a stir with those photos. None of us realised how little we knew about our town. Nothing like a fresh pair of eyes.'

By the time the receptionist had left to attend to her own duties, Margaret felt more composed. She would pretend she was still at home in the village, she decided. She would pretend she was getting ready to start a day in the classroom and just write down what she would say to the children if she were really there.

She had written four paragraphs when Anderson clumped in and dumped three books on her desk.

'There'll be more of these to come,' he declared. 'You'll have to do a fair bit of research, but don't let that idea frighten you off. Start with the Charter — that slip of paper marks the page. Find out why the merchants decided this was a good place to start trading, and write a piece about that. In your usual style. Straightforward language. Don't go all academic on me.'

Margaret nodded and waited for his parting shot. He always seemed to save his most startling announcement for the moment when he reached the door.

'Better finish the next article about your village first. That series is already in progress.'

He watched for the usual display of nerves, but this time she surprised him by giving a placid smile.

'I've almost finished that.'

'Good.' He nodded thoughtfully and returned to his office, wondering what had brought about such a surprising change. Left to herself, Margaret smiled again, confident that she had found a solution to her concerns last night. Mrs Croft's reactions had made her realise that any information about Gnujeemia would sound intriguing to an English reader; so she could continue to produce interesting articles without mentioning her own family. She would concentrate on the life style of the indigenous population. She could write about the crops, cooking methods, the markets and the source of clean water. Then she could describe various crafts that had been handed down over the centuries, the numerous languages and how the style of dress denoted the tribe to which a person belonged.

Sue came in with a tray bearing two cups of tea and a large alarm clock.

'I hear the clock is for you,' she said. 'I hope you haven't been going to sleep on the job.'

Margaret laughed. 'No. It's to make sure we all get up in time in the mornings. Robert broke our clock today and he has to get up early to deliver newspapers.'

'Well, this one has a tick that's loud enough to keep everyone awake all night,' said Sue. 'And just listen to the bell on it.'

She turned the clock hands until the alarm rang and they both giggled at the urgent clanging of the clapper above the dial.

'It sounds like a fire alarm,' said Sue, hastily switching it off. 'You won't have any excuse to be late from now on.'

She stayed for another little chat and Margaret found herself relaxing even more. Everything was working out far better than she could have hoped. Her job was safe and she need not worry about the cost of repairs to their aunt's clock for the time being. The new project that Mr Anderson had given her was going to be truly exciting. Better still, she would not have to leave the other children at home alone on Saturday morning. She could not have asked for a better outcome.

At the end of the afternoon she went out by the back door and found Tony waiting for her as promised. He led her to his car and opened the front passenger door with a flourish. Margaret settled into the seat, glad to be able to enter without rushing, and he smiled smugly to himself as he went around to the driver's side. He might make faster progress with this one than he had anticipated.

'Had a good day?' he asked as he started the engine.

'Yes, thank you.' Margaret could not resist boasting a little. 'Mr Anderson has asked me to work on a new series.'

'Good for you.' Tony drove out of the yard

and turned in the opposite direction to the one Margaret had expected him to take. 'No need to dash straight home,' he said blithely. 'We'll stop off somewhere and have some refreshment.'

'No! No, I must go home,' protested Margaret.

'Relax.' Tony took his left hand off the wheel and rested it briefly on her arm. 'A little light refreshment won't do you any harm. You need to unwind after a day's work.'

Her arm seemed to tingle at his touch and she could feel the light pressure even after he had removed his hand.

'My brothers and my little sister will be waiting for me. I must go.'

'They can keep each other company for a bit longer.'

'They'll be wanting their tea. I have to go home and cook.'

Tony glanced at her and decided it was not a genuine protest. She was just making a routine refusal for the sake of form. She could be persuaded easily enough.

'We don't need to stay long. Look, it would take you longer to get home if you were going by bus. We've got a bit of time up our sleeves.'

Margaret found herself weakening. He had a pleasant personality and it was so nice to have someone caring for her. Half an hour shouldn't make much difference. As he said, she would get there faster by car.

'I really must get home soon.'

'A quick cup of coffee,' he suggested. 'I know just the place.'

He turned into a narrow street behind a row of shops and parked in a small area reserved for customers.

'We can take a short cut through here,' he said. 'Sit tight till I open the door. There's not much room, so you'll have to be careful getting out.'

He walked around the back of the car and opened the passenger door. She edged gingerly through the small gap between the vehicle and a stone wall, then waited while he locked the car.

'Through the ironmonger's,' he said, and led the way into the back of a shop crowded with tools and household implements. They emerged in High Street and Tony guided her to a café two doors further along.

'Do you want to take your coat off?'

Margaret remembered that this was supposed to be only a hasty detour before the journey home.

'No thank you. I mustn't stay long.'

'Right.' Tony pulled out a chair for her at a table beside the window and she sat down carefully, remembering to smooth the back of her clothes.

'White coffee?' asked Tony, and when she agreed he went to place the order at the counter.

Minutes sped by as they chatted. He asked about the new series that Margaret had mentioned and then, to divert attention away from herself, she asked about his work at the newspaper. He replied that he intended to be a major writer for one of the national dailies before long, and he would soon be a leading journalist. In the meantime he was learning everything he could about the whole process.

'That means spending time in every department. The boss has great faith in me, and he hopes he'll be able to keep me here on his staff. He's grooming me for big things.'

'That's nice to know.' Margaret looked guiltily at her watch. It would be lovely to go on sitting here enjoying his company, but she had responsibilities. The young ones could be starting another fight at this very minute. 'I'm sorry, but I really must go.'

'We'll have to do this again sometime.'

'That would be nice.'

Tony mentally shrugged his shoulders. There was no point in trying to persuade her to stay longer, or to suggest going anywhere else. Her mind was fixed on those pesky kids at home so he wouldn't make much headway this time.

'If you're sure you wouldn't like another cup . . .'

They spoke little on the way to the house, neither feeling the need for conversation. Margaret was planning her activities for the evening, while he was considering ways to gain more time with her. Those kids didn't dominate her thoughts when she was at the office. Perhaps he could devise some excuse for working on that new project with her. Once he got her out on a proper date she'd switch all her attention to him, no two ways about that. He'd never failed yet with any young girl who'd caught his eye.

He drew to a halt beside the kerb at the same spot as before and leapt out to open the passenger door. Margaret accepted his hand again, fully expecting another gallant kiss, but this time he drew her closer and kissed her on the right cheek.

'Good-bye for now,' he said. 'I'll see you at the office tomorrow.'

'Oh. Yes. Thank you. Thank you for everything. Good-bye.'

Tony grinned at her reddening face and gave an elaborate farewell wave before climbing into his seat. Margaret raised her hand in response, and watched the car speed away. She had just been out for her first date with a man, she realised; only a simple occasion, not a romantic interlude, but he had expressed a desire to do it again. That meant the event had been agreeable for him as well as for her. Perhaps she should try to be more sociable — find some means of spending more time with him.

Mrs Croft hovered behind the lace curtains in her dining-room, delighted that she had chosen such an opportune moment to set the table for tea. So young Margaret had found herself a good-looking man already. She certainly was an enigma. She had turned up out of the blue looking like an orphan or a refugee — well, of course, that's what she was — a refugee. But she had looked like a woebegone little kid who needed her mother, and now look at her. She had certainly blossomed in the past couple of weeks. The new hairstyle had been a great help, she could congratulate herself for her part in that, but Margaret seemed to have hidden talents. She had walked into a plush job at the local newspaper, and now she had a male friend who drove a car. It couldn't have been just a casual offer of a lift home. He had kissed her, right there in the public street, and Margaret certainly relished his attention. She was positively glowing.

Margaret crossed the road, feeling that life was exceptionally pleasant, but her good humour vanished when she entered the house and caught sight of the charred hole in the left leg of Stephen's trousers.

'What happened?' she demanded. 'How did you do that?'

'I was only standing here,' said Stephen, taking a small step closer to the hearth. 'I'd spilt water down and I was only trying to dry it.'

'You must have been nearer than that,' scolded Margaret. 'What a dangerous thing to do! You've been told not to get too close. You know how dangerous fire is. If I can't trust you to do the right thing I'll have to lock that heater away.'

'Sorry,' he mumbled. 'But I'll earn some more money tomorrow, digging for Mrs Summers. That'll help to pay for another pair.'

'You'll have to make do with a patch. I'm not buying any others. And it might remind you to be more careful.'

'Just leave it,' said Stephen sullenly. 'It won't matter all that much.'

'I can't leave it. If people see a burn they'll say you're not being looked after properly. We've got to look as if we're competent and know how to do things safely.'

After they had eaten the evening meal Margaret hunted for some spare material. She found a bag of hexagon-shaped pieces, obviously intended for patchwork, but there was no plain navy-blue. Finally she cut a piece from inside the pocket of the same trousers.

'You won't be able to use the left pocket now,' she told Stephen. 'I'll sew it up in case you forget and put something in there.'

She pinned the patch over the damaged area and began to sew neatly around the edges. Another thought occurred to her as she worked and she turned to Stephen again.

'What time will you be going digging?'

'After school.' Stephen lifted both hands and spread his fingers to halt any objection. 'I've already spoken to Mrs Croft about that. She said that Pauline can go over to her house while I'm busy.'

'That's good of her.' Margaret smiled up at him. 'I'm glad to hear that you've thought ahead this time and that you're looking after Pauline.'

'Yeah, well . . . ' Stephen shuffled his feet self-consciously. 'We were a bit mean the other day, going off without her.'

During the lunch break next day, Margaret was alone in the room that doubled as a kitchen and meeting space for the staff when

Tony strode in. She smiled at him, hastily pushing the remains of her last sandwich into the greaseproof wrapping paper.

'Nearly finished your lunch?' he asked breezily. 'Let's go out for a quick drink.'

Margaret glanced at her watch. 'Well . . . '

'Come on, bags of time. And even if we're running late we can claim to be working. I'll tell you some interesting facts about this town.'

He did not need to exert as much pressure as he had expected before she agreed to fetch her coat and accompany him. Tony beamed with satisfaction and guided her to High Street, but instead of walking as far as the café they had visited the previous day, he turned into the front porch of the Red Lion. Margaret came to a sudden halt as he pushed the door open.

'I can't go in there!'

'Why not? What's the matter?'

'I thought you meant we were going for coffee.'

'Look, it's a hotel. You can have coffee if you insist.'

'I can't go in there.' Margaret licked her lips, trying to think of a way to extricate herself from the situation. She could not explain why she must not go in. The fact that she was under-aged was the cause of all her difficulties, the one fact that nobody must know.

'I take it that your family is against the demon drink.'

'Not exactly. But I must not frequent a public bar.'

They had to move aside to allow two middle-aged men to enter. As soon as the door had closed behind them, Tony took hold of her arm.

'Come on,' he coaxed. 'It's a respectable place. It's not one of those noisy pubs where people go to get sloshed. This is a proper, decent hotel, with rooms for travellers. They serve good meals, too. Whole families come for dinner here.'

'Well . . . '

The mention of families had given him an edge and Tony quickly took advantage of her uncertainty.

'Come on. You won't be looked down on for entering a respectable place like this. Besides, if you want to get on in the newspaper world you'll have to go to hotels. Most of your contacts will meet you in pubs, and where else are you going to interview people from out of town?'

Margaret did not aim to become a fully fledged reporter, but she gave a slight nod and allowed him to lead her inside. The saloon bar was fairly busy, but he managed to find a small table and two empty chairs in the far corner.

'You don't really want coffee, do you?'

'Er, no. Lemonade, please.'

'A lemon squash would be good. I'll get that for you, shall I?'

Impatience battled with his conscience as he made his way to the counter. He could slip a vodka into the lemon and she'd never know. That would melt some of the icy shell around her. But supposing she dropped off to sleep or something in the office afterwards? No, better wait and gain her full confidence first.

'Yep?' said the barman, making a hasty sweep with a damp cloth across the counter top. 'The usual?'

'One lemon squash . . . '

The barman looked up, his face creasing with amusement. 'You taken the pledge or something?'

'Not for me.' Tony made a vague gesture to indicate the direction of a companion. 'I'll have the usual.'

Margaret stared in surprise as he lowered two large glasses and a smaller one onto the table.

'This is what is known as a chaser,' explained Tony. 'Would you like a sip?'

'No, thank you.' Margaret shook her head

firmly and picked up the lemon drink.

Tony grinned as he downed the whisky and followed it with a long swallow of beer.

'That's better. Gives you a pick-me-up after a hard morning.'

Moments later his glass was empty, but Margaret left long pauses between small sips from her glass and he gave up on the idea of offering her a refill.

'We ought to go out together one evening,' he suggested when he came back with a second beer for himself. 'Don't you think it would be nice to go somewhere and not have to worry about the time? We can't really relax when we have to keep an eye on the clock.'

'Yes, it would be nice.'

'Well, then — how about tonight?'

'Oh, no, I couldn't possibly. The children . . . '

'How old is the biggest one? Fourteen? Big enough to baby-sit once in a while.'

Margaret looked into his eyes and her resolve weakened. The idea of going out with such an attractive man, of enjoying herself while Robert took charge for an hour or two, was hard to resist. It would be lovely to be pampered for a change, instead of running around after everybody else and worrying about all the jobs that had to be done.

'How about it then? Shall we say quarter

past seven this evening? I'll pick you up.'

Despite her longing for an evening free from responsibilities, Margaret felt a quiver of unease. Everything seemed to be happening too fast. Besides, she had to prepare lunches for tomorrow. If she were to accept an invitation, perhaps it would be better to do so on Friday when there was no school day to follow. This week she did not even have to come to the office on Saturday morning.

'Not tonight,' she said finally. 'Another day perhaps.'

'Right then.' Tony's eyes gleamed with triumph. 'I'll hold you to that.'

17

Anderson grinned when he caught sight of Tony and Margaret walking back to the office together. Trust that flamboyant young bloke to turn on the charm as soon as a presentable new female came on the scene. Maybe that was the reason for the change in the girl's demeanour this morning, the sudden blooming of self-assurance. If so, good for Tony. His rumoured success rate might be wildly exaggerated but, even so, his romantic activities could prove to be extremely useful. A flirtatious approach could be the best way to make Margaret relax and open up. There was a huge story behind the girl's unexpected arrival on this doorstep, there had to be. She'd been struggling to hide something that first day. She still was, but she couldn't do that for ever.

Anderson rubbed his hands with anticipation. Any time now he'd find out exactly what it was that she did not want anybody to know. He'd give her a few moments to settle down from her lunchtime excursion, then go in with a query as an excuse to chat.

He sauntered into the adjoining office,

putting both hands into his trouser pockets to present an air of informality.

'I've been looking at that list you made, activities for Children's Corner. What's all this about stepping through a sheet of paper? Do you mean a newspaper?'

Margaret laughed. 'No, there'd be no trick to something as big as that. You use an ordinary page; out of a writing pad perhaps. If you cut it the right way you can make a really big hole.'

'Big enough for the older kids?'

'Big enough for an adult.'

He eyed her doubtfully and then plucked an unused sheet of quarto sized typing paper from the tray on her desk. 'Show me.'

Margaret folded the paper in half then picked up a pair of scissors and began to cut deftly.

'It's the same principle as making Chinese lanterns,' she explained. 'The paper stretches out like a concertina. The children will start by drawing lines to guide them, but once you know how to do it you don't need lines.'

She held up an unbroken narrow frame and Anderson stared at the huge gap in the centre.

'Good lord. Yes, even I could get through that. Our readers will think it's really clever. I suppose you used to teach kids to do all kinds of tricks with scissors and paper.'

'We did that sort of thing at home mostly. Paper was scarce, so you couldn't do it at school.'

'Mm. You'll have to tell us more about your teaching career.' Anderson took the opportunity to press for significant details. 'More importantly, tell us how you managed to escape from the war zone. It seems that foreign correspondents still can't get around the country, which means they can't find out what is really happening over there. So, how did you manage to get away?'

Margaret frowned and pressed her teeth down on her lower lip. 'It all happened very suddenly,' she said at last. 'My father said we had to go at once.'

'Did he get some kind of advance warning?'

'He got a radio message to say that fighting had broken out.'

'So how did you leave? Was it frightening? Dangerous? How did you do it?'

'We went by plane.' She hesitated. 'I don't think I should say whose plane it was.'

'Mm. Better not to mention any names, I suppose. Nobody knows who's going to come out on top in that lot, do they?' Anderson paused, considering his next move. A wild theory had come to him in the middle of the night, but the more he thought about it the more logical it seemed to be.

'How many children did you bring out?'

Margaret frowned again, obviously bewildered by that question. 'There are four of us, counting myself.'

'And the other three really are your brothers and a sister?'

'Of course they are.'

Anderson shrugged. 'People have been known to smuggle other people's children out of war zones.'

'Well, it certainly didn't happen in this case.' Margaret pushed her chair back and stood up, too agitated to remain seated. 'I hope you're not going to print any nonsense like that. It could lead to all kinds of trouble.'

Anderson backed away from the desk, making soothing gestures with his hands. 'Simmer down, it was only an idea.'

'A stupid idea.' Rising panic swept aside Margaret's usual courtesy. 'Look, people are in real danger over there. We don't know how long it will go on, or who's going to win. When the shooting stops, the winners are going to go looking for so-called enemies. Stories like that in a newspaper could mean the difference between life and death for some people.'

'You're right, of course. I'm sorry. Of

course I wouldn't print anything like that.'

'I must not write any more about Gnujeemia. They could identify the village and that could cause trouble.'

'I'm sure a little newspaper like ours wouldn't attract attention overseas.'

Margaret clasped her hands tightly together. This time she must really dig her heels in, she told herself fiercely. She must refuse to give him any more information.

'It's a risk,' she said tersely. 'We mustn't do it.'

Anderson edged towards the door, wondering how to persuade her to reject that point of view. He had come much closer to discovering more about her, but if she persisted with her present line of thought it would only serve to make her more defensive. What he needed was a full background and more personal details. Top national papers were interested and he aimed to syndicate the series. On the other hand, he must never forget that her parents were still trapped in that war-torn country. It was hardly surprising that she was so upset now. It was even possible that he had jumped to the wrong conclusions when they first met. He'd been sure that she was hiding a great secret — but perhaps it had been plain fear that had caused her to act so strangely; fear she had experienced during the escape, or fear of reprisals for those left behind. Obviously, he would have to wait a bit longer to find out everything he wanted to know.

'Just concentrate on Children's Corner for the time being.'

He sent Sue in with a cup of tea and instructions to calm Margaret down. Sue did her best to distract the young girl with snippets of gossip and a few local jokes, but her efforts were clearly failing. When she was alone again, Margaret found she was unable to concentrate and she gave up trying to read about the town's history. Her mind was now focused on the country she had left behind. Ever since their first plane had left the ground she had been pushing unwelcome thoughts away, determined to be strong for the sake of her siblings; but now those thoughts came bubbling to the surface. What was going to happen to Mum and Dad? And what about all those children she used to see every day in the school? How long would it be before some proper news reached the outside world? If only this afternoon would end. She was longing to go home, to convince herself that Pauline and her brothers were safe. She needed to hug them all.

She looked close to tears when Anderson

entered her room again, more quietly than usual.

'Look, you're unsettled, so you won't achieve much this afternoon,' he said. 'You've been doing a lot of work outside office hours. Why don't you pack up and go early today? If you set off now you'd be in time to meet the kids at school. It would give you the chance to have a chat with the teachers, too.'

Margaret snatched at the offer. 'Yes, thank you. I will.'

He helped her on with her coat and watched as she gathered up her shoulder bag and the carry bag that held a few personal possessions.

'Have a restful evening,' he said. 'We'll talk about Children's Corner tomorrow.'

'Thank you. Good afternoon, Mr Anderson.'

She hastened past Sue's domain, giving only a half-wave in farewell, but as she opened the main door she remembered that she had been planning to go out the back way. That thought brought her to a sudden stop and she returned to the front desk.

'Oh, Sue, Tony offered to drive me home today. Would you please tell him I have left early. I don't want him to wait about for me when I'm not here.'

'All right, I'll tell him. You just get along. You don't want to miss a bus.'

The brisk walk to the bus-stop helped to settle Margaret's nerves and by the time the school bell rang to announce the end of lessons she was feeling ready to meet people again. Pauline's face lit up with astonished delight when she caught sight of her sister, but she cringed when she heard that Margaret planned to visit her teacher.

'Why, what's wrong?'

'What could be wrong? I won't be a minute. I'm only being polite.'

Miss Weston was glad of an opportunity to chat to the young guardian. Pauline was always full of praise for her big sister, but the principal had a very different opinion. Miss Chapman had said the so-called guardian hardly looked capable of looking after herself, never mind a family, and she would contact the aunt rather than the sister if any problems arose. The girl was certainly young, but she seemed competent enough, and this afternoon she looked more sophisticated than she had when she came to meet Pauline on the first day.

'I'm pleased to see you again.' Miss Weston offered her hand, still perplexed as to how the girl had managed to make such a poor impression when she met the principal. Perhaps she had been tired and stressed when she first arrived in England and had not presented herself well. 'I'm very pleased with Pauline's progress. She has settled in remarkably well.'

'I'm glad to hear it. I knew it was going to be difficult at first.'

'Well, it was bound to be. Everything here must be so different. The turning point came when Pauline showed the children how to make that toy.'

'Oh, the whirly disc.'

'Yes, everybody in the class has one now. And some of the other children as well.' Miss Weston smiled. 'Did you want to ask about anything in particular?'

'No, thank you. I just wanted to make sure that everything was going well.'

'Better than we could have hoped. I hear that Stephen is doing well, too.'

The younger children walked home in good spirits, glad to know that their teachers were pleased with them.

'I'm supposed to go to Mrs Croft's this afternoon,' said Pauline. 'Stephen's digging a garden.'

'You must go now that she's expecting you,' replied Margaret. 'I'll go with you and say hello.'

Mrs Croft's eyebrows rose when she opened the front door. 'Hello, Pauline. Margaret, I didn't expect to see you this afternoon. Come in.'

She had already prepared a small snack of orange cordial and biscuits and arranged a low table for Pauline. She invited the little girl to sit down and help herself while she and Margaret made a cup of tea.

'I hope you didn't come home early because of Pauline,' she said softly as soon as they reached the kitchen. 'I really meant it when I said she would be welcome here.'

'No, I got some time off unexpectedly,' said Margaret. 'I wasn't worried about Pauline. But it's very good of you to look after the younger children the way you do.'

'Well, as long as you know I like to do it. Now, all we have to do is get another cup. The kettle's just about boiling.'

When Pauline had settled in an armchair in the corner, engrossed in a scrapbook, Mrs Croft poured a second cup of tea and revealed the plan that she had been making.

'You know, you should take a little time for yourself, Margaret. We could look after the children while you have a break. You could have a quiet evening by yourself. Or do you have any friends you can visit? It would do you good to have an evening out.' She smiled to herself as a pink tinge crept across the girl's face. 'How about this Friday? Do you think you could organise something for then, or is that too soon?'

'Oh, well . . . ' Margaret's flush deepened as she tried to suppress the sudden surge of excitement. Tony had offered to take her out. It would be wonderful if she could accept his invitation. But what about the children's tea? Could they afford to buy fish and chips? If she didn't have to cook it would save a lot of time.

'I thought you could all come across here for a meal,' Mrs Croft suggested. 'And then the others can stay while you go out for a while. I could make sure they get to bed in good time if you're going to be late back.'

Margaret became flustered. 'It's very good of you to offer, but I couldn't possibly let you go to all that trouble.'

'No trouble at all.' Mrs Croft waved one hand airily. 'I love children, you know. I can hardly wait to have grandchildren, but there's no likelihood of that just now. So I'm glad to have your family around. How about it, then? After work on Friday, all of you eat here and then you can do exactly what you like, knowing that the children are being looked after.'

Tony went up to Margaret's office the next morning, his latest campaign clear in his mind. He would start by taking Margaret out to the Red Lion again. Getting her out of the office was the key to success. Once they were away from these premises, he'd have no trouble persuading her to spend an entire evening with him. It would have to be a staid outing of some kind to begin with.

He had planned to coax Margaret with soft words and hints of valuable information for her project, but he quickly found that no wiles were needed. She accepted with alacrity when he invited her out for a lunch-time drink, and he was humming softly to himself as he returned to his work in the basement, unaware that his success had produced a smug smile. Other employees smirked and nudged each other. Young Tony obviously thought he was well on the way to making another conquest.

Margaret entered the Red Lion without a qualm this time, and as he approached the bar counter Tony considered the advantages of lacing her lemon drink. No, he decided. Time enough for that when he had her out on a proper date.

'So, when are we going to have more time together?' he asked when they were both seated in a quiet spot. 'After work one day. We shouldn't have to keep looking at the clock.'

'I will be free tomorrow evening,' said Margaret shyly.

Tony's eyes widened. He knew he hadn't

lost his touch, but this girl was not like the others and he'd never imagined he'd make such rapid progress.

'Tomorrow, then,' he said quickly. 'You're on. Where do you want to go?'

'I don't know this town very well.' Margaret suddenly felt a twinge of doubt. Perhaps it was a mistake to spend more time with him. She might become careless and let him find out more than he should. But why let such an opportunity slip away? It would be lovely to go out for an hour or two and let someone else make all the arrangements.

'There must be something you want to do. Where would you go, given a choice?'

'I would like to see a film. I haven't been to a cinema for a long time.' Margaret bit her lip. What would Mum and Dad say about that? Would they approve if they knew? Of course they would, she told herself immediately. It wasn't as if Tony were a stranger. He and she worked in the same place. Tony was clearly a respectable person, and a cinema was a respectable place to visit.

She was undressing in her bedroom that evening when a disturbing thought entered her mind and she began to panic. What could she wear for her date with Tony? She couldn't go out for the evening wearing the clothes she had worn at work all week. But she didn't have anything else — or at least not anything that was warm enough. Tony would not appreciate her company if she shivered all evening. Besides, she must not take any risks. She had to stay well so as to look after the others.

She would have to buy something, she decided finally. She would dash into that same charity shop, and if she couldn't find anything suitable there she would ask for directions to another such shop.

She could almost believe that Mr Anderson had been reading her mind when he came into her office the next morning and placed three pound notes and three shillings on her desk.

'For the articles,' he announced. 'I assume that cash will be more convenient than a cheque.'

'Oh, thank you, yes.' Margaret's face flared with colour. 'I haven't got a bank account.'

'I thought not. Anyway, you might want to nip out at lunch-time and start your shopping, rather than wait for the wage packet this afternoon.'

'Thank you. Yes, I will do that.'

She hurried out as soon as the clock showed twelve-thirty, not waiting to eat her sandwich. The woman who had served her before was not in the shop, but another assistant proved to be just as friendly and helpful. Margaret explained that she needed something she could wear in the evening when she was out with a friend; something that would be useful at any time of the day.

'It must be winter clothing. I've been living in the tropics.'

'You poor thing. You must be feeling cold here. Spring seems to have got lost again.' The assistant studied Margaret's build and then moved towards the other side of the shop, gesturing for her to follow. 'I think we might have just the thing. It's on the model, but I can soon get it off.'

Pauline clapped her hands in admiration when she saw the bright blue two-piece outfit, and Mrs Croft complimented Margaret on her appearance when they went across to the other house.

'You look lovely, dear. An absolute picture. Are you going out with someone special?'

'Someone from the *Daily Tribune*.'

'He'll be proud to be with you.' Mrs Croft smiled at the flush that followed her words. The companion was surely going to be the young man who had driven Margaret home and kissed her. 'Now, you all go and sit down at the table with Les. Everything is ready.'

She had cooked a hearty roast beef dinner with Yorkshire pudding and four vegetables, which was followed by steamed chocolate pudding and custard.

Stephen gave a sigh of satisfaction as he laid down his spoon.

'That's the best meal we've had since we left home,' he announced.

'True,' declared Robert, and the two girls nodded agreement.

Mrs Croft gave a complacent smile, happy to receive such warm appreciation.

'Thank you. No, I don't want any of you to help with the washing up. You're my guests today. Margaret, is your friend going to call for you? You should go back now and get yourself ready.'

She accompanied Margaret to the door and patted her lightly on the shoulder. 'You make sure you enjoy yourself. And don't hurry back. I'll go over with the children when it's time for bed.'

Margaret felt self-conscious as she entered Tony's car, well aware that everybody was watching from the window across the road. Tony noticed movements from behind the net curtain and gave a flippant wave in that direction.

'Quite an audience,' he chortled.

He had consulted the programmes of both local cinemas and decided the light-hearted musical at the Odeon was the best bet for his strategy. The B film would be a simple family story; nothing to make his date feel miserable or uneasy. An usherette led them to seats in the back row and Margaret glowed with contentment. She felt decidedly grown up as Tony helped her out of her coat and then produced a small box of chocolates.

'Oh, no thank you, not just now,' said Margaret as he offered the box. 'We have only just finished a really big meal.'

'Later then,' he said calmly. 'I'll get a couple of cool drinks in the interval.'

Soon after the lights had dimmed he slipped his left arm around her shoulders. Margaret sat rigidly for several moments, not knowing how she ought to react, but gradually she relaxed in her seat. Other couples were sitting in a similar fashion, so such behaviour must be deemed to be acceptable. Two girls a few rows closer to the screen were even resting their heads on their escorts' shoulders. She would not go that far; but she could allow Tony to leave his arm around her. It was so comforting to feel cherished and close. For weeks now she had been missing her parents and the hugs they gave so freely.

Tony was exhilarated by the progress he had made in the cinema, but he sensed resistance when he led her into a bar immediately afterwards.

'I must go home,' said Margaret. 'Mrs Croft will be waiting.'

'Don't worry. This place will be closing soon, anyway. We'll only have time for one quick drink.'

He chivvied her into the nearest chair and dashed to the counter.

'One vodka and bitter lemon. One scotch and chaser.'

Margaret frowned slightly at the sight of the glass he offered her. The contents looked cloudy in comparison with the clear drinks he had bought for her before.

'Bitter lemon this time,' said Tony soothingly. 'Very popular. It's a fairly new product. Taste it and let me know what you think.'

Margaret lifted the glass and sipped cautiously. The drink certainly had a tang to it. It was different from the other; not as sweet, but quite pleasant. It would be refreshing on a hot day.

'Yes, it seems nice,' she said.

'Adults usually prefer bitter lemon. It's the kids who like the sweet stuff.'

Margaret nodded and took another sip while Tony raised his glass in a silent toast. Next time he would slip in a double. It would take too long to get anywhere with a single vodka at the rate she worked her way through a glass. Perhaps it was just as well this place would be closing in a minute. He mustn't rush his fences. If he behaved impeccably this evening it would give her confidence. Next time he'd definitely be able to get her into his flat.

Margaret left the bar feeling surprisingly carefree. It was amazing how all her worries seemed to have been put aside while she was with Tony. To be with someone a little older, someone who would protect her and make all the decisions, had relieved all her stress. She could hardly wait for him to offer another date.

Tony drove her home and opened the car door for her as before. He led her to the footpath, then slipped both arms gently around her and drew her close. Margaret's arms went around him and they stood for a moment, her head resting against his chest. She would have remained there motionless, content to be enfolded in his embrace, but he tilted her face upwards and kissed her on the lips.

She did not respond immediately, but her inhibition swiftly vanished. When they drew apart she gazed up at him in wonder. This was her first real romance. She had never been so close to a man before, had never received that kind of kiss.

'I've got to go.' Tony's words brought her back to reality. 'Look, don't bother to bring lunch on Monday. We'll go out for something. And make sure you organise a baby-sitter soon so that we can go out in the evening again.'

Mrs Croft looked eagerly at Margaret's expression when the girl let herself into the house. She was flushed with excitement, her eyes sparkling in a way they never had before.

'You enjoyed yourself I take it.'

'Oh, yes.' Margaret was thinking she had never enjoyed herself so much. If only she didn't have to wait two whole days before she could see Tony again. Monday lunch-time would be an exciting occasion. It was too soon to ask for Mrs Croft's help again, but within a day or two she must try to make arrangements so that Tony could plan another outing.

Mrs Croft nodded, guessing what was going through her young neighbour's mind and feeling only too ready to help with a budding romance.

'I said a change would do you good. You tell that young man of yours you can go out with him again as soon as he likes. Les and I will keep an eye on the children.'

18

Everybody in the family felt better for the change of routine on Friday evening. They all slept well, and awoke on Saturday with renewed energy and an eagerness to explore unknown territory. The sun was shining brightly, enticing them to forget about household chores and make the most of a free day.

Stephen came in from the back garden, shouting with glee.

'It's warm out there! You won't believe how warm it is! We won't need those heavy coats today. And I can wear my sandals.'

Robert's eyes glistened and he went out briefly to investigate. 'He's right. Good weather at last. Terrific light for photographs. How soon can we go?'

'As soon as we're ready,' answered Margaret. 'If any of you want to change a book at the library, bring it with you.'

She packed lunch while the others washed dishes and made beds, then they hurried to the bus-stop. Margaret had become used to the journey into town, but it was still a novel experience for the others. They insisted on travelling on the upper deck, and their excited comments brought smiles to the faces of several other passengers.

'Where are we going first?' asked Robert as they neared the town square.

'You have to find all those things you photographed last week. After that we'll just look for some more. We want anything unusual.'

The whole town looked more attractive on a sunny day. Daffodils were bobbing in window boxes and garden beds, their leaves and flowers fresh and bright, and many trees seemed to have burst into bloom overnight. Robert enthused over light and shade as he adjusted the focus for a crooked chimney and some intricate stone carvings, while the younger children examined closer objects such as doorknobs and leaded windows, competing to find the oddest sight of the day. When they had visited all the spots photographed the previous week, they followed signs to the central market, but they were disappointed by their first sight of the huge building. The plain brick walls looked flat and uninspiring, but Robert insisted on going inside.

'Come on. There's bound to be a good stall at least.'

Once inside they were amazed by the

magnificent Victorian architecture. Intricate iron pillars supported a balcony with decorative wrought iron railings, and most of the roof seemed to be made of glass. Shoppers were either deep in conversation or hurrying to complete their errands, apparently oblivious to their grand surroundings, and only a few paused to see what had attracted the children's attention.

'Fantastic,' said Robert after taking several shots. 'Let's go to the railway station next. It's not far from here.'

He was photographing the foundation stone when Stephen discovered an old chocolate vending machine.

'Hey, look at the badge on this thing. That will be a really hard one to guess.'

'It'll be too hard,' Pauline objected.

'It would be a good one for grown-ups,' said Margaret. 'We can't make it too easy if we want grown-ups to get interested.'

By the time they left the station the younger children's energy had begun to flag.

'Time for lunch,' said Margaret. 'We'll pop back into the market and buy some fruit, then head for the river.'

They sprawled on the grass beside the water not far from the old bridge, well satisfied by their morning's work.

'Why couldn't the weather have been like

this when we first arrived?' said Stephen. 'We wouldn't have had to bother so much about clothes.'

'It won't last,' replied Margaret. 'English weather is notorious for being changeable, so it could be chilly again tomorrow.'

Contrary to those doubts, the mild spell continued, and they explored different areas the next day. When they returned home Stephen alighted first from the bus, but his cheerful expression suddenly changed to one of alarm.

'Look out. Here comes that policeman.'

They huddled together on the pavement as the bus drew away from the stop, watching the policeman cycling towards them on their side of the road.

'Be careful what you say,' warned Robert.

The constable rode steadily on and they hoped he might pass by without speaking, but when he reached the group of children he braked and dismounted in one fluid movement.

'Hello again,' he said. 'How are you getting on?'

'Very well, thank you,' said Robert quickly.

'Is your aunt back yet?'

'No, but we're managing very well without her,' said Stephen emphatically. 'We got that window fixed. And we all go to school.'

The constable smiled. 'I know. I've seen you and your sister going into school.' They had obviously not noticed him at the time, but that sighting had soothed his guilty conscience. He knew he should have checked more closely on that first encounter to ensure that everything was in order, rather than accept a vague explanation, but his qualms had eased by now. The children were clearly still nervous about attracting police attention, but there was nothing unusual about that and they were being well cared for by the look of things. They certainly looked much smarter now than they did the first time he met them.

'No more problems with electricity or anything?' he asked.

'No, but thank you for your help that day,' said Margaret. 'The people from across the road have been very helpful, too.'

Robert was staring at the man's helmet with rising excitement.

'Do you mind if I take photographs of your uniform?'

'You want a picture of an English Bobby, do you? Go on then, I don't mind.'

The constable straightened his shoulders and posed beside his bicycle, unaware that Robert was interested only in the chrome badge on the front of the helmet and the chrome fitting on the top. Robert moved nearer to take a close-up of a shiny button, then he stepped back and thanked him for his co-operation.

'You're welcome. Be careful how you cross the road now.'

The policeman mounted his bicycle and continued on his way, leaving the children smiling at each other with a mixture of relief and mirth.

'That was clever, Robert,' said Pauline. 'Those pictures will look good.'

'A bit cheeky,' said Margaret. 'But a very good idea.'

It was warm enough to leave top coats behind again on Monday morning. Sue greeted Margaret with cheerful remarks about the lovely fine days, and Anderson seemed to be bubbling over with good humour.

'Great weather,' he exclaimed when Margaret answered his summons. 'Did you have a good weekend?'

'Very good, thank you. We all had a very good time.'

'That's what I like to hear. How did you get on with the photography?'

'We took three rolls.'

'Great. Let's send them down straight away.' He made a call to the basement, telling Tony to come up for the films, then he clasped his hands behind his head and leaned back in his chair, resting his feet as usual on the bottom drawer.

'I see you got lots of letters from children,' he announced. 'And I tried that first set of photos out on one or two other folk over the weekend. Had a very good response to those, too. They'll go well as a new series.'

Tony came in, winking amorously at Margaret as he approached the editor's desk.

'Let me know as soon as these shots are dry,' said Anderson, handing the rolls of film to him.

'Yes. I'll get on to them immediately.' Tony turned away and passed close to Margaret on his way out. 'Lunch,' he murmured. 'You haven't forgotten, have you?'

'No, I haven't.' As usual, Margaret could not prevent the sudden rush of colour. 'Thank you.'

'See you then.' Tony winked again and Margaret looked down at her feet, failing to see that Anderson was watching and grinning at the interaction.

'I'm pleased with the work you've been doing,' he said as soon as the door had closed behind Tony. 'Very pleased.'

'Thank you.' A deeper red stained Margaret's cheeks, but her eyes sparkled with pride.

'Did you take any of the photographs yourself?'

'No, Robert is much better at it.'

'Perhaps he'll think of taking up a career in photography. Your aunt has done well at it, so he'll have a good model to follow.'

Margaret nodded in agreement, and Anderson rubbed his hands together.

'You'd better start by picking out a few jokes for next Saturday. Make an outline for the next issue so you've got a base to work on. Then as soon as those photographs come up . . . ' He broke off as the telephone rang. 'Yes? Ah. Put them on, will you. Hello, this is Anderson. Yes. Yes, editor. Yes . . . Just a moment, please.'

He held one hand over the mouthpiece and looked at Margaret with an unusually solemn expression.

'It's for you,' he said softly. 'It's Allingham General Hospital.'

Her face paled and her lips trembled as he passed the receiver to her. This could only be bad news.

'Hello . . . Yes, this is Miss Barlow.'

'Ah, Miss Barlow,' said the female voice. 'Are you Robert Barlow's guardian?'

Margaret took a deep breath. 'Yes, that's right,' she answered hesitantly.

'I'm sorry to tell you that young Robert has had an accident on his bicycle. Will you please come to the hospital as soon as possible?'

Margaret could only manage a gasping groan in response. Anderson pushed himself up to his feet and took the telephone from her.

'Anderson here again. I assume there has been an accident. How serious is it? I see. Yes, I'll make sure she gets there. Within the next half hour. Yes. Thank you.'

He replaced the receiver and turned to Margaret. 'Well, Robert's not in any danger. That's a relief. But he needs medical treatment. I'll find someone to take you there.' He studied her expression for a moment and decided she was not likely to faint or go into hysterics. 'In the meantime, you'd better get yourself organised; pick up your handbag and things like that.'

'Thank you.' Margaret headed for her office and Anderson looked at the work schedule pinned to a nearby display board, to decide who should drive her to the hospital. She knew Tony better than anybody, but an older person would probably be a better choice at a time like this. Yes, Michael Fuller, a family man close to retirement age. He would understand the strain she was feeling and would be able to offer advice, if needed.

Margaret was glad her driver did not try to raise her spirits by talking too much. He merely offered sympathy and told her they would soon be there.

'Hopefully, we'll find that things are not too bad.'

He guided her to the Casualty Department, where a nurse took over and led Margaret to where Robert was lying in a curtained cubicle. He was pale and shaken and there was a swelling above his right eye, but he managed to produce a smile when he saw his sister.

'Hello,' he said.

'Hello.' Margaret looked down at him and succeeded in hiding her concern. 'How do you feel?'

'Not bad. There's nothing much wrong.'

'The nurse said you probably have a fractured arm.'

'I know. It has to be X-rayed.' Robert sighed and closed his eyes. 'I'm sorry.'

'Nobody's blaming you. It's not the kind of thing you do on purpose.'

'Fractures are expensive. If I'd landed better . . . '

Margaret broke in. 'No! Medical expenses are the last thing you need to worry about. Hospitals and doctors are free in England.'

'Are they?'

'Of course they are.' She nodded emphatically. 'That's why I have to pay National Insurance every week. I wasn't pleased about that at first, but I am now. It's a kind of saving up for this sort of thing.'

'Well, that's a relief.' Robert brightened visibly. 'They'll get this fixed in an hour or so, and then we can go home.'

'How did it happen?'

'I was riding past a line of cars and somebody opened a door.' Robert shuddered as he remembered the sickening fall. 'There was another car right behind me. He missed me all right, but he ran over part of the bike. It's in an awful mess. I won't be able to ride that for a long time.'

'You won't be able to ride it with a broken arm, anyway.'

'I came here in an ambulance,' continued Robert. 'A police car came, too. One of the policemen said he'd want to see me again later.'

A doctor came into the cubicle, putting an end to the conversation.

'Well, my lad, it's time to send you down to X-rays. I think we'll find it's a nice clean break, no complications. And hopefully, you haven't done too much damage to your head.'

He turned to Margaret and his eyebrows drew together in a frown. 'Are you Miss Barlow?' he asked in a puzzled tone.

'Yes.'

'I was expecting someone older. Robert

said you were his guardian.'

Margaret held his gaze, licking her lips and wondering how to answer. 'I'm his sister,' she murmured at last.

The doctor studied her for a moment in silence, then jerked his head towards the gap in the curtains. 'Come outside for a moment. We need to discuss this further.'

Robert and Margaret exchanged worried glances, not daring to say anything, and then she followed the doctor out of the cubicle. He looked at her appraisingly before speaking.

'I was hoping you would prove to be a responsible adult. You are nowhere near twenty-one, are you?'

'No.'

'I've had a lot of experience with young people, working in a place like this. Sometimes I have to estimate a person's age, and I'm usually spot on.' He paused briefly, but she made no response. 'How old are you?'

This was a moment she had dreaded, but she could not conceal the truth now. Even if she had the gall to try to keep up the pretence, he would guess she was deceiving him and he would be sure to demand proof. He need only ask her to produce her passport or her birth certificate.

'I'm fifteen.'

'Fifteen? And you're in charge of the whole family?'

'Yes.' Margaret sought for something positive to say. 'It's only temporary. In a week or two my aunt will be back.'

'Haven't you got any other relatives? Where are your parents?'

Margaret briefly explained about their flight from Africa and the reason for their aunt's absence.

'We think she's in South America.'

'Well now, here's a fine howdy-do.' The doctor fiddled with his stethoscope as he considered the problem. The girl was mature for her age and she seemed to have been coping admirably, but she did not comply with his requirements for the current situation.

'Robert needs medical treatment, but you can't give permission for us to do that,' he said.

'You're surely going to treat him!' exclaimed Margaret.

'Of course. But it means things will be more complicated. He might need an anaesthetic. To make sure he's fit to take that we'll have to give him a complete medical check. And he'll have to stay in hospital for one night at least. He's had a bang on the head, you know.'

'But they told me it wasn't serious.'

'It's only a precaution,' he hastened to explain. 'We'll have to keep him in for observation. Anyway, you go and sit down over there and we'll make a start.'

Michael Fuller hastened to meet her as she stumbled towards a row of chairs. She barely recognised him through her tears.

'What's the matter? Not bad news, surely?'

'No. That is . . . ' Margaret was grateful for his supporting arm as he guided her to a seat. She fumbled in her bag for a handkerchief and dabbed at her eyes. 'It doesn't look as though Robert is badly injured. But they won't let him come home. They're going to keep him here.'

'That's probably a good thing. You'll know he's in good hands.'

'Yes, but . . . ' Margaret broke off. All the things that she had been dreading would strike now. There would be questions. Lots more questions. Officials would take over and all her efforts to keep the family together would be wasted. Would she be in awful trouble now for pretending to be a proper guardian?

A woman came towards them carrying a clipboard and a sheaf of papers.

'Are you a relative?' she asked Fuller.

'No. We work in the same place. I drove Margaret here.'

'I see.'

'Is there some kind of problem?'

The woman avoided the question. 'For the moment we just need as many details as we can get about Robert's medical history.' She turned to Margaret. 'Do you know what illnesses Robert has had?'

'Last time we came to England we both caught chicken pox.'

'Chicken pox. Anything else? What about measles? Mumps? You've come from Africa, I believe. What about malaria?'

Margaret shook her head. 'Not malaria. We've all had dysentery.' She tried to remember the few occasions when any of them had been sick. 'Just a few stomach upsets, mainly. Pink eye, too. Er — that is conjunctivitis. Robert had tonsillitis once, but not seriously.'

The woman ticked off boxes on a form, writing in a few extra details as she went.

'Are you sure Robert hasn't had any major diseases, or any severe bouts of sickness? Any accidents? Broken bones? Well then, that's all I need for now. But I'm sure other people will be wanting to interview you. And the police will want to know more about the accident.'

Fuller cleared his throat. He was being treated like an outsider, but he had been sent to support Margaret so he ought to do

311

something helpful.

'There's not much point in hanging about here, is there?' he suggested. 'It will be a while before we can see Robert. In the meantime, if anybody needs to contact Miss Barlow they can call the office. Someone will bring her back here again.'

'Yes, perhaps that would be as well. Give me the telephone number of the office.'

Margaret fought back tears as she followed Fuller out to the car. Trouble lay ahead. Big trouble. How had she got herself into this predicament? She had let her pride rule her head; that was the answer. Flattery had inflated her ego. Where had she heard that? Anyway, she'd felt grown up when Dad put her in charge, and then too proud to give up that responsibility when they arrived here. Dad had only meant it to be a temporary arrangement. He hadn't expected them to be looking after themselves the way they had. On the other hand, he wouldn't want them to be scooped up and whisked away to separate Homes, would he? Wouldn't he prefer them to stay together the way they had?

'Try not to worry,' said Fuller. 'They'll let us know as soon as there's any news.'

'There's the police and everything . . . '

'Yes, well . . . Someone knocked Robert off his bike. There has to be an accident report.'

Margaret gave a slight nod. It was too awkward to explain. But there'd be hundreds of questions to come. Could she end up in gaol? She had signed official documents. The authorities would be outraged, and rightly so.

Fuller made only a few soothing comments during the remainder of the drive back to the office. He pulled up close to the back door and took Margaret's arm as they went in, escorting her to Sue's domain.

'Sit yourself down here for a few minutes,' he said. 'Sue, cup of tea needed, please.'

Sue quickly dragged a chair forward and Fuller hastened to the editor's office. Anderson looked up from the papers on his desk, his interest soaring as he noted the expression on the other man's face.

'So you're back. Well, how's things?'

Fuller gave an expressive shrug. 'The injuries don't seem to be serious.'

'But . . . ?'

'There's some sort of trouble.' Fuller shrugged again. 'I don't know what it is. They wouldn't talk to me 'cos I'm not a relative, but there's something odd going on.'

'Where's the girl now?'

'With Sue, having a cup of tea.'

'Good.'

'The hospital will be calling here with results. And then there'll be calls from the police and various other bods from the sound of things.' Fuller spread his hands. 'Perhaps the bike was pinched.'

Anderson heaved himself to his feet. 'No. Nothing like that. But I've been waiting for a break-through, and I think this is it.' He rubbed his hands and slapped them together with a satisfying smack. 'I knew there was something strange going on. Pity the young lad had to get hurt to bring it all out, but I knew we'd get to the bottom of it before long. Keep this under your hat till we know what it's all about.'

He called Sue on the internal line and told her to send Margaret in as soon as she had finished her tea.

'Do your best to keep her calm, but don't ask any questions.'

Just over ten minutes later Margaret tapped on his door, nervously clutching her bag. He invited her in and laid down his pen.

'So you're back. I gather that Robert's accident wasn't too serious?'

'He's fractured his arm. And he's had a bump on the head.'

'I'm glad it wasn't any worse.'

'They won't let him come home.'

'Why's that?'

'Because . . . they won't let him come . . . because there's only me there.'

A tear rolled down beside her nose and then she could not stop the others. Anderson wafted one hand in the direction of a chair and she sat down with her head turned away from him, fumbling in her bag for a handkerchief. Anderson pulled a large white handkerchief out of his top pocket, walked over and handed it to her, then patted her on the shoulder without speaking and went out to talk to Sue.

'What did she tell you?'

'Nothing. Not a word. She was just too upset, trying to hold everything in.'

'Well, I'd better stay out here for a while. Give her chance to have a good cry.'

By the time he returned to his office, Margaret had gained more control. She wiped her eyes fiercely as he entered, taking deep breaths and urging herself to act like an adult. She must not lose all her dignity.

'I'm sorry,' she murmured.

'That's all right. I've an idea you've been needing that for a long time.'

Margaret wiped her eyes again, then stared with horror at the black, brown and pink streaks on the handkerchief.

'Don't worry about that. Look, you nip down to the Ladies and clean your face up properly. There's another cup of tea on the way and it'll be cool enough to drink by the time you get back.'

Margaret washed her face and combed her hair, then applied a little foundation and patted powder on lightly. Her hands did not feel steady enough to deal with mascara, but it hardly seemed to matter now whether she wore make-up or not.

'Tea's ready,' said Anderson as soon as she returned to his office. He busied himself shifting papers on his desk so that he could talk to her without looking closely at her, and by the time she had finished the tea she appeared to be more composed.

'That's better.' Anderson pushed his work to one side. 'Now then, tell me all about it.'

Margaret began by repeating that Robert would be detained in hospital.

'And there's a particular reason why they won't let him go home, eh?'

She nodded reluctantly. 'They think I can't look after him. They don't think I can look after anybody.' She bit her lip and added reluctantly, 'And I couldn't sign the papers at the hospital.'

Anderson quickly realised that her main problem had something to do with signing the hospital papers, but he made no immediate response. After a moment Margaret gave a deep sigh.

'I'm not old enough.'

Anderson leaned forward eagerly. 'How old are you?'

She paused to gather courage. 'I'm fifteen,' she admitted at last.

'Fifteen! You're only fifteen!' Anderson stared in a mixture of wonder and disbelief. He'd known there was something newsworthy in this girl's background, but he hadn't imagined anything like this. It didn't seem possible.

'I'm sorry. I didn't like tricking you the way I did. But we needed the money. I couldn't think of anything else to do.'

'Fifteen.' Anderson studied her more closely. She certainly did look as young as that now, with far less make-up and her eyes swollen and red with tears. But how could she have maintained such a deception for so long?

'I'm sorry,' said Margaret again.

'Well, I knew you were pretty young — but I thought you might be eighteen, or very close to it.' He thought briefly about the consequences. 'Good lord, you're not old enough to sign anything, not even under modern laws.'

'I have signed things, though. I've been signing forms everywhere, ever since we came to this country. It's going to cause a lot of trouble. I'm sorry to let you down, but I'd better leave here right now. I don't want to bring you any trouble.'

He raised both hands to placate her. 'Simmer down. We can sort things out. Just tell me the whole story.'

Margaret gave a brief account of their journey to England, then described the shock of finding that no one had come to meet them. Finally she related the conversation she had overheard in the London hostel.

'It's true what they said. I've looked it up. Children under the age of sixteen must have a responsible adult caring for them. If not, they are deemed to be in need of Care or Protection.'

'There must be times when . . . ' Anderson broke off as the telephone rang. 'Anderson. Yes, editor. Good morning. Yes . . . yes . . . I see. Yes.' He glanced at his watch. 'How about at the hospital, say an hour from now? Yes, yes, all right.'

He replaced the receiver and gave a slight shrug. 'That was the Children's Office.'

Margaret's spirits sank. 'Oh, no.'

'Don't panic. Look, you have been coping admirably for the past few weeks. You can keep it up for one more day. Now then . . . ' Anderson jotted some hasty notes on his pad. 'Robert is going to need a few things to keep him happy overnight. You know the kind of thing, his own pyjamas, washing gear, a book. Now I suggest that you go home right now and get all that stuff. Michael can drive you. A Miss Adams is going to meet you at the hospital at twelve-fifteen.'

'Oh dear.'

'Just stay calm.' Anderson smiled inwardly at his own placatory advice. Such a thing was so much easier to say than to accomplish.

'Stay calm,' he said again. 'I know it's difficult, but you can do it.'

19

Fuller drove Margaret home, waited in the kitchen while she collected a few belongings for Robert, and then drove her to the hospital. She asked him to stop on the way so that she could buy a small bag of sweets, but apart from that they spoke very little. Fuller was preoccupied, mulling over the scanty details he had so far. According to the editor, a great story was in the offing and it was up to him to ferret out as many details as possible during the coming interview.

When they reached the hospital, however, the woman in charge at the front desk soon made it clear that Fuller's presence was not welcome.

'There's nothing you can do here. A Children's Officer is on hand. You're not a relative, so your presence can't help in any way.'

Fuller turned to Margaret. 'You don't want to be alone here, do you? Wouldn't you like me to stay with you?'

Margaret hesitated, then decided she would prefer to continue fighting her own battles. No doubt it would have made a difference had she known him better, but as things were she wanted to cling to some sense of privacy.

'No, thank you. It's all right. You go back. Thank you for your help.'

Almost immediately afterwards she was directed to a room where Robert and an adult patient were waiting for plaster casts to dry. Now that his arm had been set and the most intense pain had eased, Robert was beginning to notice numerous other sore spots. The idea of lying in a bed and doing absolutely nothing was quickly becoming more desirable, but when he saw his sister he drew himself up and pretended to feel better.

'It's stupid keeping me in hospital, just for one broken bone. What's the big idea?'

'They just want to make sure everything else is all right.' Margaret could see no point in worrying him just now; soon enough to tell him about all the fuss when she found out what was going to happen. 'You'll have a lovely black eye tomorrow. You've got a real lump there. Perhaps they think you'll get delayed concussion or something.'

'Huh! They'd better not try to keep me here too long, that's all. What did the doctor say about your age?'

'Nothing much. But he wouldn't let me sign.'

Margaret diverted his next question by picking up a holdall and showing him the items she had brought for him.

'I hope there's nothing else you need. I bought this bag of sweets on the way, too. There's nothing wrong with your stomach, so I don't suppose anyone will object to you eating those later. But make sure you clean your teeth afterwards.'

Robert immediately began to protest that he was not a baby and knew perfectly well how to look after his own teeth, but he was interrupted by a man wearing a green cotton coat. The orderly announced that Margaret must accompany him for an interview, and moments later he ushered her into a small room near the reception counter. A middle-aged woman who was waiting there rose slowly to her feet, her expression giving no hint of her thoughts as she watched the girl enter. Margaret noted the brown tweed two-piece costume, the sturdy brogue shoes and the long strand of wooden beads, and her spirits sank. This was obviously a woman with old-fashioned ideas and values.

'Good afternoon. I am Miss Adams, from the Children's Office.'

Margaret managed a weak smile. 'Good afternoon,' she murmured.

'Do sit down.' The woman indicated an

upright chair close to hers and Margaret complied, careful to keep her back straight and her knees together.

'Now then, I hear that you are only fifteen years old, and for the past two months you have been looking after three younger children by yourself.'

'It's not as long as that,' said Margaret defensively.

'A considerable length of time, anyway. We can soon confirm minor details.'

Miss Adams went on to quote sections of the Children and Young Persons Act of 1933, and to explain why juveniles should have a responsible adult to care for them. Margaret listened gloomily. She had guessed what sort of objections would be raised if anyone in authority found out about their situation, but she had not hit upon suitable responses. In her opinion they were managing their own affairs extremely well, but officials were unlikely to agree — especially this one. This woman would be very set in her ways.

'It is our duty to provide a Place of Safety,' Miss Adams continued. 'Robert is in a safe place for the present, so we don't have to rush in his case. First of all, we must concentrate on making arrangements for the rest of you. I think we had better start by going home so that I can meet the rest of the family.'

'Pauline and Stephen are at school at the moment.' Margaret fought down a surge of panic. If Miss Adams found those two at home, unsupervised during the lunch break, she would be highly critical. 'I wouldn't like to call them out of school,' she went on, seizing upon an idea of how to gain time. 'That's what happened when we had to leave home. Dad came and took us all out of school in a real rush. It's bound to upset them if that happens all over again.'

Miss Adams pondered for a moment. 'You have all gone through a very distressing period,' she agreed. 'If the same thing happened again so soon the little ones might develop some kind of nervous reaction.' She looked thoughtfully at Margaret and for the first time she actually smiled. 'So long as they are at school they are in the care of a responsible person, so we don't need to worry about them just yet. Now then, what about you?'

'Me?' gasped Margaret. 'I should be at work.'

'Mm.' Miss Adams frowned. 'You have a full-time job, I believe. Who has been looking after the younger children until you get back from work every day?'

'Robert does usually. He's quite capable. He's fourteen, you know. He didn't expect to be attending school here.' Margaret felt reckless enough to make any suggestions or promises. 'I could get someone else to do it today.'

'Who do you know who could do that?'

'There's Mrs Croft from across the road. She has been very helpful. She can stay the whole night if need be.' Margaret slipped her right hand under the bag on her lap and crossed her fingers. It was true that Mrs Croft had offered to look after the family again if Margaret were invited out. She had only intended to do that for a few hours, of course, but she might agree to stay longer for once. After all, this was an emergency, wasn't it? It would not do to give up the fight now. Mr Anderson had sounded really confident. He had seemed to imply that Margaret only had to hold the fort for this one day. It was hard to imagine what kind of help he could give, but if she could hold out until tomorrow, who knew what solution might turn up? Aunt Joan might even come back unexpectedly. No doubt this welfare woman meant well, but outsiders must not be allowed to interfere. Dad had placed her in charge and she had managed well all this time.

Miss Adams kept a sharp watch on Margaret's face and saw her lips tighten with increased determination. The girl was very young, but she certainly had spirit.

'Very well,' she conceded. 'We will postpone any action until school is over for the day. That will give me more time to make arrangements, which will be an advantage. Now then, I must check that I have the correct address. I need everybody's date of birth, too.'

When the interview was over, Margaret decided to go back to the *Daily Tribune* by bus. It would not take long, and a few minutes alone might help to settle her nerves. The afternoon was going to be filled with unpleasant incidents. She had to tell Pauline and Stephen what had happened to Robert, and then break the news about the Children's Officer coming. It was even possible that they would not be allowed to sleep in their usual beds that night.

Sue looked up with keen interest as Margaret scurried past the front desk, but she resisted the urge to detain her and ask questions. Something was up. Mr Anderson was holding space for some big story and it obviously involved Margaret. Had somebody died? Was it bad news from Africa? The poor girl looked like a dejected waif at the moment.

Anderson invited Margaret into his office and gestured towards a chair beside his desk.

'So you're back,' he said and leaned forward attentively. 'What's happening now?'

Margaret described the events as briefly as possible and he nodded.

'I see. Do you really think your neighbour will be willing to help out to that extent?'

'I hope so.'

'Me, too.' Anderson rubbed his hands together and gave a decisive clap. He had already set up a piece for the afternoon edition. All it needed was a picture. This situation was going to make a great story over the next few days, one that would arouse the sympathy of all his readers, and he was going to play it to the hilt. If the authorities went about things in a heavy-handed manner it would result in a public uproar.

'Look, I don't want you to worry too much about all this,' he declared. 'If your neighbour doesn't want to get involved, we'll find someone else.' He would get his own wife to go there if need be. 'No one can take any of you away from that house so long as a responsible adult is there keeping an eye on things. Some of those Children's Officers can be very set in their ways, so they'll argue the toss; but I reckon we'll come out on top. Now then, I want a photograph of you. Work won't stop on that new series. And I've sent out for a couple of sandwiches. When you've had a bite to eat you'd better get home to look after those kids.'

Margaret nodded in agreement, relieved to know that he was definitely on her side. He had experience and he knew how the legal system worked. It was much easier to let him take over and organise all her next moves. He instructed her to sit at her usual desk, pretending to work while a staff photographer aimed a camera at her from several angles, then he called her back into his office. She nibbled a ham sandwich half-heartedly while he talked of his plans for future editions of the newspaper.

'By the way,' he said, 'seeing as we're having all these confessions, how about telling me more about your father's paper? How big was it really?'

'It was tiny,' she admitted. 'It was all we could do to fill one folded sheet sometimes. And when Dad was away I sometimes did it all by myself.'

To her astonishment, Anderson burst into a roar of laughter, his huge body shaking, his chair creaking under the strain.

'You're priceless,' he said at last, still quivering with mirth. 'Absolutely priceless.'

He ate one of Margaret's sandwiches, rolled the greaseproof paper into a ball and aimed for the waste paper basket.

'Got it!' he exclaimed. 'Now then, if you've had enough of that sandwich, Margaret, you go home and get things organised. A quick tidy up might be called for. If you've got nothing else to do, you can work on Children's Corner for next Saturday.'

Margaret left by the front door, giving a subdued farewell and small wave to Sue as she passed. Sue quickly searched for an excuse to see the editor, eager to find out what was happening.

'There's been a delay with the stationery order,' she announced. 'And I thought you might like an early cup of tea today.'

Anderson acknowledged that suggestion with a mere nod of thanks, but she lingered beside the half-open door. 'Tony was looking for Margaret at lunch-time. He'll be coming back for her again later. What shall I tell him?'

Anderson looked blankly at her for a second, then suddenly stiffened.

'Good God! Tony! Where is he?'

'He went down to that protest meeting. You know, where they want to open the new dump.'

'Ah, yes.' Anderson closed his eyes briefly. 'He should be back any time. Send him straight in here. I want to see him the minute he gets back. And no chitchat before I see him.'

Tony strode cheerfully into the editor's office, convinced that his big break had arrived. It seemed that some important story was about to take off and the boss wanted to see him urgently. Anderson's expression signalled that something serious was in the wind, but his first words came as a shock.

'You have taken Margaret out a few times. Right?'

Tony frowned. 'We've been out a couple of times in the lunch break.'

'You've also taken her out in your car.'

'I've given her a lift home now and again, yes. What is all this?'

'You've kissed her, I suppose.' Anderson remembered all too clearly the sparkling eyes and flushed cheeks when the girl had seen Tony entering the room. 'Has there been any kind of hanky-panky?' Anderson leaned back and scrutinized the other man's face. 'You know what I mean. You've got a reputation.'

Tony reddened. 'What's the matter? Surely she hasn't complained?'

'Is there any reason why she should complain?'

'No, of course not.' Tony clenched his fists. 'Look, what is going on?'

'The Children's Department is poking about. They want to take the whole family into care. Margaret wants to keep all the kids at home, of course, so we have to prove she's suitable and competent. The last thing we need is a whiff of scandal; but if there's any danger of that sort of stuff coming, I need to know now. So tell me, straight up. For example, have you taken her to your flat?'

'I don't know what all this has to do with me. Until I know just what you're going on about, I'm not going to say a word. What is all this?'

Anderson sighed and then leaned forward, resting both forearms on his desk and watching intently for the slightest sign of guilt.

'She's under age, Tony. She's only fifteen.'

'Jesus!' Tony's lower jaw sagged and his face paled. Anderson gestured towards the chair beside his desk and the younger man sank onto it, his mind racing. He could have fallen right into that age trap. He'd had their next date all planned — an invitation to dine out, which would mean eating at his place. One or two double vodkas and she'd be putty in his hands. Talk about being saved by the bell . . .

'Where have you taken her?' demanded Anderson. 'Be exact. There's going to be a big splash with this story, and we don't want people coming with tales just when things seem to be going smoothly.'

Tony rubbed his chin. 'We went to the Bluebird Café the first time. Had coffee.'

'And at lunch-time, I suppose you took her to the pub?' A reluctant nod confirmed that notion and Anderson took a deep breath, staring briefly at the ceiling before fixing his gaze on the other man again. 'Good God, Tony. Drinking in the pub. That's not allowed at sixteen, never mind fifteen.'

'She only had lemon. That's allowed.'

'And who's going to believe that, if someone reports seeing her in there with *you*?'

Tony thought rapidly. 'You can ask the bartender — Larry. He'll remember all right. He pulled my leg about it when I asked for lemon. Wanted to know if I'd gone on the wagon.'

'Where else have you taken her? Tell me now. Her photograph's going to be on the front page.'

'We went to the pictures one evening, and then dropped in at the Royal Oak.' Tony told himself that no one would remember the shot of vodka, so no need to mention that. The bar had been busy with last orders. 'We were only there a few minutes. Margaret said she had to get back. She would only have lemon. I didn't argue about it. Thought she was a strict Methodist or something.'

'Hm. And you never guessed her real age?'

'Well, of course I didn't! She was shy, unworldly you might say. But I thought that was just her upbringing. I never dreamt . . . ' Tony glared challengingly. 'Did you know she was only fifteen?'

Anderson shook his head. 'No,' he admitted. 'She had me fooled, too. But she has produced some good work and I don't want to lose her.'

20

Margaret almost ran from the bus-stop, along the garden path and into the house. The familiar surroundings helped to calm her, and she leaned thankfully against the inside of the front door. Be optimistic, she told herself firmly. The situation was not absolutely hopeless. Things had not always run smoothly since they had left Mum and Dad, but somehow they had managed to surmount every obstacle that cropped up. They must not allow themselves to be beaten now, not after all they had gone through. There were lots of things in their favour. Now that Mr Anderson knew the truth, she didn't have to pretend she was older than she really was, or that she had lots of previous experience. More importantly, they had a great ally. Mr Anderson had greater influence than most people in Allingham. With his support, they could surely avoid being dragged away to Children's Homes. In a day or two Robert would be allowed to leave the hospital, and as soon as he came back home everything would go on just the same as it had before.

She made a quick check to ensure that

everything was safe, then hastened across the road. Until today, their neighbour had always answered the door promptly, but this time there was an ominous silence. Margaret knocked again, her confidence oozing away. Mrs Croft was out. That was a bad omen. What was she to do now? She needed Mrs Croft's help.

She returned home and telephoned Anderson, her voice rising high with desperation as she reported her new dilemma.

'Calm down,' he said. 'I know that woman is your first choice, but she's not absolutely essential. She might not be gone for long, anyway.' He briefly considered the situation. 'Give her an hour. If she's not back by then, let me know.'

His words brought scant comfort. Margaret went to the large bay window in the front room and stared at the house opposite, silently willing Mrs Croft to return. Moments later she began to chide herself for being so faint-hearted. As Mr Anderson had reminded her, only minutes before she left his office this afternoon, she had brought the younger ones all the way from Africa to Allingham. If she could do that, she could cope with the present crisis perfectly well. The best thing to do was to keep herself busy. She would fill the time by cleaning. The house must look really smart when Miss Adams arrived.

Pauline and Stephen had left their lunch dishes in the sink, together with all the breakfast cups and plates. Margaret hastily washed up and cleaned the sink and draining board, then seized a broom. Almost as soon as she started sweeping she remembered the vacuum cleaner and began to use that instead. How quick it was, she thought thankfully. Once you had assembled the pieces it was fast and easy to use. For thirty-five minutes she cleaned and tidied, then she washed her hands, re-made all the beds to make sure they were done neatly, and scurried back across the road.

This time Mrs Croft opened the door within seconds. She had seen the girl coming, and assumed from her haste and her harassed expression that something was amiss.

'Hello, dear,' she said. 'You're home early today. Come in.'

She led the way to the kitchen and began to fill the kettle, wafting one hand in the direction of the only empty chair.

'As you can see, I was just sorting the laundry ready for ironing,' she said, stretching the truth a little. She had actually been refreshing herself with her usual pick-me-up of tea and a biscuit, whilst sitting near the dining-room window and thinking she ought to tackle the ironing before any of the other jobs. 'Sit down, dear, and we'll have a cup of tea. I was just about to make one for myself. I need it before I start on all that lot.'

She had great faith in the power of tea to help in solving problems. She bustled about, chatting lightly as she took a spare teapot out of the cupboard and set out cups, saucers and biscuits, doing her best to treat the girl's unexpected arrival as a normal friendly visit. When everything was ready, she swept some freshly laundered underwear off a chair and onto the top of another pile of garments, then she sat down and filled the cups.

'Just what we needed. Right then,' she urged, 'tell me what's on your mind.'

Now that the moment had arrived, Margaret could not bring herself to begin. This woman was kind and friendly, but she was almost a stranger. How could anyone expect her to go to another house and stay overnight, especially at such short notice? Asking her to spend an evening looking after the younger ones was bad enough, but it was presumptuous — to say the least — to suggest that she might stay for the entire night. She had her own home and a husband to care for. Margaret stared down at her cup, wondering how she could have been cheeky enough even to consider making such an outrageous request. She was almost wishing that her neighbour had not come back home so soon.

Mrs Croft waited a full minute, then pushed the little plate of biscuits closer to Margaret as a means to relieve some of the tension.

'What's the matter?' she asked at last. 'I'm sure things can't be as bad as they seem to be at first glance.'

To her dismay, she saw tears gathering in the girl's eyes.

'Something's happened to one of the children, hasn't it?' she guessed. 'What's happened, Margaret?'

'Robert's in hospital.' Margaret was grateful for the prompt. It was a way to start the conversation. 'He had an accident on his bike this morning.'

'Oh dear. I hope it wasn't too bad. Is he badly hurt?'

'No. He's broken his arm. But he's going to be all right. They won't let him come home, though.'

'That's not all, is it? You've got a bigger problem, haven't you? Tell me what that is.'

Margaret shook her head, reluctant to say more. Mrs Croft helped herself to a biscuit and quietly sipped her tea.

'One thing about the National Health, it

saves you worrying about doctors' bills. You did know that, did you?'

'Yes.' Margaret managed a small smile. 'Robert didn't. He was worrying about the cost when I got to the hospital.'

'Have you got a big bill from somewhere else?'

'No.' Margaret took a deep breath and plunged into her story. Once she had begun, she found it was like releasing a dam. 'There's a Children's Officer coming at five o'clock. She says we're not allowed to look after ourselves the way we have been doing, and she's going to send us all away to Children's Homes.'

'What on earth do you mean? She can't do that! Just because of an accident? That could happen to anybody. Those children are not neglected. They're well fed and they go to school every day. Why would she say they're not being looked after properly?'

Margaret heaved a sigh. 'It's my age. I'm not old enough.'

Mrs Croft stared at her. The girl certainly did look young this afternoon. She had no lipstick, and she must have been crying before because her eye make-up was gone. Now she looked more like the frail young thing who couldn't put her hair up when she first arrived in Allingham. But she had been running the household and holding down a responsible job at the newspaper office. How could anyone accuse her of being too young to look after her brothers and her little sister?

A considerable pause followed then she asked, 'How old are you?'

'Fifteen,' whispered Margaret.

The woman stared in astonishment, momentarily unable to speak. Her daughter was a real scatterbrain when she was that age. She was in her twenties now, but she still had not settled into a steady and mature lifestyle. This young lass could show her a thing or two, that was for sure.

'Did I hear right?' she said finally. 'Did you say fifteen?'

'Yes.' Margaret could not look her in the eye. 'By law we are none of us old enough to look after ourselves. We have to have an adult.'

'I don't believe it!' Mrs Croft's thoughts were whirling and for several seconds she could not say more. Gradually her indignation grew. 'You have been doing a fantastic job with those children. How could anybody find fault?'

'I've been signing things, things I had no right to sign,' said Margaret. 'And Robert's not allowed to come home because there's no adult to look after him.'

A long silence developed while Mrs Croft drained her cup and thought about the situation. The family seemed to have settled in so well over the road. They had learned how to use all the electrical equipment, they kept themselves clean and they were always polite. It would be a shame to take them away when they were managing so well.

'There's children with both parents in the house who're not looked after as well as your young brothers and sister,' she exclaimed. 'If the authorities got after them instead they'd be doing more good in the world. It's ridiculous, saying you're not able to do it. I assume you do want to go on looking after them?'

'Oh, yes. That's why we had to get away from London quickly and try to make me look older. We didn't want to be separated.'

'I should think not.'

Mrs Croft picked up another biscuit and absent-mindedly broke it into small pieces. What could she do to help? That family had gone through a terrible time lately. They shouldn't have to go through any more upsets. Anyway, the upheaval would hardly be worth it. Miss Wheatley would be back soon, and that would be the end of the emergency.

'This Children's Officer is coming this afternoon, you said? And the only complaint seems to be that there is no adult in the house?'

Margaret nodded mournfully and Mrs Croft drew herself up with sudden determination.

'Well, that's soon fixed. I'll come over and stand in *locust parentisis* — or whatever it is they call it.' The girl looked at her with renewed hope and she gave an encouraging smile. 'What time is this person coming did you say?'

'Five o'clock. She's called Miss Adams.'

'Well, I'll tell this Miss Adams a thing or two. You'd better get yourself home. The others might be back from school by now. Put your make-up on properly so as you look mature and well able to take care of the family, and make sure everybody looks neat. I'll come over in a little while. We'll get this sorted out.'

Margaret managed to apply fresh make-up before the others arrived home, and she was able to stay calm while she explained that Robert was in hospital. They stared at her dolefully, and Pauline's eyelids grew pink.

'Is it hurting him a lot?' she asked.

'I expect so, but he's being very well looked after.'

'We'll go and see him after tea, won't we?' said Stephen. 'We'll soon cheer him up.'

'Oh, I don't know yet. It all depends.' Margaret took a deep breath and broke the news about the Children's Officer coming to see them. The other two listened with dismay, quickly understanding the possible outcome of the visit.

'All because some stupid man knocked Robert off his bike,' grumbled Stephen. 'Fancy that happening when we were getting on so well. I thought we'd heard the last of people like Children's Officers when we sent those clothes back.'

Margaret sighed. 'Well, now we have to do our best to look as if we can manage everything properly. First of all, you two had better change into clean jumpers.'

Stephen moved to obey, but another thought occurred to him and he turned back. 'What about Robert's job? I can do that for him, but I'd better not change until after. I'd only get messed up.'

'The newspapers!' Margaret's hand darted to her mouth. 'I'd forgotten all about Robert's job. I should have gone to the shop and told the newsagent he couldn't come.'

'I can do it,' said Stephen again. 'I know where the shop is, and there must be a list of all the customers.'

Margaret shook her head, trying to think clearly. 'You mustn't do that. For one thing,

343

there's a law against it. I had to sign to say that Robert was fourteen. Oh dear. I'm not old enough to sign.'

'We won't get the money if we don't deliver the papers,' declared Pauline.

'We've got more than money to worry about just now. Oh dear. Perhaps I can manage to do the job, just for today. Anyway, I'll have to go and tell them that Robert won't be able to do the job for a while. If at all,' she added under her breath.

'I'll come with you,' said Stephen. 'I know where the shop is and you don't.'

'I'll come too,' cried Pauline.

'No, you go and stay with Mrs Croft. You can tell her where we've gone. She said she would come over here soon.'

The newsagent almost groaned aloud when he heard about Robert's accident. It always caused a problem when delivery boys failed to turn up, but the timing could hardly be worse than it was today. The baby had been sick in the night so his wife had scarcely slept, and neither had he. They had ended up spending almost three hours at the hospital.

'Well, I'm sorry to hear about Robert,' he said, managing to sound as if he were genuinely sympathetic. 'He's one of the best lads I've had and I'm going to miss him.'

'I'm sorry I didn't think to let you know

sooner.' Margaret hurried on before he had time to complain. 'If you can give me a list of addresses, I'll deliver the newspapers for you today.'

'Well, that's very considerate of you, but I don't think that's a good idea. You don't know the area for a start. By the time you found the right houses I'd have people here grumbling because the paper's late.' Perkins heaved a sigh and pressed one hand to his spine as he straightened up. 'My wife will have to look after the shop. I'll go out in the van and deliver the papers myself.'

'I'll come with you,' offered Stephen. 'You can just drive and I'll hop in and out with the papers. It'll save a lot of time.'

'We'll both come,' said Margaret when she saw the man wavering. 'I can do one side of the road and Stephen the other.'

'Thank you. That would be a great help.'

They completed the newspaper round at a brisk pace, and in gratitude for their assistance Perkins drove them home. A small black car was parked outside the house and Stephen gave a little moan of despair as they pulled up behind it.

'She's early!' he exclaimed. 'That woman's here already. It can't be five o'clock yet.'

Margaret glanced at her watch. 'It's just after five.'

She dug Stephen in the ribs to remind him of good manners and they thanked Perkins for driving them back. He nodded and departed as soon as they had alighted, too anxious to rejoin his wife to worry himself about their affairs.

'We're not that late, are we?' said Stephen. 'Will it make a lot of difference?'

'I hope not. Oh dear. Fancy keeping her waiting. That's not a very good start.'

Miss Adams was sitting in an armchair in the front room, nursing a cup of tea that Mrs Croft had pressed upon her as soon as she arrived. Pauline rushed down from upstairs to hug Margaret, and all three children gathered forlornly in the doorway of the room, not sure what they ought to do or say.

'Ah, here you are,' said Mrs Croft with a serene smile. 'I lit the fire because I know you always feel cold without it.'

'Thank you,' answered Margaret. That response seemed inadequate, but she dared not say more. Their neighbour must have carried some coal over from her own house, because they had run out and they had not ordered a fresh supply. She didn't even know where to buy coal.

'I'm sorry we came back late and kept you waiting,' she said to Miss Adams.

'That's quite all right. Mrs Croft explained

that you were doing Robert's job for him.'

'I forgot to tell the people at the shop that he couldn't come.'

'That's understandable after such an upsetting day. I was pleased to hear that you were so considerate and didn't let the newsagent down. Besides, it was a chance for me to have a little chat with Mrs Croft.'

Mrs Croft offered tea and biscuits as though she were quite used to acting as hostess in her neighbour's house. The three children quickly declined to have anything and she replaced the biscuit barrel on the occasional table, chatting on in her usual friendly manner while Stephen and Pauline followed Margaret to the sofa.

'I've been telling Miss Adams how well organised you have been. I couldn't tell her everything, of course, so she has a few questions to ask you.'

Miss Adams asked first about their financial situation, then delved into details such as what time they went to bed and what kind of meals they had been eating. She jotted notes on a sheet of foolscap paper clipped inside a folder, then asked if she could see the rest of the house. Margaret showed her around, congratulating herself for having tidied up so thoroughly that after-noon. A large pan was simmering on the gas stove and an appetising savoury aroma filled the kitchen. Mrs Croft had not only put the stewing steak on to cook, but added some herbs or spices of her own. The refrigerator and the larder were well stocked with food Margaret had bought that weekend, and she could not help feeling a little smug.

'I must agree that you have been coping very well,' said Miss Adams when they returned to the front room. 'And Mrs Croft has assured me that she and her husband will stay here in the house, so we don't have to rush into making other plans for tonight. However, that is only a temporary solution. That state of affairs cannot go on indefinitely.'

'I don't see why not,' said Mrs Croft with a touch of asperity. 'After all, my own house is only just across the road. If anything needs to be done there I can go over and handle it quite easily.'

Miss Adams suppressed an impatient retort. 'You have no legal standing. Taking responsibility for a whole family is not a matter to be treated lightly, and it is far more serious when that family is not related to your own.'

Mrs Croft leaned forward, certain that she was about to make a telling point. 'Supposing their aunt had been here when they arrived.

And then supposing she was taken ill, and she was in hospital right now. What's the difference? In a case like that I would have come over to lend a hand, wouldn't I? Nobody would meddle. It would be a perfectly natural response. Miss Wheatley will be back any time now. There's no need for all this fuss.'

The other woman squared her shoulders and drew herself up to express indignation.

'This fuss, as you call it, is a means of covering all eventualities. At present, nobody has the legal right to make any decisions on behalf of these children. In the mythical case you have just mentioned, the aunt would still be accessible and able to be consulted.'

Margaret's spirits plummeted and Pauline edged even closer to her. The Children's Officer closed her folder and rose to her feet to indicate that the meeting was over and she would not permit any further discussion.

'As I said, we will let matters stand as they are for tonight. Tomorrow we can look deeper into the situation.'

21

Les Croft was accustomed to finding his wife eager to greet him and the kettle near to boiling when he returned home from work. Today, however, no one came to the hall to welcome him and no one answered his call. A note on the kitchen table produced a sense of mystery rather than an explanation. He read the message a second time then went to the dining-room to look at the house across the main road. Nothing seemed to have changed. No obvious signs of disaster there. What kind of problem could that family have that needed neighbours to stay for the night? Had Margaret gone away for some reason to do with her job? According to the local newspaper, young Margaret was carving out a real career for herself in journalism. They'd even got her picture on the front page today, and she'd had something to do with the unusual photographs on the centre page. Those photographs had had half the passengers on the bus arguing about where they were taken.

He washed as quickly as possible and changed his clothes, then went across to the other house. Everybody was in the kitchen, but as soon as they had exchanged greetings Margaret shepherded the younger children away to the front room.

'So, what's going on?' demanded Croft.

As briefly as she could, his wife explained the circumstances.

'I couldn't leave them in the lurch, could I? So I said we would stay here overnight,' she ended.

Croft pursed his lips. 'Do you think that's a good idea? You might have let us in for a real legal problem. Who knows what might happen?'

'What could happen? All we have to do is make sure the fire's safe and the door's locked. Same as at home.'

'But . . . Four children, Betty. Just think of all the cooking and everything.'

'Margaret wants to go on looking after everything, same as before. I won't be running the show. It's just that an adult has to be on the premises. And it's only for one night.'

Croft nodded doubtfully. One night, indeed. He could see this stretching on into an indefinite future.

'I hope we haven't taken on more than we can chew. We were right when we said Margaret looked very young, weren't we?' He paused to consider the situation and then gave a resigned shrug. 'But you're right. We

351

couldn't leave them in the lurch, could we?'

The Barlow household was calmer than usual the next morning. Robert was not there, clattering about in a vain attempt to keep quiet as he rushed to his job at the newsagency, while Mrs Croft had been determined to get up first and make breakfast for everybody. Her husband had started on his eggs and bacon by the time Margaret reached the kitchen.

He looked up and nodded. 'Good morning. I hope you slept well.'

'Fairly well, yes, thank you. Oh, Mrs Croft, you shouldn't have gone to all this trouble. We could . . . '

'No trouble to me, dear. I've had a lot of practice, so it doesn't take me long to do things. Now, you sit yourself down and have a decent breakfast. And don't worry about any of the household chores today. You just keep your mind on your work at the office and follow the editor's advice. I'm sure he has your best interests at heart.'

Anderson could barely contain his impatience and he called to Margaret as she passed his open door on the way to her office.

'Well, how did it go? How did you get on with Miss Adams?'

Margaret gave a short description of events and he grinned.

'That's the first hurdle over. How much did you do for Children's Corner yesterday?'

Margaret blushed. 'None, I'm afraid. We went to see Robert, and then Mrs Croft was rather chatty when we came back. I thought it would be rude not to talk to her when she was being so helpful.'

'Quite right, quite right. Plenty of time, though. Before you do anything else, I want you to write another article about your village. Same style as the others, but this time I want you to tell us about some of the cases your mother dealt with as a nurse. Especially ones where you helped.'

Margaret hesitated, wondering what the future held. If the Children's Department really did take over the family, would she be allowed to stay with the Crofts and go on working here as before? And would the Crofts be willing for her to stay with them? More importantly — what about all those forms she had signed? No one had even mentioned that problem yet. How much trouble was going to come?

'Look at this,' said Anderson. He grabbed a folder and pulled out a letter with an ornate heading in black and red ink. 'Look, a national newspaper is going to reprint your first article. They'll want all the others, too. That war is still red-hot news, even though it's been pushed off the front pages of most papers.' He slipped the letter back into the folder and smiled gleefully up at her. 'I told you they'd be interested. That will mean extra payment for you, and this paper will gain some valuable publicity, so we're all happy.'

'Oh. I hope . . . '

'Don't you worry your pretty little head about the other business. That's all under control. Those welfare people should be in the office by now. I'll give them a ring in a minute.'

Margaret gave a doubtful nod and he directed her to a small room along the corridor.

'Hang the engaged sign on the door. No one will disturb you in there. Wander about, if it helps. Go down the street if you like. But bring me a good article by twelve o'clock.'

Margaret was closing his door when he called her back.

'By the way,' he added casually, 'we're running a story on your family this week, starting today. We'll go home at lunch-time and take photographs of you and the kids.'

Margaret did not welcome the idea of having their private affairs splashed across the pages of a newspaper, but she could not bring herself to protest. Mr Anderson had been so kind and understanding, and they needed his help. She hesitated for a moment longer, then gave a resigned nod and went away to begin the article. She wrote in longhand on foolscap paper and after two false starts the words began to flow. There were plenty of incidents to choose from, such as the one in which a man had a bad fall, just a few weeks before she left home. He had suffered multiple fractures and Margaret remembered all too clearly the consequences of that. All his limbs had to be immobilised for the journey to a distant hospital over rough roads, and his family had been left to survive without a breadwinner.

She handed the article in just before noon and the editor sent her home by car with a reporter and a photographer. Mrs Croft hurried out of the kitchen when she heard voices in the hall and Margaret quickly explained what was happening.

'Well, I suppose Mr Anderson should know what's best,' the woman sighed. 'Come in, all of you. I haven't heard a word from that Miss Adams, so I presume that business is all under control.'

Stephen and Pauline were thrilled to find a reporter and a photographer waiting when they returned home for lunch a few minutes later. Pauline was too shy to speak to either of them, but she always enjoyed having her photograph taken so she posed willingly with her brother. By contrast, Stephen was delighted to find himself the centre of attention. He began to chat eagerly to the reporter, telling him how exciting it was to be in another country where everything was so different. Margaret worried in case he said something that would upset the authorities and harm any favourable results that Mr Anderson might have achieved.

'Stop talking and come for your lunch,' she said anxiously. 'You have to go back to school.'

'One more shot.' The photographer clicked the shutter once more and packed his camera away. 'If you're ready to go, Margaret, we'll drive you back to the office.'

The first edition of the paper left the press twenty minutes later than usual, and Sue rushed to show Margaret as soon as she received a copy.

'What do you think of that?' she asked, dropping the newspaper onto the desk.

Margaret flushed and gasped aloud as she looked down. On the front page, spread across its entire width, glared a headline in bold print.

MUST THESE CHILDREN BE SEPARATED?

Beneath it were two large photographs. One showed Margaret with the two younger children, while the other was of Robert sporting a vivid black eye.

Sue stood motionless beside the desk, waiting for some comment, and at last Margaret managed to murmur: 'It's a bit startling.'

'Wait till you read it,' chuckled Sue. 'You haven't seen the best part yet.'

She hastened back to her own desk to read the piece again, while Margaret snatched up her copy of the paper. All she wanted to do was to hide. The whole town was going to know about her. How could she face anybody again? All the shopkeepers and the librarian and everybody . . . what would they think? After several moments of indecision, she hurried to the room where she had been working that morning and hung the engaged sign outside the door. No one must come near her until she had found out what had been said about the family. She also needed time alone to gather courage.

The further she read, the more embarrassed she became. The local reporter was obviously on her side, but he seemed to have exaggerated everything beyond belief. He claimed that she had outstanding ability, far greater ability than could be expected for one of her tender years. He laid great stress on the fact that she had been employed as a full-time teacher, and emphasised the experience she had gained with the newspaper in Africa.

Miss Barlow is responsible for our new-look Children's Corner, and regular readers will recognise her name as the author of the much-discussed articles on tribal customs in the war zone. A further article about life in Africa appears on page 5. That account should clear away any remaining doubts about her ability to care for the family.

Margaret gulped and flicked over the pages to find her article. What changes had Mr Anderson made? No doubt he had wanted everything to sound far more dramatic than they really had been. She read quickly to the end and then leaned back, sighing with relief. Her words seemed to have been left untouched. At least that segment did not glorify her skill and importance.

She quailed at the thought of meeting the editor again. He was sure to ask for her reactions, and she could hardly tell him what she really thought. Eventually, she began to feel calmer and she went back to her regular office, doing her best to concentrate on background material for the series about

Allingham. Nobody interrupted until a few minutes before five o'clock, when a light tap came on her door. She looked up, warning herself to behave with dignity, and saw the door open a few inches. Immediately afterwards, Tony's head appeared.

'Hello,' he said.

'Oh. Hello.' A bright flush spread rapidly over Margaret's face and neck and she felt an urge to disappear under the desk.

'Can I come in?'

'Well, of course. Yes, come in.'

He sauntered into the room and gave a little bow, followed by a lop-sided grin. 'I thought one might need to make an appointment now — seeing as you're such an important and knowledgeable person.'

'Oh, don't, please. It's embarrassing enough.'

Tony nodded. She just didn't know how embarrassing and dangerous it might have been, he thought. A day or two later and he could have been in a nightmare situation right now. They had both been lucky.

'I was surprised,' he said, struggling to convey his customary cool approach. 'And impressed, too. I must say I took you for an older person.'

'I'm sorry about that.'

'Yes, well, I wasn't the only one, was I? Anyway, I'm sorry I took you into pubs. I wouldn't have, not if I'd known.'

Margaret smiled faintly. She knew perfectly well that he would not have invited her to go anywhere if he had known her true age. He would have looked upon her as a mere child.

'Are you ready to go?' he asked. 'I've finished for the day. I could drop you off at home.'

The offer did not have the usual ring of enthusiasm and Margaret guessed he was trying to back graciously out of their relationship. Not that there really had been a relationship, she reminded herself sharply. One kiss on the lips hardly constituted a great romance and she could not expect another date with him, not even for a simple drink of coffee. A clean break now would be the easiest way out for both of them.

'No thank you,' she said. 'I have a few things to do before I go home.'

'Ah, well then.' Tony edged away, hoping he had managed to conceal his relief. The excuse was just what was needed right now. At least he had faced her and cleared the air. Now they should be able to work in the same place without fear of embarrassment, neither feeling the need to avoid the other. 'I'd better take my leave and let you get on with things.'

Les Croft bought a newspaper as usual on his way home from work, and his first reaction to the front page was one of consternation. There was going to be no quick end to the Barlow situation. The male passenger beside him on the bus noticed his interest and gestured towards the report.

'Amazing kid, that.'

'Yes.' Croft decided it was safer not to mention that he had become involved with the family.

'They're all amazing by the sound of it. They should be left alone. What do you reckon?'

'They seem to be doing pretty well.'

'They're doing a better job than lots of so-called normal families. I reckon the Welfare should back off and let them get on with it.'

At the first opportunity, Croft took his wife aside from the younger children and showed her the newspaper. Neither knew whether they should feel pleased or threatened by the account. Margaret was obviously a special child, someone to be admired; but would all this publicity harm their cause and encourage the Children's Department to act?

'I hope that editor really does know what he's doing,' muttered Mrs Croft. 'Miss Adams won't like this.'

'She hasn't called you today, has she? I reckon she's a bit wary. She won't do anything in a hurry, and I bet that's exactly what that editor has in mind.'

'Yes, well if she does call, I'll tell her we'll stay on here.'

Stephen and Pauline were delighted to see their photograph on the front page, and Robert greeted the news with enthusiasm. He met his brother and sisters at the entrance to the hospital ward and led them to a small public lounge.

'That'll fix them!' he exclaimed, skimming quickly over the account. He tucked the newspaper away inside his sling so that he could read it more carefully later. 'They won't keep me here much longer now. And don't try to fool me with stories about delayed concussion. I know why they kept me in here.'

'Why aren't you in bed?' asked Pauline.

'You don't stay in bed with a broken arm,' he retorted. 'Anyway, I've been too busy to stay in bed. I've been helping.'

'How can you help with just one arm?' asked Margaret.

'I've been in the little children's ward most of the day. I've been helping to look after them. Fetching things, reading stories and that.'

Margaret chuckled. 'That might not have the effect you're hoping for. They might find you're so useful they won't want to let you go.'

★ ★ ★

362

Anderson anticipated a heavy mail delivery the next day and he was not disappointed. The second post brought a further batch of letters from all parts of the town, some agreeing with the reporter's comments about the Barlow family, others criticising and saying that professional child minders should know best. Several people offered to give a home to the four children, and a few had sent money.

'We can't accept money,' Margaret protested. 'But how can we send it back if they don't give an address?'

'Just ignore all that for the time being. Things will settle down soon enough.' Anderson rubbed his hands together and slapped them twice. 'Things will start moving now. Just you wait. Did your Miss Adams call yesterday?'

'She made a quick visit last night, but Mrs Croft was the only one there. We went to see Robert at the hospital and Mr Croft came with us.'

'So what did Miss Adams say?'

'Nothing much.'

'I bet she didn't! Now then, we'll wait till after doctors' rounds, then we'll telephone the hospital. I wouldn't be surprised if they discharged young Robert today.'

He proved to be right again, and he had

already arranged for a reporter and a photographer to be on hand.

'They've agreed that Mrs Croft can sign the release forms,' he said. 'Now you go home with them, Margaret, and keep young Robert company.' He heaved himself to his feet and Margaret lingered near the door to hear his final instructions. She was used to his habits by now and was prepared for him to make some unexpected announcement.

'A television team will be coming to interview you this afternoon,' he said. 'They'll start as soon as the young kids come home from school, but the crew will arrive earlier to plan the lighting and things like that. Make sure you give a good impression, won't you?'

Margaret was too nonplussed to answer. She merely nodded and Anderson strode off to another part of the building, taking it for granted that neither she nor the Crofts would object to his arrangements.

Robert was still moving more slowly and stiffly than usual, but he asserted that he felt fine when he left the hospital. He had no qualms about wider publicity, and he smiled happily for the camera.

'The authorities know about us now, so there's no point in trying to keep it quiet,' he declared.

The thought of a television programme did

not disturb him either, and he could not understand why Margaret was so dubious about its effect.

'Mr Anderson must know what he's doing. He wouldn't have fixed it up unless he thought it would help.'

'I hope you're right,' said Mrs Croft. 'But don't mention it to the others yet. They won't settle at school this afternoon if they know anything about it.'

Pauline and Stephen gasped with excitement when they turned a corner into Ridgeway Drive at the end of the school day and caught sight of a television unit parked outside the house. They hurried towards the vehicle, forgetting they were supposed to go to the bakery to buy bread, but they hesitated as they drew closer. Several neighbours had gathered to watch the preparations and two of them pressed forward as soon as they recognised the youngsters, calling out questions.

'What do we do?' cried Pauline.

'Run!' Stephen grabbed her hand and they fled to the house, to find a tangle of wires leading to most of the rooms on the ground floor and running up the stairs. Two men were wandering about, erecting lamps and talking through microphones to the crew in the vehicle outside.

'Wow, isn't this exciting?' gasped Stephen.

'Are they going to take photographs of us?'

'Yes,' answered Margaret. 'You'd better have a quick wash and tidy yourselves up a bit. Put your blue dress on, Pauline.'

'No,' interrupted the man who seemed to be in charge. 'Don't do anything. We'll take shots of them arriving home first. We want everything to be absolutely natural.'

Margaret and Mrs Croft exchanged rueful smiles, remembering all the changes that had taken place in the house. Chairs and tables had been pushed into positions more convenient for the cameras, a vase filled with artificial flowers had been moved into a prominent position and white screens had been carefully placed to throw more light onto the filming areas.

'All set,' announced the director. 'Now then, children, all you have to do is behave quite naturally. I just want you to go out to the street and pretend you're coming home, just like you do every day.'

They could not forget the group of spectators watching every move, but after two poor attempts, Stephen and Pauline managed to walk in by the front gate in a way that satisfied him.

'Right, now you, Robert. No bike, so you'll have to walk today, won't you? We'll pick you up coming in at the front door.'

When Margaret had made her entrance they all moved to the kitchen, where the director wanted the children to prepare a meal. He planned to show how the children had organised their affairs before the accident, and Mrs Croft was not to appear until later. Some potatoes were waiting on the table, but Robert was unable to peel them because of his injured arm and Stephen thought he was too slow and clumsy to do that job in front of cameras.

'Don't fuss, we have rice more often than not,' declared Margaret, suddenly asserting her own authority. 'You and Pauline can shell some peas, and Robert can set the table for us.'

They went through a performance of sitting down to eat, then they moved into the front room, where the three younger ones were filmed watching television while Margaret sat typing at the table. Stephen and Pauline changed into pyjamas and pretended to go to bed, after which they were allowed to change into their weekend clothes. Then came the part that Margaret had been dreading.

'Don't look so nervous,' called the director as the interviewer sat down beside her. 'If you want to convince viewers that you can look after yourselves, you'll have to speak up for yourselves.'

The interviewer began by questioning

Margaret about their journey to England.

'You said your father gave you some money when you left home,' the interviewer went on. 'Have you got any of that money left now?'

'No, we spent that quite quickly.'

'What on?'

'Warm clothes mainly. Especially shoes.'

'But you said you were given clothes at the hostel.'

'We sent those back about three days later.' The man raised his eyebrows and Margaret hastened to explain. 'We didn't want anything that didn't belong to us. We were arranging everything just as though Aunt Joan were here.'

'So you have been living entirely on your wages. Tell me how you spin the money out.'

Robert noticed that Pauline was biting the tip of her thumb. He gave her a discreet nudge and she sat on her hands, hoping the man would not expect her to say anything. He led Margaret on until she had described some of the meals they had eaten during the past week, then he questioned Robert about his schoolwork, his chores and his newspaper round. He asked Stephen about the jobs he did in the house and how they spent the weekends, and Pauline began to stiffen with fright. She was now certain the man would not leave her out.

'Pauline, you are very quiet,' he said. 'Do you think Margaret is looking after you as well as anybody else could?'

She nodded emphatically and he gave an encouraging smile.

'You have been going to a different kind of school here. Do you like it?'

Pauline began to shake her head, then remembered they were all trying to make a good impression. If she admitted to disliking the school she might ruin everything. She quickly nodded her head and the interviewer smirked.

'You don't seem too sure about that. Now then, England is a strange country to you, and people are worried in case you don't know how things work. What would you do if you were alone in the house and it suddenly caught fire?'

The rest of the family stared at Pauline in dismay, but for once she was not afraid to speak up. She had suggested that kind of question for the children's competitions, and she was sure of the answer. This was no worse than being in school and having to talk to the teacher.

'I'd close the door and run down to the telephone box. That way.' She suddenly swung one arm in the direction she would take. 'I'd dial nine, nine, nine and tell the operator I wanted the Fire Brigade, and I'd tell them there was a fire at number one four nine Ridgeway Drive.'

Margaret and Robert smiled at each other and the interviewer nodded, obviously impressed.

'Well, you seem to be prepared for emergencies,' he said. 'What about English money? Can you work out pounds, shillings and pence?'

'I'm still learning that,' Pauline admitted.

'I see.' He introduced Mrs Croft to an invisible audience, then asked her what help she had given to the family so far and how much responsibility she was prepared to take on if the children stayed in the house. Soon afterwards he spoke a few sentences alone in front of the camera, displayed a variety of facial expressions while he pretended to listen to some other person, then signalled that he had finished. The lights died and the two men who had set the scenes began to roll up the wires, pack their equipment and return pieces of furniture to their proper places.

'Thank you,' said the interviewer, shaking hands with them all. 'If you want to see yourselves, switch on at six-thirty tomorrow and watch *Pinpoint*. Good luck.'

The following afternoon Margaret looked through an early edition of the *Daily Tribune* and found that her family was still the centre of attention. Reporters had interviewed officials from the Welfare Department and the Education Department, but received only cautious responses. Letters from readers revealed that public opinions differed sharply. Some people thought there should be regular supervision by an official, a small minority thought the children should be left alone to continue as they had been doing, while others declared the present arrangements were far too haphazard and the children should be removed immediately to be looked after properly in an authorised Home.

Even the Editorial contained a segment about the Barlow family. The editor referred to the article he had published the day before, pointing out that Margaret had often helped her mother to care for seriously injured patients.

If she could cope with emergencies in a remote area of Africa, surely she can manage in Allingham. Here she need only lift a telephone to summon help.

Anderson lumbered into the office and grinned when he saw Margaret reading his column.

'Ah, so you've seen that, have you? I kept it back until today so that it would coincide with the television programme. Just wait till people have seen that programme tonight. Then you'll see what a controversy we've started!'

When she was alone again Margaret turned to the inner pages, and there she found a description of their escape from Africa. She grew hot with indignation as she read the account of their supposed exploits. The journey certainly had been long, tiring and sometimes uncomfortable, but it had certainly not been dangerous. According to this report, four brave children had undertaken a very risky endeavour, and were fortunate to have emerged unscathed.

Mrs Croft had already begun to prepare the evening meal when Margaret arrived home.

'I thought we'd better make an early start tonight, dear. We don't want to miss that programme on the television, do we?'

'I hope it's not like the newspaper reports,' said Margaret. 'Everything has been terribly exaggerated.'

They all gathered in the front room in good time to watch *Pinpoint*. The novelty of seeing themselves on the screen was enough to excite Pauline and Stephen, but even they grew angry as the programme unfolded. A narrator described their situation in such a way that the youngsters appeared to be struggling against overwhelming odds. Several close-up shots showed Pauline looking frightened and forlorn, and the camera lingered on Robert's plaster cast and bruised eye.

The interview was interspersed with scenes of the children carrying out domestic chores, and frequent shots of price tickets to indicate financial struggles. Pauline's response to the question about fire was given as 'I'm still learning that', while Mrs Croft scarcely appeared. Despite the detailed explanations she had given the day before, her contribution consisted of only one comment, in which she said she would give the children independence to make their own plans. The programme ended with a female member of the local Borough Council, who declared vehemently that the children were in immediate need of Care or Protection.

As the final credits appeared on the screen, Mrs Croft strode to the television set and switched it off.

'That was disgusting. A really one-sided version.'

'That wasn't what I said!' Pauline objected for the fourth time. 'I knew the answer to that question.'

'They made it look as if we're almost destitute!' protested Margaret. 'They haven't given people the right impression at all.'

'It was awful,' muttered Robert. 'It looks as though you were right when you said it wasn't a very good idea. What do you think, Mr Croft?'

Their neighbour took a deep breath, holding back a string of expletives.

'I didn't like it,' he said at last. 'It's the most disgraceful thing I've ever seen. Really biased, that's what it was. In fact, I don't agree with the way any of this has been handled. If you ask me, that editor is only interested in stirring things up, just so's he can sell more newspapers.'

22

The sudden peal of the front doorbell interrupted rowdy complaints about the *Pinpoint* version of events. The Crofts turned to each other, instinctively aware of a need for caution, but before they could think of warning the children, Margaret jumped up and hurried to the front door. The short, plump stranger who was standing on the doorstep smiled cordially and offered his hand.

'Good evening. I'm Fred Goss from The *Daily Chronicle.*'

Margaret drew in her breath. He was from the rival newspaper in the nearby town. What was she to do now?

'I'd like to know your reaction to the *Pinpoint* programme,' he said. 'Did you see it?'

She gulped and slowly nodded. 'Yes, we saw it.'

'Would you say it was accurate — a true representation of your affairs?'

'Oh.' Margaret frowned and clutched the latch on the inner side of the door, sensing that she must not let the man enter the house. 'I — er — I don't think I ought to say anything just now.'

'You can surely tell me what you thought of the programme.'

Croft suddenly tapped Margaret on the shoulder and took control of the situation.

'Don't you start pestering anybody here,' he snapped. 'We've got nothing to say.'

'I was merely asking Miss Barlow for her opinion.'

'Well, I'm in charge just now, and I'm telling you she doesn't want to give an opinion. Good night.'

He closed the door gently but firmly and took Margaret's elbow to urge her back to the front room.

'You'd better let me answer the door in future,' he said. 'I'm afraid we're not going to get much peace until all this commotion has blown over.'

Less than half an hour later another reporter arrived and Croft turned him away. He refused to answer the door after that, and callers gradually gave up, but when he drew back the bedroom curtains the next morning he saw that a small knot of reporters and cameramen had gathered by the front gate. He gave an exasperated sigh and turned to his wife.

'We're in for a hectic time. The Press. Here in force.'

She peeped out of the window and shuddered. 'Just look at them! You'd think there was nothing important happening anywhere else in the world.'

They had finished breakfast before Robert noticed the group of men waiting outside.

'Come and see what's going on out here,' he shouted.

The others left what they were doing and ran to look, Stephen with his mouth full of toothpaste and Margaret still holding her hairbrush.

'Reporters!' gasped Margaret.

'I'm not going to school today,' mumbled Pauline.

'Oh, yes you are,' retorted Robert.

'It's all right for you — you're not going, anyway.' Pauline's mouth drooped and the ready tears welled in her eyes. 'I don't want to go out while all those men are there.'

Mrs Croft heard the dispute and hastened into the room.

'If you don't go to school you might ruin your chances of staying here with us,' she said. 'Don't worry, Pauline, I'll go with you today, and meet you at lunch-time. I'll give them a piece of my mind if they don't keep out of our way.'

Her husband had followed close behind and he nodded emphatically. 'Yes, you'll be all right, Pauline. You go with her. Margaret, if you can get ready in fifteen minutes, we can go for the bus together. You'd better not go by yourself today.'

As they approached the front gate he warned Margaret to stay close to him and not to utter a single word.

'Don't even nod or shake your head. We'll be through in no time. Try to imagine there's nobody there.'

She kept her head down as Croft silently forced a passage through the group of newsmongers. Thank goodness he was there, she thought fervently. She couldn't have left home without him. She would never have dared to face this mob alone.

Anderson was waiting for Margaret and he called her into his office as soon as she reached the premises.

'What did you think of that programme last night?'

'It was dreadful. It didn't give the correct impression at all.'

He smiled at her indignation. 'An important lesson for you — never believe everything you see and hear on television. It can be deceptive, the way things are presented.'

The television producer had purposely devised a programme to create dissent, and he was gratified by the response. The first mail delivery brought several letters to the studio and he knew there would be many more to follow. The insertion of that single comment by Mrs Croft had given some viewers the impression that she was not supervising the children adequately and many letters were abusive, the writers demanding that government officials take over at once.

During the day, dozens of letters arrived at the *Daily Tribune*, some delivered by post and others by hand. Anderson was prepared for the outcome of publicity and relished it, but Margaret was taken aback. She could not resist reading several letters, her spirits rising and falling according to each writer's point of view. Some said the youngsters should be praised for their courage, but others were highly critical about the lack of official action. A few people claimed that the children were under-nourished, their evidence being that the children looked thin and had admitted to feeling cold, while two alleged that a local newsagent had been employing the nine-year-old boy to deliver newspapers.

'Stephen was only helping out that once,' exclaimed Margaret, looking up from the first of the accusations. 'And Mr Perkins drove us everywhere.'

'I told you to expect a storm.' Anderson rubbed his hands together with intense satisfaction. The controversy had certainly drawn attention to the *Daily Tribune*, and now the national newspapers had taken up the cause. 'Don't you worry, Margaret. One thing we can be sure of, the authorities won't move too rapidly. They'll face too much criticism if they break the family up without real necessity.'

All that day reporters tried to waylay members of the family, hoping for some newsworthy comment, but Mrs Croft guarded the younger children well and Anderson arranged for a staff member to drive Margaret home. The journalists drifted away after Croft came back and told them they were wasting their time, but Margaret's relief was soon shattered. The councillor who had appeared on the television programme was still pressing for action, and the following evening she announced in a radio news bulletin that she was taking the case before the Juvenile Court.

'I am astounded that no immediate action was taken when the situation first became known,' she declared. 'Here we have a clear case of a family being in need of Care or Protection. The parents intended to delegate reponsibility to an aunt, not to an unknown neighbour. As neither the parents nor the aunt can be contacted, the authorities must take control. We must not allow sheer sentiment to overrule commonsense.'

Margaret felt shaky with apprehension when she went back to work the next morning but, as always, Anderson seemed unperturbed.

'Don't worry. One woman won't be able to persuade the court, not without some kind of firm evidence.'

'But we can't deny it, can we? The law says I'm too young.'

'A lot has changed since you overheard that conversation in London. You didn't know a single person in the country then, and you were just about penniless. You're living in your aunt's house now. That's a safe place, isn't it?'

Margaret warily agreed and he gave a complacent smile. 'So that's one of their main arguments shot down.'

'But what about all those forms I signed? It wasn't lawful for me to do that, was it?'

'Don't worry — they won't make a fuss over that little matter. After all, your father appointed you as guardian, didn't he? It's not as though you stole from somebody or claimed money you weren't entitled to.'

Anderson leaned back, exuding confidence. The way he had it figured out, there were no grounds for a court case. He mentally ran through the reasons listed as a cause for action. The kids were obviously not running wild. There were no signs of neglect, nobody's health had been endangered and, if Tony were telling the truth, there was no moral danger involved. Even if the case did go against them, the result could merely be an Order placing all the children in the care of a fit person. And who would the Magistrates name as a fit person, when Mr and Mrs Croft were already there on the premises, doing a good job?

Rather than go into details, he heaved himself to his feet and patted Margaret's shoulder.

'Cheer up. The next Juvenile Court won't be held until next Thursday, and anything might happen before then.'

Margaret dipped her head, not wishing to argue but still dubious about the consequences, and he patted her shoulder again. 'It's Saturday. Go home early today and do something interesting. Don't let that silly council woman spoil your weekend.'

She wanted to believe, but she had little faith in his assurances, and Mrs Croft shook her head despondently when Margaret confided in her.

'I don't know. I must say it all sounds ominous to me. Going to court will be a

382

terrifying experience for the little ones, even if that woman doesn't prove her case. I wonder what Miss Adams is thinking?'

The Children's Officer made another of her regular visits when they were clearing the table after lunch, but she would not be drawn into giving an opinion about the councillor's action.

'I'm sure every effort will be made to keep the family together,' was the most she would say, but her tone was not convincing and Margaret's spirits sank lower.

'Just try to forget about her and enjoy the weekend,' said Mrs Croft when the woman had driven away. 'Now then, would you like me to cook this evening, or would you rather just do your own thing?'

'No thank you, Mrs Croft. I'm sure you must have lots of things you want to do. We can look after ourselves.'

'As you like, my dear. Les will be doing a few odd jobs around the back of our house all afternoon, so if you need anything just come across.'

'I thought we might go to the cinema for a treat this afternoon — just in case this turns out to be our last weekend together.'

'Better hurry up then, dear. And enjoy yourselves. Les and I will be back here this evening.'

The cinema programme could have been specially devised to cheer up the Barlow children after the anxieties of the previous few days. Both films were in technicolour, the first following the exploits of a large family who lived on a farm in Scotland, while the main film was a comedy with a well-trained dog as the major star. Ice cream during the interval added further enjoyment and they came out to the daylight feeling light-hearted and full of optimism.

'That was a lovely afternoon,' said Pauline as they let themselves back into the house. 'Will you make chips for tea? Please. I like chips.'

Margaret smiled. 'We all do. Yes, all right, I'll make chips. You set the table.'

Pauline pulled out all the things she thought would be needed for cooking and then arranged tablemats and cutlery, while Margaret set a pan of dripping on the stove to heat and quickly sliced potatoes. It had not taken her long to peel them, she thought with amusement. She had certainly developed some useful skills since they first arrived in England. But it seemed as if all that might be about to end. If only they had been left alone . . . The authorities would surely be the winners in a court case.

She turned back to the stove and quickly

realised she had put too much fat into the pan. Never forget Archimedes and his theorem, she scolded herself: the reason why things overflow. She couldn't put that amount of chips in there.

'Pass me that bowl, Pauline,' she instructed, and the little girl pushed the clean green bowl towards her. Margaret carefully poured excess dripping out of the pan, and they both stared in horror as the bowl immediately collapsed into a shapeless mass. Hot fat streamed over the edge of the table, and Pauline shrieked as it splashed across her leg.

'Oh, no!' gasped Margaret.

She put the pan down on the stove and quickly turned off the gas, then reached for a clean tea towel. The screams brought the two boys running to the kitchen and she shouted at them to stand back.

'Don't come any closer. Pauline, stay where you are.'

She soaked the tea towel in cold water and wrapped it around Pauline's leg, then pulled a chair away from the table.

'Sit down and hold that on firmly to keep the air out,' she ordered. 'I'll wet another one.'

When the first shock had passed Pauline decided she must be brave.

'It's not hurting so much now.'

'Good. Keep holding that on. I'll soon have it fixed up.'

'What's all that stuff?' asked Stephen, staring at the mess on the floor.

'Hot fat. Stay well away. We'll put newspaper on top in a minute and leave it till it gets cold. We can scrape it up when it's set. That will be safer, too.'

The prompt First Aid had saved Pauline from more severe pain, but the spilt fat had left angry red blotches on her lower leg. Margaret covered them with lint and a bandage and praised the little girl for her courage.

'That's a bit conspicuous,' murmured Robert, as Margaret tied the bandage.

'Yes, that's all we needed,' she sighed. 'Everybody's going to be convinced that we can't look after ourselves when they find out we get burnt making dinner. And they'll want to know why Mr and Mrs Croft weren't here.'

The couple noticed the bandage as soon as they came back to the house and Margaret tried to explain what had happened.

'I don't understand it,' she said. 'The bowl just seemed to fall apart.'

'Ah, it must have been a plastic one,' said Croft. 'Perhaps you've never seen that modern stuff before. It can be very useful — doesn't break if you drop it. But you can't let it get too hot.'

'Margaret wouldn't be the first to make that mistake,' said his wife. 'I've known other people do exactly the same thing.'

'We won't be able to hide that bandage, unfortunately,' said Croft.

'No.' Margaret sighed, then she lifted her chin defiantly. 'Still, we're not going to stay in tomorrow, just to hide a bandage.'

The sun was shining warmly again the next day so Margaret took her brothers and sister to the river, where she bought tickets for a cruise. The fine weather had enticed hundreds of people to the river banks and the pleasure boat was crowded, but the children had arrived early so they were able to find four seats together on the upper deck.

'Wow, we've had a marvellous weekend!' exclaimed Stephen as they waited for a bus to return home. 'Just imagine how we'd enjoy ourselves if we always had plenty of money.'

'You wouldn't appreciate it so much then,' responded Margaret. 'Everything would lose its novelty.'

While they were out Mrs Croft had visited a relative, and she had procured some antiseptic cream and a pair of knee-length socks.

'This will make your leg feel better,' she told Pauline, smearing cream onto another piece of lint and bandaging it into place.

'Those blisters are only tiny and all those marks will soon go.'

'It doesn't hurt now.'

'Good. But you must keep it covered until there's absolutely no danger of infection.'

'Miss Weston will want to know what happened. She'll say we shouldn't be looking after ourselves.'

'She doesn't need to know. Look at these socks. Nobody will see that bandage if you wear these on top. Look, there's a cute little dog on the side, and I bet everybody in the class will want socks just like these.'

Pauline's doubtful frown soon changed to a happy grin. 'Yes, I've never had socks like these. And I think that dog is lovely. It's just like the one we saw at the pictures yesterday.'

On her way to work the next morning Margaret caught sight of a newspaper being read by a passenger across the aisle of the bus, and she almost gasped aloud. She had feared that someone might notice the bandage on Pauline's leg and send a letter to the local editor, but she was not prepared to see a photograph of it splashed across the front page of a national newspaper. She slumped down in her seat and lowered her head, hoping that no one would recognise her. Was there no end to their trouble? This was like living in an endless nightmare.

One or two people stared at her in a puzzled fashion as she hurried along High Street, apparently unsure whether or not they knew her, but nobody spoke and she reached the office without incident. Anderson called her into his room and her gaze immediately went to the newspaper on his desk. The photograph seemed larger than ever and, now that the whole page was on view, she could see there was a second photograph showing a close-up of the bandage.

'How's the patient?' asked Anderson, and chuckled at her reaction. 'Don't let any of this get you down. All kids have mishaps from time to time. And don't worry about that interfering old busybody from the Council. Thursday is a long time off yet and there should be a change for the better before then.'

He reached for a letter and handed it to her.

'You need to be ready in case this subject comes up. I wouldn't show you this — but it would come as a nasty shock if you weren't prepared, and then you might say the wrong thing.'

Margaret's face flushed and then paled as she skimmed the letter. She took a deep breath, then read it again more carefully. The writer alleged that she was clearly exposed to moral danger; that she kept bad company and had been seen drinking at the Red Lion.

'This is terrible. It's really serious. It will really count against us.'

Anderson eased the letter away from her fingers. 'Don't take it to heart.'

'But it's against the law for me to drink in a hotel. Who will believe that . . . ?'

'Don't worry. The bartender remembers. He knows you only had lemonade.' Anderson fervently hoped that Tony had been honest about that. If the situation did become sticky and ended with a court case, they might have to call the bartender as a witness. Being seen in a pub could be the one thing that turned proceedings against them. He shrugged off that possibility and handed her another batch of letters.

'Forget that other business and enjoy these comments instead,' he said. 'Our regular readers are thrilled to bits with the new column about Allingham.'

Margaret blushed with pleasure and he gave a nod of encouragement. 'I told you, didn't I? Did you manage to find out any more about that tithe barn you were telling me about?'

'Yes, it's mentioned in the church records.'

'Good. Deal with Children's Corner first, then concentrate on the barn. I've got some letters here about some more odd spots, so you'll have plenty to be going on with during the next few weeks. People have already started to take more notice of their surroundings.'

Robert had insisted on returning to school that day, anxious to tell everyone that the television programme had not given the true story. He had to face intense curiosity from members of the staff as well as the students, but he put on a brave front, determined to prove that he could not be intimidated by adverse publicity. During morning recess the class bully strutted up and flaunted the front page of the newspaper with the photograph of Pauline.

'Sure you fell off your bike?' he taunted. 'Or did your big sister beat you up? Says here it's suspicious. How come you all end up in bandages?'

Robert did his best to convince himself that size did not count as much as dignity and confident words. 'You won't have so much to say when I get rid of this sling and the cast,' he retorted.

Cronies warned the bully he would be in serious trouble if he attacked when his victim could not retaliate. He blustered until he thought his tough reputation was safe, then sauntered away to find an easier target.

Robert drew a deep breath of relief and smiled gamely at the onlookers, telling himself the worst was over.

By Wednesday morning the fuss seemed to have abated and Robert only had to deal with the frustration of not being able to use his right arm. The pain of the fracture had dwindled to a mild ache, and the bruises on his face had faded. The plaster cast gave him the perfect excuse to avoid written work, but school was a real bore when he could not use any of that wonderful equipment in the workrooms. Worse than that, a thorny situation lay ahead. What would happen at court tomorrow? Would he have to say anything, or would lawyers do all the talking? Pauline and Stephen didn't even know yet that such a thing was going to happen.

At the newspaper premises, Anderson was putting the finishing touches to some plans of his own. He told Sue to send Margaret to his office as soon as he had finished his next telephone call, and when she went in he wasted no time on small talk.

'*Pinpoint* is following up your case,' he said. 'They're going to interview me. Do you want to get involved?'

Margaret immediately shook her head, repulsed by the suggestion. 'No, thank you.

I'd rather not see any of those people.'

Anderson rubbed his hands, smiling and nodding in whole-hearted agreement. He had been banking on that response. Now he could use his experience to exert some control over the direction of the interview. He had insisted on a live broadcast from the studio so that his words would be complete and unedited, and he had rehearsed answers to likely questions.

'I agree that it's better for you to keep out of sight,' he said. 'The team will only be taking background shots here so they won't be around for long. Go and work in the public library in town if you like. I'll say you're out on a job. If you want to see the programme, switch on tonight.'

That evening the Crofts and all the children gathered in front of the television set, anxious to see how their affairs would be dealt with this time. They chattered and wriggled impatiently during the advertising session, but as soon as the *Pinpoint* signature tune began they shushed each other and leaned forward. The same announcer as before outlined the 'Barlow Case' to remind viewers of the previous programme, and stated that the situation had aroused great public interest. A few of the earlier scenes were repeated, followed by shots of Pauline and Stephen being escorted to school, and then of Robert kicking a football about with a group of friends.

'Hey! I didn't see anybody taking that,' he complained.

'Trust you to be seen when you weren't looking after your arm very well,' retorted Margaret. 'Thank goodness you didn't fall over.'

The scene switched to the newspaper office and Margaret tensed at the sight of Anderson working at his desk. Moments later came typical shots of newsprint rolling off machines, then Anderson was shown seated in the television studio. He appeared to be as unruffled as ever, but the interviewer seemed determined to needle him.

'Wouldn't you agree that you took advantage of this family's situation, merely to obtain a good story?'

'No, I would not.'

'But you wouldn't take on just any inexperienced young girl. You must have decided the scoop was worth it.'

The editor shook his head and began his version of events, refusing to be diverted despite efforts to interrupt.

'You seem to misunderstand the situation. Miss Barlow is not an inexperienced young girl.' Anderson gave an expressive shrug. 'Maybe she did leave school at an earlier age than we usually expect nowadays — but who's to say that is wrong? She had been living in a country where that is customary. Miss Barlow answered my advertisement in the usual way, and I found that she had worked on a newspaper before. She impressed me enough to give her a fortnight's trial, and before that fortnight was up, I was convinced that we couldn't afford to lose her. She's a natural, and if you would take the time to read a few copies of our paper, you'd see just what I mean.'

'But you didn't employ her as a reporter. All those articles and so forth didn't appear until this publicity started.'

Anderson tilted his chin, telling himself it was time to show signs of irritation.

'That is incorrect. Check the dates. Anyway, I didn't advertise for a journalist. Miss Barlow applied for a job in the office. I arranged the switch when I found out what she could do. Naturally, that didn't happen overnight.' He leaned forward and wafted one hand towards the interviewer. 'You're in a similar line of business yourself, so you must know it takes time to develop a series. Miss Barlow was working on background material for quite a while before anything came into print. As for exploiting the family, none of this would have been publicised if young

Robert had not been knocked off his bike. You can blame a careless driver for that.'

'You must have known that Margaret — er — Miss Barlow, was looking after the whole family.'

'Of course.'

'You didn't think that was unusual?' A lack of response forced the interviewer to press for an answer and he rephrased the question. 'Didn't you think she was far too young?'

'I thought it was unfortunate that she had to take on such great responsibilities.'

'But you thought it was perfectly all right for her to look after a family by herself? A young girl, barely fifteen? She's only a child.'

'I didn't know her age then.'

The interviewer appeared to be flabbergasted by that reply. 'You didn't know her age? How do you explain that?'

'Because I didn't ask.' Anderson gave an expressive shrug. 'She was mature enough to do the job, and I didn't need to know her date of birth. I was more interested in the quality of the work she was likely to turn out.'

The interviewer probed for a few more details about Margaret's employment, then suddenly pounced with a question about the impending court case. Anderson rested his left forearm on the arm of his chair and leaned casually to that side, determined to show that a court case posed no great challenge.

'Don't you agree that a court case is the most appropriate way to deal with this problem?' suggested the interviewer.

A satisfied smile spread across the editor's face. 'No, I don't. But in this particular instance, the case is unlikely to go before the court.'

The interviewer was visibly shaken. 'What gives you that idea?'

Anderson beamed with triumph. 'The case will be adjourned tomorrow. And very soon afterwards, the so-called problem will have ceased to exist.'

'Why is that?'

'Let us say I have received some useful information.'

The interviewer waited for an explanation, but eventually he was obliged to ask, 'Where has this information come from?'

Anderson only shook his head silently and the other man frowned.

'Have you told the authorities?'

'Not yet. I have to wait for confirmation.'

'So when do you expect to share this private information?' The interviewer fought down his frustration and assumed the pose he always adopted when he wished to display care and sympathy for the downtrodden and unfortunate members of society. 'Mr Anderson, the public are very concerned about these young children. They must not be exploited. The public must be assured that these children's interests are being safeguarded. So, there should be no secrecy.' He raised his voice. 'The public needs to know.'

Anderson nodded slowly before he spoke. 'I cannot say any more just now.'

'Is this a genuine development? Or is it merely a delaying tactic to hinder the court case?'

'Absolutely genuine. But I cannot say any more just now.'

Anderson steadfastly refused to add to that statement and the interviewer attacked from a different angle.

'Why the sudden decision to seek an adjournment? Is there an ulterior motive? Is this an attempt to hide an injury to yet another child in the same family?'

'Of course not.'

'Do you deny that the youngest child has an injured leg?'

Anderson waved both hands in a disparaging gesture. 'A mere mishap. Happens all the time with active children. Yes, Pauline injured her leg this week, but the bandage was a mere precaution. There was no serious damage.'

The interviewer brought the segment to an

end by stressing the fact that a large majority of viewers believed the family should be taken into care immediately. Margaret gripped her hands tightly together and clenched her teeth, while the other children shouted angry protests.

Croft switched off the television set and turned to his wife, hoping his expression did not reveal the intensity of his feelings. 'Well, what did you think?'

'I don't think that was very helpful, do you? That editor might be making things worse rather than better.'

Croft shrugged. 'He's a newspaper man. It suits him if things get worse. He's not really interested in the family. All he's interested in is how many newspapers he can sell.'

23

The telephone rang scarcely ten minutes after the close of the television programme. The children's chatter ceased immediately and Pauline clutched Margaret's arm for comfort.

'Reporters,' she gasped.

'Leave it,' Croft commanded. 'We don't want to be harassed by them again.'

The bell continued to ring for so long that when it stopped the silence seemed unnatural. They all looked towards the door of the room with the uneasy feeling that some sinister incident was about to occur, and then the ringing started again.

'Let me get it,' said Mrs Croft, rising quickly to her feet. 'I'll give them a piece of my mind, then leave the phone off the hook.'

She stalked out to the hall and lifted the receiver. 'Yes?'

'It's Anderson here. Is that Mrs Croft?'

'Yes.' She felt too indignant to give a more friendly response.

'I want to come and see you — give you some news. Will that be all right?'

'Oh. Well, yes, I suppose so. Can't you tell me over the phone?'

'I want to see you all. But I'm in Birmingham. It will take me about an hour and a half to get back there. I'll call through the letterbox. Don't open the door to anybody else. Okay?'

Mrs Croft sighed. 'Yes, I suppose so.'

'Cheer up, Mrs Croft. Things are not all that bad.'

She returned to the front room to find Pauline in tears and Stephen pouting rebelliously.

'Oh dear,' she said. 'Now what?'

'Pauline doesn't want to go to school,' her husband explained. 'Stephen does want to go. But I just told him none of them will be going to school tomorrow.'

'I'm not going to let a silly old television programme frighten me,' declared Stephen. 'I'll jolly well show them. I don't care what those silly people say.'

Mrs Croft smiled gently and went back to her easy chair. 'It's got nothing to do with the programme, love. The teachers aren't expecting to see you at school tomorrow. Even Mr Croft isn't going to work. We all have to go into Allingham.'

Pauline looked up suspiciously. 'Why? What's happening?'

'We have to go to an office in town.' Mrs Croft had decided it would be better to avoid all mention of court cases until it became absolutely essential; but that night's programme had brought the matter to the fore, and when Pauline had time to think about what had been said she would start asking awkward questions. 'It will probably turn out to be a very boring day, but it can't be helped.'

'Are we going to the place where Miss Adams works?'

'No, but she will be there.' Mrs Croft stood up again, feeling the need to keep herself busy. 'I'm going to put the kettle on. Mr Anderson is coming, but he's a long way off so it will take him a while to get here.'

Almost two hours passed before an imperative knock sounded on the front door, followed by a man's deep voice calling through the letterbox.

'Are you there, Margaret? Open up. It's Anderson here.'

She rushed to answer and he stepped into the hall, grinning cheerfully.

'Took me a bit longer than expected, but I'm here now. Where is everybody?'

'In the front room.'

Without waiting for her to close the door and lead the way, he strode ahead of her. The children stared up at the huge man, clearly apprehensive, while the Crofts glared with displeasure. Anderson nodded and smiled as if he had received a friendly reception.

'Well, you obviously saw the programme.'

'We did, and we were not impressed,' said Croft.

Margaret hastily invited the editor to sit down and he walked across to a vacant armchair in a leisurely fashion. He then began to rub his hands together, and a smile flickered across Mrs Croft's face. She exchanged a quick glance with Margaret, then looked down to hide her amusement. The young girl's description of her employer had been remarkably accurate. Any moment now he would make an announcement. As expected, a little clap preceded his next words.

'I'd better tell you straight away — put you out of your misery. None of you has to go to the court tomorrow.'

'Are you sure?' demanded Croft. 'We don't want to be up for . . . '

'There's nothing to be concerned about. It will be a straightforward adjournment. Our solicitor will be there. I've already spoken to the other side. They've agreed. There's no need to produce the children. Miss Adams sees them regularly and knows they are in good health.'

'What else should we know? Something is

in the wind,' said Croft.

Anderson nodded and gleefully hitched himself forward. He then rubbed his hands again. 'I got some fantastic news this evening. Just before the programme, too. It was all I could do not to tell that fellow in the studio. I would have loved to drop a real bombshell on him.'

Croft scowled. The man was running true to form, he decided. The only thing that mattered to Anderson was selling newspapers. If there had been any new development, he wanted to be the first to publish it, and in his own paper.

'Yes, it was tempting,' Anderson continued. 'I would have loved to drop it on him. But I wanted to tell you first.'

An aggravating pause followed and Robert groaned with frustration.

'Well, go on then.'

Anderson sat back in his chair, relishing the moment. 'We have managed to contact Miss Wheatley. Your Aunt Joan,' he added, to make sure all the children understood the significance of his words.

They stared at him and then at each other, hardly daring to believe they had really heard what he had just said.

'Is that true?' demanded Robert.

'Do you mean you have actually spoken to

Aunt Joan?' whispered Margaret.

'Not directly. But I know where she is. And she's on her way home.'

'Aunt Joan is coming home!' That momentous news made Pauline lose her usual timidity and she jumped up. She jigged excitedly from one foot to the other, then she dropped onto Margaret's lap and flung her arms around her neck. 'She's coming home! We're saved!'

'Don't get too excited just yet,' warned Croft. 'Things might still go wrong.' He turned to Anderson. 'We don't want any red herrings, just to excite your readers. Is this genuine, or just a rumour?'

'That television bloke put ideas into your head, didn't he?' said Anderson placidly. 'No, this is genuine all right. We found the children's aunt, and she is on her way home.'

'How did you do it?' asked Margaret.

'Your aunt is a well-known photographer, you know. Once I realised who she was, I guessed she must be off on some kind of assignment. So I found out which magazine she was working for.'

'How long have you known all this?' Croft still distrusted the editor's motives.

'I've known which country she's in for several days. But I didn't want to raise anybody's hopes until we had a definite result. It has been difficult to reach her.'

'Are you really sure now?' asked Mrs Croft.

'Absolutely. She is in a remote area in Bolivia.' Anderson raised one hand to discourage questions. 'It's going to take time. It takes two days to walk to the road, and then at least a day from there to reach La Paz. After that she will probably have to go to Lima in Peru. And then she might have to go to California.'

'Sounds a bit like our trip,' mumbled Stephen.

'Exactly. You know what it's like, travelling in a country with few roads and so on. Anyway, the important thing is — the end is in sight.' Anderson leaned forward again, his expression now serious. 'Mr and Mrs Croft, are you willing to continue caring for the family?'

'Of course we are!' Mrs Croft stretched out her arm and gave Pauline a comforting pat. 'Just let anyone try and stop us!'

'Are we going to have reporters from Miss Wheatley's magazine pestering us now?' her husband asked.

Anderson grinned. 'It's a scientific journal. They don't run human interest stories.'

'Well, thank goodness for that. But it won't stop the others, will it?'

'I suggest that you stay out of sight. A

couple of days off school won't hurt, and Margaret can work at home. Next week we could be down at the airport meeting Aunt Joan.'

'What about her assignment?' asked Margaret. 'She won't be very happy if she's had to leave it half done. And the publisher won't be, either.'

Anderson clapped his hands in triumph. 'She'd finished it. That's why it took so long to trace her. She'd gone off to do a bit of exploring by herself in the mountains.'

24

Margaret sighed with frustration and pushed the typewriter away. It was all very well to tell herself it was time to forget all the excitement of the past week and to get on with some work, but she just couldn't concentrate. She had intended to write a complete article this morning, and there was nothing to stop her from doing so. The others had gone back to school, so there was nobody to claim her attention or start an argument. Aunt Joan wouldn't interrupt.

She scowled at the sheet of paper in the typewriter. What had she achieved? Two paragraphs that would be of no use at all. Perhaps she'd get back into a more workmanlike frame of mind if she went to the office. It was difficult to think here, listening to the occasional clink of dishes and the sound of cupboard doors opening and closing as Aunt Joan pottered about in the kitchen. Handing over responsibility for the family had not been as easy as she had imagined during all those weeks when she had been in charge. Now she felt out of place, superseded. She often thought she should be doing more to help with the cooking and cleaning and everything, but she mustn't try to take control in Aunt Joan's own home. If she were to keep any self-respect she would have to hold on to her job at the *Tribune*, at least for the time being. But to do that she would have to prove her worth. In other words — write some good articles.

Margaret sighed again. Perhaps Mr Anderson had already started to ease her out. He had told her not to come back to the office for another week, and she could not forget Mr Croft's early suspicions. Was it true that Mr Anderson had only been interested in selling more newspapers? In that case, he would no longer want her. Where would she find another job now, after all that awful publicity? And how long would their current arrangements last? Aunt Joan was very kind and she kept saying she loved having them to stay, but she had to earn a living. Supposing her next job turned out to be overseas again? That possibility did not seem to have occurred to any of the others yet. They were lucky. Things had not changed much for them, except that they had fewer chores to think about. Pauline and Stephen would be coming back for lunch very soon. How had they got on this morning? Pauline had been reluctant to go back to school, but that was not surprising. Stephen had been keen to see his classmates again, longing to tell them all about the exciting trip to London Airport.

Margaret rested her elbows on the edge of the table and cradled her chin in her hands. It was hard to resist thinking about everything that had happened recently. Going back to the airport had stirred a mixture of emotions. Again they had been met by a hostess and taken away to wait, away from the crowds in the main hall. This time, however, they had been accompanied by Michael Fuller and a local cameraman, and there was no uncertainty about where they would spend the night. The prospect of seeing Aunt Joan at long last had been both exciting and daunting by turn. So many years had passed since they had last met. She only had vague memories of her aunt, helped by photographs, while Pauline and Stephen had been so young they could not even remember coming to England. Would Aunt Joan be pleased to see them, or annoyed because her trip had been cut short? They had been living in her house without permission and treating her belongings as if they were their own. What would she think about that?

Margaret smiled as she thought of their first glimpse of Aunt Joan. She was taller and sturdier than Mum, but she looked very much like her, especially as she was wearing khaki drill trousers and shirt. Judging by her outfit, she had come straight from doing field-work in the bush. She had walked in quickly, smiling a greeting and ignoring camera flashes.

'You poor dears!' she exclaimed, putting her camera case and cabin bag down on the floor and holding out her arms. 'I had no idea what was happening while I was away.'

She tried to envelop the whole family in one fond hug, then hugged each of them individually and gave them a light peck on the cheek.

'You poor dears. Fancy coming all this way by yourselves, and nobody here to meet you. I didn't know anything about all that fighting. I never saw a newspaper or heard a wireless. We were quite cut off from the outside world.'

They travelled back to Allingham in the same car that had taken them to the airport, endured a few more poses for photographs to record their homecoming, and then at last they had been left in peace. Mrs Croft had worked hard to prepare a suitable welcome, vacuuming carpets, laundering bed linen and making a casserole dinner that could be heated whenever they felt ready to eat. However, she had not stayed to greet them personally.

'This is a time for family,' she had said. 'There've been too many outsiders around here lately. You need some privacy. I'll catch up with your aunt later when you've all had time to be together.'

Joan Wheatley paused in the midst of setting out plates for lunch. There had been no clacking of typewriter keys for several minutes. The timing couldn't be better. Margaret would probably welcome an excuse to give up for a while.

She went to the back room, tapped lightly on the door and went in without waiting for an answer.

'Would you go to the Post Office for me, love? It would save time later. And perhaps you would like to meet the children from school, seeing as it's their first day back.'

Margaret agreed instantly. 'Yes, I will do that. I think the exercise might do me good.'

'The brain's feeling a bit rusty is it?' Joan chuckled softly. 'Don't panic, love. It will come. But a change of pace will probably help.'

She moved towards the door then turned back as if she had just had an idea.

'I thought we might go to town this afternoon, just the two of us. You have to think about getting ready to face the big wide world again, so you're going to need some new make-up.'

Margaret blushed. 'I'm sorry I used yours. I know it's not right to go into people's private drawers and things, and it's awful to use really personal things like make-up.'

Joan laughed and wafted one hand dismissively. 'That's not my private stuff, love, so don't worry about it. It's theatre make-up.'

'Theatre make-up?' gasped Margaret.

'Yes, that's why there's so much of it, all those different shades and that.' Joan chuckled again. 'I'm a photographer, Margaret. I do portraits as well as scenery and action shots. And I usually do the publicity shots for the local drama group, so I help out with their make-up, too.'

'I see.'

'Now you've started using make-up there's no reason why you shouldn't carry on. But what you need is something light. By all accounts you did a pretty good job with that stuff in the drawer, but it's not intended for ordinary use.'

'Mrs Croft helped me. I made an awful mess at first.'

'Dear Mrs Croft. She's one of those who just can't help looking after other people. She's like an angel in disguise.' Joan headed for the door again. 'I'll just make sure I've put a stamp on everything. And I need some more Air Letters please.'

Anderson waited until Margaret had left the Post Office and begun to walk towards the primary school before he started his car. He drove along Ridgeway Drive and parked outside the Wheatley house, where Joan was waiting to lead him to the kitchen.

'How's it going?' he asked.

'Quite well. Not so hectic now.' Joan filled two mugs with tea and pushed one towards him. 'Before anything else I have to thank you for arousing all that interest. If it hadn't been for publicity on television and in the national papers, they'd have never gone to so much trouble to find me. But I must say I didn't enjoy being the centre of all that fuss.'

Anderson shrugged and spread his hands. 'It'll be good for you — help to boost your career. Publicity's never harmful. Just think of it — increased fame without having to exert yourself.'

'Perhaps.' Joan gave a wry smile. Only the prospect of publicity for his own business had made him pursue the matter so diligently. 'Anyway, all I can say is, thank goodness for that gaol break last week. It took the spotlight off us.'

'It will stay off, too.'

'Are you sure?'

Anderson nodded. 'There's a whiff of

scandal in Whitehall. That will occupy everybody's attention for days, if not weeks.'

Time was short, he reminded himself. The children would come storming in very soon and he wanted to learn more about Margaret while he had the chance.

'So tell me. How did Margaret manage to fit so much into such a brief life? I couldn't believe she really was so young. She told the truth about teaching, didn't she?'

'Oh yes.' Joan smiled reminiscently. 'She's an unusual child, always has been. Of course, they've all had an unusual upbringing. The family was more or less stranded out there all through the war. They were safe from the blitz, but it was sometimes difficult to keep in touch, and supplies were often hard to get. I used to worry that they'd all go down with some horrible disease and not be able to get medicine.'

'What about Margaret's education? A village school couldn't have taught her everything she knows.'

Joan gave a snort of amusement. 'You wouldn't believe how patchy her education has been. She's had a lot of practical experience, because everybody had to look after themselves and make do with whatever materials they could get hold of. The rest of her knowledge comes from newspapers and programmes on the wireless. Plus a few books. She was only eleven when she started to help out at the local school. They couldn't teach her anything more, you see, so they made her a monitor. She did so well with the little ones they promoted her the next year, and from then on she was a full-time teacher.'

'Remarkable.' Anderson drained his mug and shook his head at the offer of more tea. 'No thanks. Well, down to business. You're the guardian of the family now and Margaret's not desperate for money. Do you agree that she should continue to work at the *Tribune*, or have you got other plans? We could take her on as a trainee, you know. She shows more promise than most.'

Joan considered that proposal, but quickly decided against it.

'I don't think she should commit herself to anything just yet. She needs to feel that she's doing something worthwhile, but she mustn't be rushed into a long term arrangement.'

'What about the parents? Did they have any plans?'

'They were going to bring the whole family back to this country.' Joan shook her head regretfully. 'They left it too late, though, didn't they? A remote place like that was not suitable for teenagers and they knew it, but Bob was working on something important and he wanted to get it up and running before leaving. They were planning to come back here in June, just in time for the summer.'

'What did they expect Margaret to do once they came back?'

'Improve her education, first of all.' Joan sipped her tea, recalling the discussion yesterday evening. After the other children had gone to bed, she and Margaret had settled in the front room with mugs of cocoa, talking softly in the muted light of a single standard lamp. It was the first time they had talked so intimately.

'I've already suggested night school, or taking private tuition.'

'What's the purpose of that?'

'She's got huge gaps in her education and she'll need help to fit into a normal class. She'd never pass GCE at the moment, and she's going to need that if she still wants to train to be a qualified teacher.'

Voices sounded in the hall and Stephen clattered into the kitchen, followed by his two sisters. Pauline's smile quickly faded, and Anderson noticed how Margaret tensed as soon as she caught sight of him.

'Hello,' he said, raising one beefy hand in greeting. 'I thought this might be a good time to catch you all in. Is everything going well?'

'Yes, thank you,' said Stephen defiantly, treating the query as yet another challenge. 'Nobody can complain about anything now.'

'I'm glad to hear it.' Anderson leaned sideways and lifted his briefcase off the floor. 'Are you feeling ready to think about Children's Corner, Margaret, or would you rather leave it this week?'

'Oh, no! No, I'd like to do it.'

He cast a quick glance at Joan before delving into his briefcase, grinning with satisfaction.

'I was hoping you'd say that. I brought some of the competition entries with me. Just in case. You'll do a better job with them than anybody else.'

Margaret glowed with pride as she accepted the bulky folder. It was lovely to know that he really valued her efforts. It seemed that her job was safe after all.

'There's sure to be another batch tomorrow. You can do everything at home, if you like. Makes no difference to me. I'll let you decide where you want to work.'

'I think it will be better to do it at the office.'

'As you like. Now I must go and let you people get on with lunch. I know there's not much time before school starts again.'

Margaret felt awkward and self-conscious

when she first entered the newspaper premises the next day, but Sue welcomed her back as if she had merely been away for a short vacation, and other members of staff acted as though nothing unusual had occurred. Before half an hour had passed she became engrossed in her task, and no longer cared what anybody else might be thinking about her or her family.

Anderson said he wanted Robert to continue taking photographs, which sparked his enthusiasm and spurred him into making new experiments. Aunt Joan gave some useful advice and, with the aid of a tripod, he found he could handle the camera well despite the plaster cast on his arm. Once that cast was off he would really branch out, he promised himself. Aunt Joan was sure to let him use the darkroom, and he aimed to become a world famous photographer. It would be great to go off on scientific expeditions like Aunt Joan.

He was out taking shots one cloudy Saturday morning when the front doorbell rang. Pauline rushed to answer, assuming it was Robert coming home for lunch, but she found Anderson standing on the step. She stared up at him in awe. He was the biggest man she had ever known and she still felt slightly scared of him.

'Hello, Pauline. Is everybody at home?'

'Er — nearly everybody. Margaret's here, and Aunt Joan.'

'Good. Can I come in?'

When Margaret heard his voice she felt a twinge of alarm. Had she made a mistake, forgotten to do something? One glance at his expression dispelled all those thoughts. Mr Anderson obviously had some announcement to make.

Joan put a dish back into the refrigerator and turned towards him. 'Perhaps we should go into the other room.'

'No, no. I don't need to sit down.' Anderson rubbed his hands briskly and smacked them together. 'I've got something to tell you. I wanted you to know right away. Couldn't wait till Monday.'

He waited, enjoying the anticipation of his audience. Margaret willed herself to remain silent, but Stephen had no such patience.

'Go on then, tell us.'

'I've got news about your Mum and Dad.'

They stared at him, hoping desperately that it would be good news, and he added, 'They're coming to England.'

The three children began to fling questions at him, all speaking at once, and he held his hands up in mock protest.

'I don't know when they'll get here. We'll have to wait and see. But they're safe. That's the important thing. You'll be seeing them soon.'

Margaret felt an almost irresistible urge to hug him, but she reached out to Aunt Joan instead.

'Oh, thank goodness. They're safe. Oh, thank goodness.' Tears of joy and relief rolled down her cheeks, but she was too excited to notice or care.

Pauline and Stephen jigged about with whoops of delight, while the two adults exchanged looks of greater understanding.

'I suppose you'll want another picture now,' said Joan, when the first burst of glee had diminished somewhat.

'Well, of course. We've got to round the story off. I hope you'll all be here at half past one.'

'We've got to tell Robert.' Margaret brushed her tears away. 'I know where he is. He hasn't gone far. We've got to go and tell him.'

'Yes, let's go right now,' shouted Stephen.

'Thank you, Mr Anderson. Thank you for coming,' cried Margaret as all three children rushed into the hall.

Joan and Anderson followed them to the front door and watched them race to the gate. For once Margaret had given up all attempts to look dignified and her true age was clearly evident.

'What's the full story?' asked Joan, when the children had disappeared from sight beyond the neighbour's privet hedge. 'Were Bob and Kath attacked? Have they been wounded?'

'They're not injured, but they're both in a field hospital. Over the border with the Red Cross. Food poisoning, bad water — or something.' Anderson spread his hands. 'They've been pretty sick by all accounts, but they're both recovering. The children don't need to know all that yet.'

'What about the village? Has their village been saved?'

Anderson shook his head. 'It doesn't sound like it. Their house has probably gone.'

'And all their little treasures. Oh dear.'

They returned to the kitchen, where Anderson accepted an offer of tea.

'I've got some good news that can keep for a while,' he said. 'They're going to need a bit of a boost to their spirits when they realise they've lost just about everything they've ever owned.'

'Are you going to tell me?'

'No reason why I shouldn't.' Anderson grinned. 'You know Margaret's been researching Allingham's history. Well, we're going to put all her articles together in a book. Not a bad start to a career, eh? A full-length book at her age.'

'You're determined to keep her in the newspaper world if you can, aren't you?'

'If that's what she wants in the end.' Anderson sat back, thinking about the recent scene in the kitchen and the excited scramble as all the children tried to reach the gate first.

'There's plenty of time for making choices,' he murmured.

'That's what I keep telling myself.'

'Yes. That's one thing we've all got to remember. She's still only fifteen.'

THE END

We do hope that you have enjoyed reading this large print book.

Did you know that all of our titles are available for purchase?

We publish a wide range of high quality large print books including:
Romances, Mysteries, Classics
General Fiction
Non Fiction and Westerns

Special interest titles available in large print are:
The Little Oxford Dictionary
Music Book
Song Book
Hymn Book
Service Book

Also available from us courtesy of Oxford University Press:
Young Readers' Dictionary
(large print edition)
Young Readers' Thesaurus
(large print edition)

For further information or a free brochure, please contact us at:
Ulverscroft Large Print Books Ltd.,
The Green, Bradgate Road, Anstey,
Leicester, LE7 7FU, England.
Tel: (00 44) **0116 236 4325**
Fax: (00 44) **0116 234 0205**

Other titles published by
The House of Ulverscroft:

MOVING ON

Audrey Weigh

The sequel to *Hester's Choice*. Hester Carleton's husband died soon after the tragic death of her baby. Now she has to find a new home and some means of providing for herself and her two young children. The problems are daunting. Relatives help her to move to St Kilda and are ready to give practical advice, but where is Bruce? At the time of the tragedy Bruce had been attentive, so why does he seem to be avoiding her now? Times are changing. The threat of war looms over Europe and thousands of young Australians are rushing to enlist. Soon Hester's whole family becomes deeply involved in ways she could never have imagined.

WHAT HAPPENS NOW

Jeremy Dyson

When fifteen-year-old Alistair Black gets a part in a children's TV series everyone says it will change his life. Having spent most of his teenage years hiding in his bedroom, surely things can only change for the better? But Alistair's so-called 'opportunity' leads to a dark and terrifying event, which threatens to ruin his own life, and the life of Alice, the girl he has befriended and secretly loves. Twenty years on, Alice and Alistair are still struggling to live with what happened that terrible night — and fate hasn't quite finished with either of them.

THE SAFFRON KITCHEN

Yasmin Crowther

On an autumn day in London, the dark secrets and troubled past of Maryam Mazar surface violently with tragic consequences for her pregnant daughter, Sara, and her orphaned nephew Saeed. Racked with guilt, Maryam is compelled to leave her suburban home and mild English husband to return to Mazareh, the remote village on Iran's north-east border where her story began. There she must face her past and the life she was forced to leave behind, when her father disowned her for a sin she did not commit, in the days when she was young, headstrong and beautiful.

THE TOUCH

Liu Hong

Lin Ju works as an acupuncturist, work that involves close contact with her patients. Yet her life, in a southern English town, is solitary. After a failed marriage, her estranged husband and her daughter, Tiantian, live in China . . . When she and Lucy, a patient, become close friends, Lin Ju's world is transformed. But soon, Lin Ju finds herself in a dilemma that stirs painful memories. For twenty-eight years she has tried to bury a secret — how, during the confusion of the Cultural Revolution, she betrayed the man who defied family and tradition to teach her his craft: her grandfather.

THE WIFE

Meg Wolitzer

Joe and Joan Castleman are en route to Helsinki. Joe is thinking about the prestigious literary prize he will receive and Joan is plotting how to leave him. For too long Joan has played the role of supportive wife, turning a blind eye to his misdemeanours, subjugating her own talents and quietly being the keystone of his success . . . This is an acerbic and astonishing take on a marriage and the truth that behind the compromises, dedication and promise inherent in marriage there so often lies a secret . . .

THE VALLEY

Barry Pilton

It is the 1980s and in mid-Wales the inhabitants of the Nant Valley are holding out against the modern world. Then outsiders discover the valley, and wrongly believe it to be an idyll. Mysterious Stéfan buys a derelict manor house and sets about becoming a squire. Jane and Rob, poor arty urbanites with an enthusiasm for alfresco nudity, buy a tumbledown farmhouse. Meanwhile, Dafydd the postman doubts the valley is ready for outsiders — and as they struggle with sexual scandal, hostile artisans and a corpse, the omens are not good.